D0345546

CARMICHAEL'S DOG

ALSO BY R. M. KOSTER

The Tinieblas Trilogy:
The Prince
The Dissertation
Mandragon

with Guillermo Sánchez Borbón
In the Time of the Tyrants

CARMICHAEL'S DOG

–

R. M. KOSTER

–

W · W · NORTON & COMPANY

NEW YORK

LONDON

The text of this book is composed in 12/14.5 Bodoni Book with the display set in
Gill Sans Bold Extra Condensed and Gill Sans Condensed Roman.
Composition and manufacturing by The Maple-Vail Book Manufacturing Group.
Book design by Margaret M. Wagner.

Library of Congress Cataloging-in-Publication Data

Koster, R. M., 1934–

Carmichael's dog / by R. M. Koster.

p. cm.

I. Title.

PR9295.9.K67C37   1992

813'.54—dc20   91-42767

ISBN 0-393-03391-0

W.W. Norton & Company, Inc., 500 Fifth Avenue, New York, N.Y. 10110
W.W. Norton & Company Ltd., 10 Coptic Street, London WC1A 1PU

1 2 3 4 5 6 7 8 9 0

To P.

The Onlie Begetter

CHIEF CHARACTERS

FURFANTE a small dog

CARMICHAEL a writer of science fiction

NICOLE his wife

DAVY their son

MRS. SNED a neighbor

WICKERSHAM an imaginary butler

ORCIS
HIFNI
AGLA
ODVART
GONWE
} *Demons
(of pride, envy, wrath,
sloth, and lust,
respectively)*

CARMICHAEL'S DOG

ONE

1 "Lord Orcis Was on One of His Tours of Inspection

—

Lord Orcis was on one of his tours of inspection. With Duke Agla his next in command, and Hifni his expert on authors, and a trio decked out like sirens strumming on lutes, and his humble servant (and yours) hobbling hindmost. We'd just come into Carmichael's motor cortex, lit up by the spasmodic flashing of synapses directing his index fingers to poke at his typewriter, when the whole place went more or less dark, even the neuron chains hooked up to his eyeballs, leaving nothing but the regular dull flicker of his autonomic nervous system. The bank that worked his lungs surged in a sigh. Then muscle controls began to pulse all around us as Carmichael pushed back his chair and heaved himself upright.

His Nosiness went topside to see what was breaking. With the rest of us trailing, of course. Gonwe's bunch were securing from Mode "C," Solace, so the lute players doffed instruments and decostumed. The officer of the day presented her compliments, still tarted up like a Bithynian belly dancer.

"He needs something from his bedroom, Your Cleverness." That was Gonwe's standard form of addressing him, aped by everyone in her department. "I don't think he means to stop working, but I took the precaution of standing us down." With that she got rid of allure and outfit but kept humanoid form and female gender. Most of Gonwe's folks preferred the latter. "Do you want me to order an alert?"

His Cleverness grew a buzzard beak and sneered nastily. "What I want," he croaked, "is officers who make decisions. It's your watch. Come or quit humping!"

She took the form of a toad and crouched in obeisance. I didn't wait for her to get up and turn around. She'd order an alert just to be on the safe side, and from there it was only one step to Mode "A." Ergo, I bolted. There wouldn't be a calm cell in Carmichael's body if the infestation went over to Torment.

I'd been through it ten thousand times. Never got used to it. The racket! The crowds! The expense of energy! The insufferable glee of all the others, none of whom was of my branch. The point wasn't simply to make Carmichael suffer. Keeping up morale was a major part. So invariably it kicked off with a generalized rampage. Just having that go on around me would have been bad enough. I had to participate. I was there before them all, but that counted for nothing. All His Pomposity cared about was enlarging his command and our host's celebrity, and go ream your seniority in residence! So here would come platoons of screaming demons, in every sort of outlandish form and getup, rubbing my face in their disgusting enthusiasm, expecting me to join their senseless pranks, making me the butt when I showed reluctance.

Everyone on Odvart! Bugger the lazybones! Let's take

him down to the bladder. We'll turn ourselves to sharks and
tear him to pieces!

The time was when Carmichael's person was a paradise.
Tracts of empty protoplasm to lounge in. Long siestas
underneath his pancreas. Placid evenings in his upper
bowel. No big shots, no discipline, no orders. No grandiose projects, no Mode "This" or "That." I had him to myself
for seven months, my first virgin after all those eons, and
then for years new settlers arrived one by one. Low-grade
spirits like myself, perfectly content to reside in a nobody,
and if now and then they took fever and ran amok, there
were still wilderness crannies to hide out in.

Those days of ease and quiet were long over. Carmichael
had become almost uninhabitable for a demon of my inof-
fensive persuasion. But I wasn't leaving, oh no. I was there
first. Inertia was what I showed them, passive resistance,
and whenever Mode "A" threatened I sneaked off, and hoped
I wouldn't be missed in the commotion.

I nipped out to the porch of Carmichael's left ear. That's
how I happened to be on hand when the dog first entered
the picture.

2 ‖ Not Carmichael's Dog

—

Not Carmichael's dog back then, his wife Nicole's.

Their son had gone away to college. Not right in town to
Sunburst like his mother, where Carmichael had taught till
he got rich, or even to some other school in the region, but
all the way north to Cawdor in Racebury, Quagantic. As
far as Nicole was concerned, he might as well have been

on the polar ice cap, and the spatial separation, cruel as it was, hurt less than the proof it gave that he'd grown up. She decided she wanted a dog as a somewhat replacement. Not just a dog to have around, a puppy to baby.

She mentioned the matter to Carmichael. Carmichael grunted. This was in the living room of their house, at ten-thirty or so that mid-September morning, when Carmichael sailed unexpectedly from his study. He beat firmly out into a fresh gale, towing the stately hulk of his fourth novel. Nicole hailed him when her chair was off his port beam.

"Now that Davy's gone I'd like a puppy."

Carmichael did not acknowledge. He did not alter course or reduce speed. He beat on into the hall.

In a bit he sailed back out. Nicole hailed him again. But now he was running before the wind. He grunted once and plunged on into his study.

3 "Nicole Got Up and Stood Staring at the Closed Door

Nicole got up and stood staring at the closed door. Her stare, or glare, bit nearly through the oak panel but would have slid by the back of Carmichael's head as he sat, hunched forward, preparing to poke at his typewriter. She didn't know that Carmichael's books had two presences, a visible bulk that grew in a bin in his study and an ecto-plasmic hulk he towed around. She had never had one of the latter cabled behind her, and thus had no sense of its mass, or of the mystical force it exerted on everything—on the elements, say, between his bedroom and study.

During most of a book's construction the hulk engen-

dered off-study winds. These tended to rise in strength as
the day grew older. Carmichael was thus well advised to
cast off early, to plow straight across, to tie up stoutly, to
have ample stores of provision already laid by, and not to
venture out till he cared to stop working, lest he find himself unable to beat back in.

At night the wind dropped. He might easily slip in after
dinner, to touch up the day's work or even extend it, though
whatever he built while fatigued would likely have to be
dismantled later, and weary tinkering could cause serious
damage. Night visits were best spent reprovisioning: coffee
and cigarettes, typing paper for his machine, toilet paper
for his midget bathroom. Carmichael often overlooked the
last item, which was why so much of his library lacked
title pages. Food was not needed. Book-building was a
sacrament to Carmichael. Accordingly, he performed it
fasting.

Now and then the hulk boiled up tropical tempests of
the sort that only a madman would put to sea in. Carmichael qualified. He was insane. Not because he often thought
of himself as a vessel. As a cutter or patrol boat when he
was driving (calling "Come right [or left] ninety degrees!"
at corners, and "All ahead full!" when preparing to pass).
As a submarine when he was in his bed. But mainly as an
oceangoing tug, a wide-beamed, low-sterned, seaworthy old
bucket, built for endurance not dash, able to hold its blunt
prow up in all weathers and to wallow firmly along with its
deck awash, with rust on its fittings and brine streaks on
its wheelhouse and every bit of its elegance hidden below,
down where the powerful engines throbbed. Imagining
himself a craft (and its crew and its captain) wasn't lunacy
but the knack of converting pain into fantasy, one of Car-

michael's few healthy human traits. His actual madness came of demonic possession. There were more than twelve hundred of us inside him that autumn, commanded by an ex-cherub pride fiend called Orcis, who all by himself could have driven most people nuts.

Waking on hurricane mornings, Carmichael might know a brief term of sanity and prudently resubmerge to the depths of his bed, but soon clamorous mobs would go atroop through his person, piss acid in his bile, take craps in his blood-stream, line up to tear plump chunks of his brain for breakfast, and then streel off for duty in Mode "A." He didn't know he was possessed, but he knew the effects of it. Only the ordinance of book-building appeased Orcis, got the demons to desist from active torment, and if Car-michael could perform it with perfect attention, loathsome hoods transformed to lissome houris, an effect that might persist for several hours. So he would heave himself up and fling on some clothing and plow out into the teeth of the storm.

On such days every sort of disaster was possible. He might begin taking water on entering the hall and be forced to heave to in Davy's room till the seas slackened. He might be driven aground in the living-room shallows and languish marooned on a couch browsing *Soignée* and *Môde*, while inside him demons whooped and buggered each other. He might be capsized by a squall and washed into the kitchen, and have to spend the morning there careened, or be swept right out of the house to wander all day. Merely to stay afloat was an achievement. Actually reaching the study required the pluck and luck and seamanship of a Sinbad. And if, barnacled and battered, he at long last made port, no width of hawser nor weight of anchors fore and aft gave the slightest security against his being blown back out in three minutes.

But when a book was nearing completion, the fresh, on-study gale blew all day long. The passage over was speedy, the anchorage sure. From waking to the point of exhaustion he might dwell in the sanctified trance of book-building, while comely demonesses fondled his thoughts. Leaving before dark, however, was tricky business. Beating up to the bedroom demanded full power, and alert hands at the helm lest he be broached broadside. Running back down to the study asked for the same, or he might lose steerage, or have the cable go slack and foul the propeller. And the whole affair was complicated by the tendency of his wits to remain in the study while the rest of him was tossing on the high sea.

This last was the case that morning. In his haste to set out on waking, Carmichael had neglected to load vital cargo, a note he had made to himself during the night. With only a skeleton crew, he ventured back for it. Even if he had heard Nicole's first hailing, he could scarcely have afforded to pay it attention, and had he so much as slowed down when she hailed him again, the huge, invisible hulk would have kept plunging onward, thrust by momentum, the wind, and the following sea, until it crashed against him and stove him under. But Nicole, Nicole knew nothing of his predicament.

4 " Nicole Did Know, However

—

Nicole did know, however, by lengthy experience, that there was no point nursing anger and hurt with her husband. He was unbeatable at being miserable. By day-long, daily practice she believed, though actually by demonic intercession. The devil dung in his blood, the fiery acid sprayed each dawn on his liver, and mainly Mode "A," its memory and expectation, goosed him to a pungency of ill humor beyond the reach of unbedemoned humans.

I have here a deposition by one Theron Bishop, some-time lifeguard at the Tarpon Harbor Municipal Beach, who on August 14, 1966, leaped from the tower where he was stationed, abandoning the comfort of bench and umbrella, and sprinted eighty feet, mostly over hot sand, to snatch Davy Carmichael, six, from the maw of a breaker. Note the exchange when Carmichael heaved up:

BISHOP [expecting gratitude, if not gratuity]: "Is this your son, sir?"

CARMICHAEL: "Think I go around picking up little boys on the beach?"

Such was Carmichael's normal response to benefac-tion—as numerous witnesses would eagerly testify, but let us call Mrs. Jeannette Sned of 3372 Marston Road, Sun-burst, who on the day the Carmichaels moved into 3370 baked and brought to their door a spinach quiche. Apolo-gists for Carmichael will leap to point out that this act was liberally smeared with ulterior motive, that Mrs. Sned was atwitch to inspect her new neighbors, to browse their fur-nishings for defects of taste, to view their effects before disreputable items might be secreted away in cabinets and closets, and generally to collect intelligence of them, for her own files and for peddling to her crone cronies, and that, besides, she craved first crack at Nicole to bad-mouth other residents of the vicinity before they had a chance to bad-mouth her. But Mrs. Sned is not the defendant here. Attempts upon her character must not be allowed to obscure the facts:

First, her quiches were of excellent quality.

Second, the quiche in question, had it achieved delivery, would have relieved Nicole of the burden of cooking on a day when she had many other things to do.

Third, its baking and bringing constituted *prima facie* evidence of decency, as yet unimpeached by hints of Sned's actual character.

And how was the gesture received? To Mrs. Sned's unspeakable chagrin, Carmichael answered her knock, scowled at her blackly, sneered at the proffered treat as he might have at a basin of lemur droppings, snarled that he and his family weren't on welfare, and slung the door shut in her face with a thundering fwap!

Even flattery was powerless against Carmichael's ill temper. Let us leave aside the fans who wrote to thank him for enriching their lives and sent copies of his books for him to autograph (in whose consideration he employed a girl part-time to open and garbage their letters and ship their books to a seondhand dealer for sale). Let us likewise omit mention of the professors and graduate students who strained the lexicon of sycophancy to beg answers of him to questions regarding his work. Their missives too were destined for oblivion. Nor need we make reference to the critics and journalists who flattered him by long-distance telephone with petitions for interviews or attempts to conduct same, only to have the instrument crunched down in their ears. Let us instead present one simple instance. Edgar Finn, Ph.D., director of research for the Aerospace Unlimited Corporation, Tres Tigres, Golconda, and an author of note himself on technical subjects, recognized Carmichael in the Green Hat in Willowy Dales, at lunch with a quack of film people, and made the mistake of going up to his table to tell him he'd read his book *Vama* seven times.

"Fuck do I care? Come back when you've bought seven copies."

Which of Carmichael's students, when he was teaching, escaped his abuse? "Yes, thimblehead, I see your flipper flapping. What's on your alleged mind?" "Did I hear you say 'I think,' little Miss Porridgebrain? I have yet to see evidence that you pursue such activity."

Who among his erstwhile faculty colleagues had not felt the sting of his contempt? "With baboons like you getting tenure at this diploma mill it seems that evolution is reversing itself."

What repairman ever returned to Carmichael's house after Carmichael had happened upon him at work? "What's this idiot doing, Nicole? How long has he been here? A monkey could fix that thing in two minutes."

Was there a waiter who had ever served him who did not pray never to see him again, even among the waiters at the Sheldrake, where he stayed at his publishers' expense and wrote tips as if to put the firm into receivership? Where was the stewardess who had not dreamed of strangling him with his seat belt, or even hoped vaguely for a midair collision, provided that he might perish in it too?

And Carmichael's crabhood was democratic. It clawed at powerful and weak alike, without care of consequence, unrestrained by fear of punishment or hope of reward. Here, in this photograph I shall pass around, is Marion Quease, sheriff of Elmore County, Verdura. Note the five-pointed star and .44 magnum, the campaign hat, the uniform, the boots. Regard the hogshead chest and nail-keg forearms, the razor lips, the ittey-bitty eyes.

Question: Who would mess with this specimen anywhere, let alone on his home ground?

Answer: Only a lunatic possessed by demons.

At 5:44 P.M., January 10, 1965, Sheriff Quease found himself on the Pecan Tree Turnpike, supervising three deputies in the disentanglement of a multivehicle smash-up that had blocked both northbound lanes and backed up traffic for the best part of a mile. Thus engaged, he observed an aged green Knauser sedan, piloted as it turned out by Carmichael, proceeding toward him at speed along the well-kept mall that divided the highway, in the process gouging deep ruts in the turf. Quease stopped it as it was regaining the pavement, very nearly getting run over in the process. He slouched to the driver's window, put one hand on the roof and the other on his pistol butt. The following colloquy ensued:

QUEASE [peering down at Carmichael, as if at a rat that had fallen into a cesspool]: Just exactly where in hell you think you're going?

CARMICHAEL [squinting up at Quease, as if at a chimp in a tree]: To Spring Glades, and I'm late, though it's none of your business.

QUEASE [nodding almost imperceptibly back at the twin lines of immobile vehicles stretching southward into the distance]: You see all those folks? They're waiting on me and my men to open this highway. Now why is it, do you think, that none of them did what you done?

CARMICHAEL [snorting]: How in hell do I know? Maybe they're stupid.

The remark, compounding his outrageous vehicular comportment, cost Carmichael a night in the Elmore County slammer, and a fine of two hundred thalers.

This drawing, on the other hand, shows a scene from the infancy of Carmichael's life in letters. He is easily recognizable on the right, as yet unpaunched and un-grog-blossomed but already balding, with baggy eyes and loose jowls as displayed on book jackets, wearing the chino pants and elbow-patched sport coat of an obscure assistant professor of biology. The gentleman on the left, who has just taken the telephone and slung his wingtips on his desk, is Everson Tordle, editor, at the moment the picture depicts (1968) the chief cheese at Frauther & Fust. On the other end of the line is Blanchard Thorne, whom storers-up of literary trivia will remember as that year's best-selling author.

Prior to the intercom's buzz and his secretary's burble, Tordle has told his visitor that he will be proud and happy to publish *Vama* (the first production of Carmichael's magical bookyard), has passed him a check for thirty-five hundred thalers as advance against royalties, and has been offering certain editorial suggestions. Prior to lifting the receiver, he has inquired rhetorically as to whether Carmichael minds his taking the call. Carmichael, you will notice, has risen to his feet—abruptly enough to send his chair toppling backward. His jaw is clenched, his eyes blaze fury Tordleward. He is ripping the check into minute scraplets. When done, he will fling them in Tordle's puzzled face. Not because he deems the sum insufficient: it is more than he expected and in his financial state represents a small fortune. Not because the suggested revisions impeach artist's honor: they are minor, few, and well conceived. Not because a better offer is pending: he has had no other offer, and *Vama* will dangle for months before someone else bites. Not from any sort of cognition, wise or foolish, but from plain and mindless, rash, foul-tempered spite. How dare Tordle break off discussing a gem with a genius to coo and cluck to an overpraised hack! A swarm of hornets reasoned its actions more deeply than Carmichael when the fit of spleen was on him.

World-class curmudgeons acknowledged him their master. Eleanor Schreig made a name and a splendid living insulting the famous on live network TV. Carmichael gave her her own back and had her in tears before the commercial break. Karl Kuhn, the movie producer, was known throughout the industry as Genghis for the savagery with which he browbeat associates—players, directors, agents, and above all writers, whom he classed as so many disposable doormats—but when he and Carmichael went tantrum to tantrum on the set of *Outcasts of Vama,* it was Kuhn who backed down, and later said he would rather have three teeth pulled than dispute with that maniac.

What, then, could be the posture of Carmichael's family? Imagine a tribe of primitives settled on the slopes of an active volcano. What rites and propitiations do they not celebrate in hope of keeping the demiurge from erupting? Or think of villagers out of some dark-age legend, in whose precincts a dragon has made its lair. They go about on tiptoe and speak in whispers for fear of rousing the monster to its wrath.

5 " Not Always

Not always. This was not always their stance. Carmichael was not always an ogre. While building his books he was mild, endlessly patient, and bountiful as mines of Golconda, a caring father to his creations. True, he performed this sacrament alone (and woe to the wretch who disturbed him at it!), but sometimes in the echo of its celebration some of this generosity of spirit—and that, by the way, is what talent is—was suffered to spill from his art into his life to sweeten his relations with actual people, as in the days before he was fully befiended.

In the happy childhood of our infestation, before His Flatulence brought the mobs on board, Carmichael began consorting with a figment concocted from solitude's pain. This was Wickersham, an Anglian butler. He was a spin-off of sorts from a serial daydream that ran during Carmichael's tenth to fourteenth years, in which Carmichael starred as the lost heir to an earldom. The cast included an evil usurper great-uncle who had murdered the rightful earl and countess, a retainer who saved their small son from the same fate, and a sad slum couple named Carmichael into whose care the babe came by a happenstance goof. The thing ended, of course, with the hero restored to his birthright, and what Carmichael did the year he began boarding demons (and thereby deepened his native loneliness) was take up the thread and invent Wickersham to converse with. Later on, when love seized him, and he became a husband and a father, he extended and externalized the fancy for the benefit of Nicole and Davy. So while the three of them eked on his miserable salary, and what Nicole managed to make baking and sewing, they disposed of an imaginary estate and the ghostly attentions of four phantom domestics: Wickersham the butler, Fang the chauffeur, Cook the cook, and Fifi the chambermaid.

See the family assembled for supper in the cramped dinette of their bungalow, addressing a macaroni casserole. Nicole isn't to blame for it. She has been in bed all day with the flu. The casserole is the gift of a neighbor, whose family Nicole has fed in similar circumstances. Four-year-old Davy forks gingerly at his portion, as if to test whether it's dead or not. Nicole's face tightens in annoyance. At which Carmichael smacks his lips, dabs them with his napkin, and beams at a point above her head to her left.

"My respects to Cook, Wickersham. The squab is delightful! His Young Lordship, it seems, prefers fillet of mongoose, but that is merely because his tastes haven't matured.

"Davy, is that what you'd like, fillet of mongoose?" Gray eyes go green, flood Davy with mirth and affection. Rollers of love foam through Carmichael's person. "Or what about an anteater sandwich? What about some beaver paw pâté?"

Davy giggles in reproof. "People don't eat that, Daddy."

"Oh, no? Wickersham, pray enlighten His Young Lordship. Wasn't it Baron O'Droul who had his chef horsewhipped for putting thyme in the beaver paw pâté?"

Carmichael gazes expectantly at Wickersham, then lets his grin decompose, then shrugs in defeat.

"See, Daddy?"

"I guess so," sighs Carmichael. "But all the same, the squab is very tasty, and I'm sure your mother agrees you ought to eat it. You never know, there might be a revolution, and you'll have to settle for squab like everyone else."

The point of Cook was not that she bested Nicole in the kitchen but that she had better ingredients to work with. She transformed Nicole's meat loaf to Médaillons de Veau, her tuna fish to Truite Amandine—treats Nicole could and would have prepared had her budget permitted. Fifi fetched Her Ladyship's sable, a great improvement on Nicole's cloth coat. Fang brought the Bromhead Specter around from the garage, though what Carmichael had out front was a third-hand Knauser.

Fang had a way of replacing Carmichael at the wheel when Davy was riding. At the start of trips, for example, calling out, "Ellyone leady?" On glimpsing the rampant white bear of the Polar Lick on Verdura T-5 at Wahola: "Prease, Rung Rordship, stoppee gettee ice cleam?" Or when shooting across two lanes of traffic to nip through an intersection on the amber, a "Ho!" of satisfaction, a toothy nod, a slit-eyed grin at Rung Rordship beside him, and then the fruity tones of an announcer: "And so the wily Cathayan survives again!"

The last was a reference to a serial drama in which Fang supported a hero called His Young Lordship in frustrating the wicked schemes of El Scorpo, a secret agent of an alien race. An installment was broadcast each evening around seven in the bathroom between the bungalow's two tiny bedrooms, with Carmichael wreathed in mist aseethe in the bathtub, acting the announcer's and characters' voices, and pajama'd Davy crouched listening against one door.

"The wily Cathayan . . ."

Here Davy sees an orientalized Daddy, a Daddy with slanty eyes and black hair in a pigtail, with skullcap and baggy-sleeved blouse, silk trousers and sandals. This personage can operate every sort of conveyance, can kill with a single blow of hand or foot, but is not as wily as the announcer bills him. Our typical episode finds him strung up by the ankles, along with an endless line of hog carcasses, on a conveyor cable in a meat-packing plant in Asgaard. His hands are thrust in his sleeves, his features composed in Confucian impassivity, as the cable hauls toward him the throbbing machinery that will skin him, bone him, mince him, and pack him in tins.

Above, in a glassed-in control booth, gloats El Scorpo, a nine-foot upright crustacean in a pink jumpsuit, with two pairs of crab-clawed arms and long outrigger feelers and a segmented stinger projecting behind. He jerks a lever speeding up the cable. Fang's body swings and lurches toward the skinner. But here, bursting through the skylight, comes His Young Lordship to wing one shoe into a pulley, jamming the cable, to hurl the other through the glass of the booth, to bounce on the cable and slingshot himself at El Scorpo, butting the evil menace in his soft underbelly!

But now the shoe gives way, the cable jerks onward. Dodging a stab from El Scorpo's stinger (its venom is paralyzing), His Young Lordship wrenches off one of his claws (El Scorpo will grow a new one for the next episode) and slings it to Fang—who catches it and wielding it like a pincer cuts the bonds at his ankles. Down he floats, somersaulting, to land on his feet.

"And so the wily Cathayan survives again!"

———

An idyll, in short, compared to the state of things later. Carmichael, of course, was often grumpy, raised his voice to Nicole, raised his hand to Davy (albeit to drop it at once and grow properly shamefaced as his own father's image swaggered into his mind). One mustn't forget the man was possessed by devils. A mere nineteen imps, all of low rank, and cruelly enfeebled by fumes of love billowing through him, but devils nonetheless and hence to be conjured with. He grumped and grouched and mini-tantrumed, but daily, often twice daily, he stepped from his trollhood to live generously with his wife and child.

Nicole and Davy repaid him. They never forgot. They bore gently with his ill temper and established funds of affection for him that he drew on for years yet never exhausted.

The idyll was brief, though. Carmichael was demoted to teaching night school. Orcis came on board and took command. Mobs and big-shot demons swarmed after him. Devil dung and Mode "A" made Carmichael insufferable for almost every minute when he wasn't working. Now and then, it is true, as a reward, in the glow of his sacrament's perfect celebration, he was allowed to live generously with his family. At Davy's farewell dinner just a week earlier, on knocking back his second or third vodka, Carmichael had produced Wickersham for their amusement, ending so: "My dear Davy: I should let you have Wickersham keep your rooms at Cawdor, but Cook and Fifi can't bear to part with him." Had the business of getting a puppy been on her mind then, Nicole might have successfully broached it.

Such episodes could not be predicted, however. Months might pass before another occurred. Nicole, therefore, dispelled her hurt and anger. Nursing them alone would poison her day. Displaying them to her husband would enroll her in a snapping match with a pit viper. Another sort of favorable moment would surely come sooner.

6 ⏤ *Carmichael Housed Upward of Two Hundred Lust Devils*

—

Carmichael housed upward of two hundred lust devils, of all grades and every rank except ex-seraph. They were not the most populous faction. Both pride and anger fiends outnumbered them clearly. But Lord Orcis had come to consider it useful to let them rule our host for short periods daily, fifteen to eighty minutes in most cases, usually around dusk or late in the evening. During these intervals, called Mode "D," Carmichael was transfigured.

Relaxed, alert, expansive, open to life. Uncaged from himself, attuned to others. His smiles grew frequent, lost their cynical twist. His wit improved and sloughed its mordancy. Men who moments before were grinding their teeth at him suddenly found him pleasant to have around, and he was the most charming companion imaginable to any adult woman this side of decrepitude not blatantly disfigured or diseased.

Women became tremendously interesting to him, spiritually, intellectually, physically interesting, like saints to a mystic, birds to an ornithologist, ice cream cones to a toddler all at the same time, worthy at once of reverence, study, and gobbling. As a class, but as individuals also. He was instantly aware of the unique personhood and special appeal of every bedworthy woman in his vicinity, so that to each he became a man who liked women and who was especially attracted to her. In this guise he made women feel immensely desirable, and that, with him, they would be in good hands. The women he approached had trouble resisting this. Few bothered.

Carmichael's impromptu leaping companions came in all makes and models, in all states of repair, were acquired in every sort of condition and circumstance. Germaine Roult, twenty-two, a tourist from Francterre, was about to board an elevator at the Royal in Powhatten when Carmichael came out of the bar from a business meeting, squadrons from lust having just seized control of his person. She was clear-skinned and trim, ordinarily fetching enough, but wilted by August heat and the department stores, empty of desire except for a shower. Carmichael glimpsed her in profile and wheeled to the right, following her into the car. All his life he had been longing for this special woman. That was what he always felt when lust attacked him, and what caused the electric glow that, in this case, cleansed the inmost zones of Germaine's spirit.

They got off together, he holding her key and her shopping bag, she feeling herself the most lovable woman on earth. He confirmed as much to her in her room three minutes later, and reconfirmed it twice in the following hour. Allow that Germaine was booked on the twenty-first floor, that the elevators at the Royal are inordinately languid, that no one else got on during the ride, and that her accent ignited a special radiance in Carmichael. He loved how Frankishwomen chirp during a wank: *"Ah, oui! mon amour! Comme ça, mon ange!"*—that sort of thing. It was nonetheless an improbable score for them both, an unsmashable record for brevity of acquaintance, so that, later on, Carmichael found himself thinking he'd dreamed it, even with Germaine's scent still on his body, and her delicate chirps still echoing in his mind's ear.

Constance Lilywhite, on the other hand, he'd known for years, but had never thought of bedding, not even in a nightmare, until he bunked into her in Baronial Liquors a few seconds after the onset of an attack. She was a large, incredibly plain woman who headed a department at Sunburst U, an inch taller than he and probably heavier, with a face designed for a steelworker or a drill sergeant. The only thing intriguing about her was that she kept replacing her husbands with younger ones. Well, there were plenty of morons running around loose. But coming on her that afternoon in full letch, Carmichael was captivated. Unconsciously he had divined her appeal. She was housing as many lust devils as he was, but very few of any other branches. In consequence she loved swiving and all its works, and had mastered the art in a lifelong course of study a great deal more assiduous and intensive than ever she'd made of Ibero-Ultranian history, or whatever field it was she had degrees in.

They stumbled along the checkout line together in a fever of mutual lubricity, stung and singed by their respective demons, groping at each other's flesh with their ogles, and ended up in the back of her station wagon, rear seat kicked over, bundles shoved aside, under a tree on the shoulder of the turnpike. The ensuing bout went two brisk rounds, with devils from both cavorting through their merged privates. Carmichael held his own during the first, but in the second crushed the dome light on a backswing, nearly destroying his coccyx in the process. At which Dr. Lilywhite flipped him like a fritter and went into a combination swivel and grip that shucked the poor man dry in thirty seconds and left him goggle-eyed like a beached flounder. He never enjoyed anyone more, but afterward, whenever he saw her, he felt like slapping his brow in amazement. To think he'd wanted that woman! To think he'd actually humped her, and with delight!

Adele Ainsley, in contrast, was lovely but seven years frigid, a fact that would have astonished her early lovers. Not just frigid, anesthetized. Not just anesthetized, dead. At twenty-six she went to Skandia for the title role in Alfstrand's *Saint Beatrice, Martyr* and acquired a congregation of religious scruples that exiled every joy from her sweet body. Her quiet thoughts were ambushed by fancied sinfulness. Her attempts at love were anguished by tremors of guilt. A dozen clerics and medics had counseled her. None made the least headway. She had in fact given up when she met Carmichael.

This was in Eldorado, at a party given by Myron Myrick after the premier of the movie version of *Vama*. Nicole had stayed home in Verdura, suspecting her husband would find the film disappointing and be more than usually obnoxious. Sure enough, he blustered to all who would listen about the atrocity done to his book, giving his host, who'd directed, all manner of insults. But then, just before midnight, he abruptly turned affable. Lust had come to him like sunshine to Smogville. He smiled at people, listened to what they were saying. He praised Myrick and confessed jealousy of filmfolk for being able to reach and move people he couldn't. Then he gave an uproarious account of what movies had meant to the slum kids he grew up with. Twelve-year-olds trying to wiggle like Lara Lamont and speaking her lines in a Pohuncus accent. Benny Cain, the subsequent racketeer, galloping around the schoolyard swatting his butt, a cowboy and his horse at the same time. He drew laugh upon laugh from a ring of people around him, then announced that, for him, it was three in the morning. He looked at Adele, whom he hadn't been introduced to, and asked if she would drive him to his hotel. She agreed at once. She'd noticed him playing to her and found him interesting. What surprised her was that when they'd arrived, she agreed just as easily to come to his room.

For the next twenty minutes, on subliminal guidance from his presiding demons, Carmichael achieved perfect tenderness and patience while maintaining maximum ardor and good humor. This was as well, for the instant the door closed behind her, Adele's scruples showed up in full force, turning her into a most difficult companion. She fluttered for a while, and then she snapped at him, then mewed tearfully, then snarled, then howled, then hissed, play-acted a bestiary of unease and unpleasantness, finishing on the bed in bovine inertia. Nothing disturbed him. He continued to find her appealing, attractive, exciting, till Adele began to accept this estimate. She forgot to feel crippled. She forgot to be anxious. She forgot herself and considered the man she was with. He was caressing her gently, and making her laugh. She decided he deserved a reward for effort, and though feeling no sexual interest began to pretend some.

Adele was a trained and talented actress. Carmichael's ego was ten stories tall. He bought her performance without the least haggling and began, with continued gentleness, to unwrap her, and to shed his own clothes as calmly as he could manage—a perfectly reasonable course but potentially disastrous. Her scruples had merely been playing possum. The closer Adele came to love, the more strongly they reasserted themselves, so that by the time she and Carmichael were naked, her brain was seething with guilt and her body englaciered. All the tenderness in the world would have been useless.

At this point a clever imp named Enyeh, who once dormed in the Tuscan cocksman Scoparoni (famous in his time for seducing nuns), assumed tactical command of the engagement. Without the slightest conscious calculation, Carmichael drew Adele up and turned her around. Opposite the bed was a Formica counter, desk-cum-dressing table. He seized her bum and pushed her there like a shopping cart, wedged her legs open with his, bent his knees and empronged, dropping his head to bite her nape.

She cried out, "Stop!" and "Leave me!" Neither cry was heeded. She struggled but was firmly gripped and impaled. In the half-light from the sitting room all the mirror showed was Adele's face and torso, so that Carmichael seemed not just altered in mood but invisible. In concord with her seven-year obsession, the thought entered her mind she was being enjoyed by an incubus—not an untoward idea, when one comes to think of it, considering the power of devils at work inside Carmichael. She felt instantly absolved of all complicity. With that pleasure engulfed her, radiated to the tips of her toes and fingers, then flowed back to its point of origin and condensed there, in much the way that the cosmos itself is expanding, in response (as some physicists hold) to a seminal bang, and will someday concentrate back in unbearable density, thereupon to go off again.

After an uncertain number of detonations, Carmichael's face appeared near Adele's in the mirror. To no ill effect: her scruples were crushed. Two bouts later she left him asleep, smeared with her tears and kisses. When she called the next morning to thank him, he was himself again. He grouched at being wakened and hung up.

Such, though, were mere targets of opportunity, handy havens when lust's storm caught him abroad. His partner of preference was his wife Nicole.

This was, first of all, simple good taste: Nicole was adorable. She had, besides, the spectacular merit of loving him, even when he was his normal, unlovable self. And there is nothing the lust-crazed crave less than uncertainties as to with whom and whether. Nicole was usually nearby when lust attacked him, and far from being coy encouraged his pounces. She knew what women just meeting him merely suspected: Carmichael was a phenomenal lover.

How could he not be? He had hordes of lust fiends inside him goading and coaching, a number of them sometime lodgers in laureled fickmeisters, ancient and modern, western and oriental, male and female, hetero-, homo-, and bi-. There were no lengths to which they wouldn't drive him, no yens however obscure they didn't divine, no tricks they hadn't seen in action, no hang-ups they couldn't arm him to dissolve. Prone or supine, sitting, kneeling, or standing, on a bed or a chair or a couch or a rug or a table—the fluffy pink rug in Nicole's bathroom, the motorized adjustable massage table she had installed for an unneeded slimming program—Carmichael delivered demonic ardor refined by centuries of human art.

Nicole didn't know the cause, but she liked the effect. It blotted all memory of slight and rudeness and caused her to warm wonderfully to her husband, to caress his nape, to nibble his lower lip, to call him "Bay" (for "Baby"), or "Des," or "Desy," or even "Desmond," (since when Carmichael was in rut his loathing of his first name was briefly suspended and its use countenanced instead of "Mr. C."). She also liked the aftereffect on him. He was approachable. Also good-natured. And open-minded, no matter what subject was raised. And nineteen times out of twenty even agreeable. Thus thoughts of the puppy she wanted crept into her mind when, at eventide that same day, he invaded her bedroom, a goblet in his hand, a grin on his kisser, and at the helm of his person the agents of lust.

The thoughts seeped out, however, a short time later, along with every thought of anything else, and stayed out till after the favorable moment had passed. As often occurred in the wake of her husband's attentions, Nicole stepped from her body and watched it rise slowly and float out through the closed window, into the garden behind the house, mantled in an azure-green halo that bore and laved it softly like sun-warmed salt water. It lay in placid delight and glimmering nudity eight or ten feet above the tulips while the nimbus surrounding it pressed against the dusk and dripped seaweedy streamers among the flowers. Then, still reclining in air, face smiling starward, pallid hands crossed limply over its abdomen, her body began to turn, and with each turn to rise, as if caught in an indolent, warm, upside-down whirlpool, till at great length it was absorbed by the darkling sky. Then time, which had been getting vaguer and vaguer (like the voice of a dispirited door-to-door salesman who knows he has a product nobody wants), gave up entirely, and Nicole rejoined her body somewhere in oblivion.

When she returned to this world, Carmichael was in the kitchen fixing his dinner, and (by the crashing of pans) sullenly drunk. Approaching him would be both unwise and impossible. She decided to interpret his morning grunt as agreement. The next day she began to look for a puppy.

7 " Nicole's Quest

Nicole's quest led in widening gyres through her numerous kinfolk and was duly chronicled by Iscilblost. This midranking gluttony fiend was her daily companion, assigned years before to tempt her from her diet, to snoop her movements, and to watch for signs of incipient pact-making. Orcis dreamed of getting a detachment aboard her and souring her nature. Idiot dream; Nicole was at peace with existence and therefore not in the market for devils. He also hoped to dig up filth about her to sift into Carmichael's mind and turn him against her. Empty hope; Nicole's life was limpid of scandal. As for her diet, from time to time she broke it, but always then returned to it with such vigor that though she was pressing forty she was still shapely.

The supposed point of all this was further to weaken the withered tendrils of love still clinging in Carmichael. They were no real threat to our infestation. Old love (say, for Nicole) would not flower in him unless and until new love prepared the ground. But like many commanders, Orcis prepared to counter the previous threat and thereby missed the threat on the horizon. He kept a spy on Nicole as a matter of policy, then failed to appreciate what his spy reported.

Dogs abounded in the homes of Nicole's relations, but none of them had puppies that fall, no proper stand-in for Davy anyway. Two weeks passed in bootless searching. Then her Aunt Betsy recalled a tale from off on the clan's less fortunate fringe involving a commoner doggess and her morganatic union to an aristocrat. Scraped of romantic touches, it went like this:

Early in July, Dr. and Mrs. E. K. Talbot of Titangel, Avalon, were motoring north from the Royal Kennel Club Summer Nationals (held that year in Tamami), where Mrs. Talbot's Thuringian, Prinz Günter, had won best of breed. They detoured to inspect the Sunburst campus, where Dr. Talbot's daughter would soon be freshmanning. En route back to the turnpike, they erred into the shabbiness of East Clyde Street and stopped to ask directions across from the home of Ruth Ann Tomlinson Sledge.

This lady, Nicole's cousin and coeval, her confidante from preschool into college (from which both ejected to wed in their sophomore years), was the once-but-no-longer-unbearably-proud wife of Sid "Runaway" Sledge, All-Ultranian halfback. (He signed to great fanfare with the Hornburg Werewolves but broke a leg in camp, played no pro ball, and had since, at lengthening intervals, held jobs as a beer salesman.) She was also the modest owner of a mixed-breed terrier, Colette. The latter, in her first heat, was chained in the front yard. The gate of the picket fence was shut. A levee of suitors mooned and moaned beyond it.

The least of these was twice Prinz Günter's size, but when waftings of Colette's charms reached his nostrils, his noble blood was stirred past all confining. He shot from his mistress's lap out the car window, scampered the street, squirted beneath the pretenders' bellies, and squirmed through a slot in the fence too small to admit them. Before Mrs. Talbot's shriek of horror faded, he grappled aboard

Colette's lowered poop and presented her with a dram of premium semen.

Three hundred thalers' worth, baritoned Dr. Talbot. That was Prinz Günter's minimum fee in stud. He demanded the sum of Ruth Ann (whom the shriek had summoned), along with return of the champion, whose titles and quarterings his wife supplied in recitative. Nor was Talbot unconnected in Verdura. He had, he announced, probed Prince Nestor Nepomucene's prostate, and cystoscoped half the sovereignty's parliament. Meanwhile, Prinz Günter dismounted and (unable to disengage) formed a two-headed monster with panting Colette, who hoisted him up by raising her hindquarters so that only his front paws were on the ground. Yet withal his face bore no wisp of postcoital sadness, but rather a lank-tongued foxy grin.

Dr. Talbot was repeating his demand, his wife was rehearsing the drama of Prinz Günter's latest ribbon, Ruth Ann was recalling her own devirgination (achieved with a brusqueness not unlike Colette's) while refusing to pay any three hundred thalers, when "Runaway" Sledge reeled out of the house, clasping a sample of his last employer's product. He emptied the beaded can over the canines, scooped the unplugging Prinz Günter up in one hand, and shovel-passed him over the fence to Talbot.

"That your Cranston over there with the M.D. plates?"

Talbot nodded.

"Well, you'll need a doctor your own self if you don't stick your ass inside it and drive on out of here."

Sixty-one days later, Colette pupped. The last of the litter, a male, arrived just at sunrise on the day that Davy left for Cawdor.

Nicole and Ruth Ann had not spoken in nineteen years, but the pups sounded too promising to ignore. A meeting was arranged by the ladies' Aunt Betsy. Nicole reached East Clyde Street at 3:05 P.M. on October 1. Ruth Ann waited nervously inside the front door. Colette was nursing her pups on the site of their engendering. As Nicole opened the gate, the smallest, least favorably placed, interrupted his meal, lifted his head, and gazed up at her soulfully. Then time, which had been plodding in regular paces, rewound some eighteen years in an instant, and there welled in Nicole the warm salt tide of protectiveness she had felt when newborn Davy was first laid beside her. Her quest was over.

Orcis merely sneered when this item was related, but the dog himself determined Nicole's choice and, as it were, elected to move in with Carmichael.

He then eased the reunion of the estranged cousins by allowing himself to be fussed over for a few minutes. Five of negotiation followed. Nicole opened with an offer of one hundred thalers. Ruth Ann countered by declaring the puppy a gift. Both held for a while to these positions, but a bargain was finally struck at seventy-five. An hour of coffee, crumb cake, and old times ensued, dissolving in sobs of reconciliation.

The dog had healed an ancient family schism. All Orcis noted was that Nicole slipped from her diet.

A quarter hour went by in sniffled leavetaking and arrangements for lunch the following week. The drive to the Carmichael manse consumed eighteen minutes. The dog reached it, then—in a cardboard box lined with the Otranto *Sentinel*—at 5:51.

Inside, in his study, Carmichael had just achieved the

demolishment of Vama, and with it the completion of his tetralogy begun thirteen years, eight months, and five days before. For weeks the binary suns Omë and Narga had been gulping and regulping chunks of the planet. Noiselessly (there is no noise in space), but with spectacular ingestive paroxysms. Now, at last, Carmichael had these right. As Nicole lifted the box from the car seat, he laid the final page on the visible bulk. With that, the cable parted. The ectoplasmic hulk cruised off on its own, through the study wall, out into the world. It cleared the house just as the dog entered.

Orcis gave this synchronicity no significance.

Neither did I, not at the moment, but I wasn't in charge either, was I? I wasn't an ex-cherub viscount. I didn't wear silver horn tips on parade and rate all manner of fawning and bum-licking. I didn't bray and bluster and boss spirits around, or encourage them to address me as "Your Cleverness." All I was (am, and shall be throughout eternity) was a low-rank sloth demon. All I wanted was not to be annoyed. There was no reason on earth (or in hell, or in heaven) why I should have glimpsed the dog's significance. But since my mind isn't fungused with pride, I caught on a lot sooner than our leader.

8 ‖ The Dog Proceeded Box-borne to Nicole's Bedroom

—

The dog proceeded box-borne to Nicole's bedroom, where he was promptly joined by a saucer of milk, a crushed cookie, and an ancient alarm clock. This last was manufactured in Angstrom, Oswegan, and shoplifted in Pohuncus, New Guernsey. It was Carmichael's companion at Quire College, Cawdor, then at the Bovingham Institute, then in Sunburst. It roused him, all told, to two decades of classes, counting those he gave and those he took, but fell into disuse when he became wealthy and did not return to Cawdor that autumn with Davy because Davy complained that it ticked louder than it rang. Which tick was now its meal ticket, the reason why Nicole fed energy to it, a simulation of Colette's heartbeat to make the pup feel at ease in an alien world. It did this very well for a couple of days, until Carmichael noticed it and had what Nicole and her kin called a conniption fit.

"WHAT'S MY GODDAM CLOCK DOING IN THAT BASKET?"

"You haven't used it for years, since you stopped teaching."

"WHAT'S THAT GOT TO DO WITH IT? THAT'S MY GODDAM CLOCK! YOU THINK I WANT A GODDAM MUTT PISSING ON IT?"

But this is getting events out of right order. Let's go back into the study with Carmichael. He lays the final page on the visible bulk. He reaches beside his typewriter and opens his notebook—a green pasteboard-bound ledger, to be precise, the latest of many in which he does drafts of sentences, plans sections and chapters, gives himself pep talks, and so forth, also from time to time recording progress. He rummages back of the typewriter and finds a pencil. He writes the date and under it, "#4 finished!" He sighs, he pushes his chair back, he heaves himself up. Now he gets under way, steering for the living room:

And lurches ahead and nearly rams the closed door. He gives Stop Engines! Momentum carries him forward. Then the on-study breeze arrests his headway. It is dropping, but he is so light it broaches him around and blows him back, rolling vertiginously, till he beaches in his chair. There he stays, immobile, hands adroop, staring vacantly at his typewriter, trying to come to terms with the odd draglessness of having no book cabled behind him.

He knows there was a time before he towed any, but he can't remember what things were like then. He towed *Vama* for years. Before it was launched, he was towing *Outcasts* too. Then, with *Outcasts* half-built, *Lightbringers of Vama* attached itself to him. Then this last book, whatever he'd end up calling it.

At a point in his life, dream books began to haunt him, sought him out, wanted him to build them. The best inveiglers cabled themselves to him. Till they were built he had to tow them around. So, for a time, he found himself towing three, one of them almost completed, two for which not a single phrase had been fashioned. Then two books, then one, but now no book at all. How had he maneuvered when he was bookless? No doubt with no trouble, but now he doesn't know how. The lightness of it is unnerving.

Well, a phantom hulk would float by tomorrow. Maybe tonight he'd hear its foghorn groaning, glimpse its stately superstructure looming in the gloom. Meanwhile, the thing to do was run at dead slow, to avoid going aground or ramming something.

With that, he gets underway again, puts gingerly out from the study and across to the kitchen. Grog for all hands, as much as they want.

But no book will hail him tonight. When he sails for the study tomorrow, the sea will be empty. The unnerving draglessness will go on and on. Worse, when his tenant demons surge off in Mode "A," Carmichael will have no way to calm them, and (unlike your servant Odvart) nowhere to sneak to.

Carmichael is in for difficult times. The dog has joined him, but a crucial point has been reached in his life and enfiendment.

TWO

1 " I Entered Carmichael's Person
—

I Entered Carmichael's person at five in the morning, on
June 27, 1956.

This was at the Royal Army Fourth Training Facility,
Fosgood Barracks, Jude's Lick, Foxpotamia, three weeks
after Carmichael's graduation from Cawdor. He'd attended
through the largess of the penitent rich, and on personal
hustlerships in pool and poker, earning himself first-class
honors and a Crown Fellowship. Before taking this up, he
was called to the colors.

Briefly. Most fit Ultranians soldiered for eighteen months.
Crown Fellows, however, served as civilian researchers after
a single summer of primary training. This was as well.
Carmichael did not like the army.

That his head was shaved was no bother. His vanity was
exclusively intellectual. He suffered no homesickness. He
loathed his slum home. What hurt was that King and Country
valued him lowly, abused, reviled, and berated him in the
persons of chevroned anthropoids as churlish as his father,
put him to scouring implements for use at one end or the
other of the alimentary canal, showed him no more respect

or consideration than they did the dolts who shared the barracks with him.

A pampered lordling might have borne it better. As a novelty, as a character-building experience, as an adventure. To Carmichael, though, squalor was familiar, and empty alike of virtue and romance. At an early age he'd grown heartily sick of it and acquired the knack of converting its pain to ambition. Since then he'd been trying to climb from the social trash bin through cleverness, hard work, and nerve. On receiving his Quire College sheepskin he'd thought he had made it. Abrupt reconsignment to garbagehood stung him cruelly.

Worse, the attributes he had nurtured now worked to his detriment. In the peacetime army, preferment is not achieved but rather impeded by exercise of intelligence, expense of energy, and exposure to risk. Individuals rise like balloons in accord with their lightness. The clever, industrious, and ballsy are held back, lest they corrupt the others by example. So was it with Carmichael. Merely for being himself he found his pain doubled. Rage was the result. But rage, too, is of no use in the peacetime army. Instead it is a handicap to its possessors. Therefore his rage turned inward and became self-destructive. Howled out of bed before dawn for yet another daylong session of scouring, he was pitched by rage to a state of unconscious willingness to make a pact with whatever power would relieve his pain. This was enough to permit diabolic infusion, which never occurs except by human will. I entered him a few moments later.

Fans of pop demonology will be accustomed to hear of big-time devils. Astaroth, Balberith, Calconix, and so on. This droopy nun or mustached mother superior is possessed, one reads, by none other than Pruflas, a great prince and grand duke of the infernal empire, who commands forty legions. That verminous clerk or half-wit friar endures temptation at the hand of Belphegor, a demon of ingenious discoveries and inventions, who assumes for the nonce the shape of a lovely young woman. And the other (priest, monk, almoner, sacristan, beadle; housewife, spinster, seamstress, chambermaid, scullion) emits during exorcism a stream of ex-seraphim celebrities from Adramelech to Zebulon. As if no one were ever befiended by anything less than hell's nobility or *haute bourgeoisie!*

That is not the way it happens in practice. Your devil of note picks and chooses among the celebrated or promising. Carmichael was a nonentity. Hindsight reveals he had promise, but it would have taken an imp of great wit to discern it as he stumbled to the latrine, dull-eyed and bullet-headed, in his unlaced boots and dung-colored fatigue trousers. No such demon was present, nor did any great figure answer his call. I rank no higher in the infernal service than he did in that of the A.S. of U.

I'd been loitering about the post for days following the demise of my previous landlord, an alcoholic lance corporal of sixteen years' service. How I came to miss that fellow! He hadn't a particle of pride or greed or envy. A less wrathful specimen never bore arms. And his only commerce with lust came the night before payday, when all his money was gone and he couldn't get soused, in the form of an indolent pull at his pogo. He was so poor in spirit six devils were all he could welcome. Two were of the Drink Division of Gluttony. The rest of us were from my branch. We took care that none of us was molested. A happy home, in short, till our host died a drunk's death, drowning in his own vomit.

I might have found a new one quickly enough among the prisoners in the post stockade. It was twenty miles off, though. I couldn't be bothered to make the trek over. A place opened in the spare frame of a major's wife, but she was housing sixty lust demons already, along with a dozen of greed and a dozen of envy. I dallied in the lobby of her left nostril, considering the likely push and shove, till another fiend knocked me aside and claimed the vacancy. I drifted morosely to the nearest barracks and camped in the latrine feeling sorry for myself. It was only by undeserved good fortune that I happened to be lounging on one of the flush levers when Carmichael clomped in, publishing by scowl his ten-second-old willingness to deal his person to the power of Sloth. I slipped between his nearly clenched incisors and settled snugly in his large intestine.

For six idyllic months, the loveliest of my many-eon existence, followed by eight years of relative quiet and ease. He took in other devils, and they were annoying. He fell in love, and that was a searing pain. But all in all he remained a superior residence till Orcis, the ass, turned him into a tenement. And what did Carmichael get from his bargain with me? He got three traits of body, mind, and spirit useful (up to a point) in bearing the army.

Sixty to eighty percent deadening of the senses. After I joined him, Carmichael took little note of the howls of sergeants, their insults, threats, and manic exhortations, the curses, groans, and sighs of fellow recruits, the smells put forth in ninety degrees of heat by day-old garbage, unscoured excretoria, his comrades-in-arms, and himself, the sliminess of mess-hall grease sumps and of his own flesh most of the time, the insipidity of army cuisine and the pungent freshness of certain army locutions, the vistas of ugliness that stretched at all points of the compass and those few of charm he might otherwise have enjoyed—the unsmogged brilliance of the evening star, the stately glide of dawn-patrolling cranes.

Profound intellectual torpor. My presence gave him the life of a mobile vegetable, disinclined from all attempt to make sense of his circumstances. This lightened him of much care. His circumstances were senseless by civilian standards.

Complete moral coma. This involved the snuffing (as of so many candles in the barbaric night) of pride, responsibility, and initiative and their replacement with half-assedness, don't-give-a-shithood, and fuck-itism, the disposition to aim for and rejoice on attaining the lowest level of performance he could scrape by with, the inability to care, and the conviction that, after all, nothing matters.

Most of the sting went out of being in the army. What remained Carmichael could bear. Meanwhile, his brain got a long-overdue vacation. In fact, though he never knew it, much less said thanks, it was during that summer of army primary training that Carmichael's brain (recumbent and adoze, as it were, in a hammock, dreaming vaguely of a military encampment) concocted the theory that a species so unfit as human beings could never have evolved through a natural process but must instead have been bungled into existence by a lunatic creator from some other planet—the germ, in short, of his Vama tetralogy, not destined to sprout in his consciousness for years.

Still, having me on board was not always useful. I incited him to inexplicable offenses. Inadvertently, but that made no difference. Not because I wanted him to suffer. All I ever want is not to be bothered. But the presence of devils is always offense-provoking, irrespective of what they desire.

Offenses of omission, to be sure. Inertia is my branch's watchword, slackness our countersign. In response to my presence within him, Carmichael omitted salutes and sir-rings, for which he was berated, abused, reviled. He omit-ted to attend a parade formation on the day the commanding general inspected his unit—this although he was the pen-nant bearer, marched beside the first sergeant when they were in column, stood to front and center when they were in line, and thus was certain to be missed. It cost him a weekend pass, and a sixteen-hour Sunday of scouring fish pans. And one afternoon, when the company was bound for the mortar range and the first sergeant had dropped back along the column to howl at someone in the last pla-toon, Carmichael omitted to guide left or right around an expanse of fresh cement in the roadway. He clomped straight through it, taking eighty booted double-timers with him.

For that he was nearly court-martialed, and before sum-mer's end many times wished that he had been. When his apoplectic captain demanded to know what he had thought he was doing, Carmichael (in response to my presence within him) achieved a dispirited slump and a flaccid stammer and an answer worthy of a legion of sloth fiends. The first sergeant, he said, had told him and the others repeatedly that they weren't paid to think but to follow orders. The only order he'd had was "Double-time, march!" Nothing about guiding left or right around anything. He couldn't be blamed, he was only following orders.

The first sergeant lost a stripe and his job with it. He

was reassigned to lead Carmichael's platoon. He found a number of ways to make Carmichael suffer.

And my excretions in his bile and bloodstream precipitated the ill humor that became chronic with him. And my sluggishness, afflicting the organ where I made my nest, gave him chronic constipation. And, worst of all, my presence was to blame for his becoming infested with other devils.

Unwittingly, but what did that matter? Against my intent and interest, but that didn't count. I lost by it too, but it couldn't be helped. We had no personal grudge, Carmichael and I. We were both disposed to a symbiotic relationship. But enmity had been put between my kind and his. We had no choice in the matter, we damaged each other. As it were, I bruised his heel, he bruised my head.

2 ‖ The Process of Bedevilment
—

The process of bedevilment is self-perpetuating. Your fiend fulfills up front, provides instant if mainly illusory solace. The discomfort of housing him accrues over time, compounds like interest. Since you tend to recall with nostalgia the seeming relief experienced on admitting a devil, you soon turn to contracting new ones to ease the burgeoning bother caused by the old.

So was it with Carmichael. His Odvart-inspired accidie, useful (up to a point) in bearing the army, did not let up when he mustered from Fosgood Barracks. It brought poor performance when he took up his fellowship at the Bovingham Institute. Which wised him up to the fact that he wasn't himself. Which spurred him, in turn, to attempts at reformation. Which were futile. I was lodged inside him without his knowing. He kept responding to my presence. The frustration of his attempts to regain his ambition pitched him into a state of unconscious willingness to make a pact, et cetera, et cetera.

The purport of the pact defines the demon, its urgency the number piped aboard. Four devils of pride joined Carmichael immediately. They caused me no end of personal inconvenience and more than counteracted the pull of my presence, except in my home borough, Carmichael's bowel. But not by quelling temptations toward half-assedness, don't-give-a-shithood, and fuck-itism. By tempting him toward opposite extremes, subjecting him to different tugs and pushes, warping him to new disbalancements. His ambition returned redoubled, but now he was too clever and nervy by far. He would take no advice, much less direction, even from authorities in his field. He had to do everything his way, no matter what. Most of his hard work was accordingly wasted. The consequent annoyance pitched him into a state. . . .

He acquired two devils of lust and two of gluttony, the latter specialists in drink, and temporarily put his annoyance aside. But the behavior they encouraged was as swinish as his father's, so that at the deepest regions he loathed himself. He also got deeply in debt, anxiety over which, plus his self-loathing, pitched him . . .

The advent of five robust greed demons made him so merciless at pool and poker that in a short time his finances were sound. But the demons' influence persisted, drove him to the tables night after night, chained him there in helpless compulsion, cueing rack after rack, playing hand after hand. He took in an envy fiend and five more of pride. They broke the thrall, they drove him back to his studies. The greed demons, though, had set up house in his liver. From then on Carmichael was incurably stingy, a vice he'd never suffered in deepest poverty, and later, when money rolled in, he took no joy in it, remained merciless at minging more and more, and couldn't bear spending except in spasmodic blowouts.

All his devils incited him to offenses, but the pride fiends had a plurality, they provoked most. Of commission, to be sure. Along the themes of arrogance and rudeness. Soon he was friendless. Worse, in response to the pride demons' presence, he adopted the view that he didn't need friends, and got used to not having any, and even took pride in it. When he craved company, he talked to Wickersham. Wickersham put up with his defects phlegmatically. But meanwhile they antagonized flesh-and-bone people who might have helped him in his career and could certainly cause him trouble when given the urge to. As a result he had bitter disappointments. These pitched him . . .

He took in some anger devils, two experts in resentment and two in fury. They taught him to savor bitterness. They showed him how to nurture disappointment into inward-seething vengeance rages.

There you are. By the time he received his doctorate, and his third-rate appointment at Sunburst University, Carmichael had collected two dozen devils representing all seven departments of hell.

3 "Carmichael's Devils Met in Irregular Council

—

Carmichael's devils met in irregular council on the shelf of bone over his right eye. None was of high order or public spirit. All were fiercely divided according to branch. But to manage their collective interests they met.

I say "they" because I never attended. I couldn't be bothered. Still, I was aware of what went on. Deliberations were raucous and unruly. Acrimonious harangues, dilatory motions, endless raising of points of personal privilege. Moonings of the speaker, barrages of excrement, insults and accusations, whistles and hoots. Sessions usually broke down before much got done into mingled fisticuffs and buggery. Still, the forces quartered in Carmichael maintained a government.

Despite their small number the anger fiends tended to run it. They joined with the pride contingent, on the latter's request, when the factions of greed, drink, and lust formed an alliance. The pride-anger coalition had a majority. The anger side bullied it. Partly by vociferousness, mainly by blackmail of a sort common to parliamentary assemblies: the reiterated threat (backed up by action on particular votes) to bolt the alliance and throw in with the minority. Meanwhile they cut a deal with the envy fiend Mingo. He shuttled between the two groups, telling tales and sowing discord, to prevent a combination between pride and greed. Carmichael, then, came to Sunburst ruled nominally by pride in collusion with anger but actually by anger in false council with pride.

The department he joined was stocked with incompetents, most poorly trained to begin with, the rest lapsed from their training through laziness or want of stimulation. Not one was truly a teacher, eager to pass knowledge on to new generations. Not one. was a scholar, curious to know any more than was needed to stay on the escalator to rank and tenure. Not one was a scientist, able to wonder at things and question current doctrines of explaining them. Few were even human in point of energy. These devoted themselves to university politics. The department head, Dr. Siwash, was the most practiced. He chaired the university committee that allocated spaces in parking lots and was a power on campus, a notch above the president in influence, and no more than two below the football coach.

Siwash hired Carmichael out of snobbism. Sunburst had never had a Crown Fellow. None had ever succumbed to its blandishments, much less answered its ad in the Powhattan *Banner*. A warning light went on in Siwash's cortex when Carmichael's application reached his view. Siwash ignored it. He omitted to check with anyone at Bovingham Institute. He likewise omitted an interview and even a brief nibble at Carmichael's thesis. Had he done either, he would have looked elsewhere at once. Even if Carmichael had remained civil—and that, in itself, is assuming a lot—he could not have concealed his training and drive to excel, while his dissertation displayed on every page an inquiring mind and an unorthodox viewpoint.

Any one of these attributes would have sufficed to set Carmichael apart from his new colleagues and disturb the lethargy they happily wallowed in. All combined were a recipe for disaster, even before one added in his arrogance, his rudeness, his ill humor, and his contempt (since he himself was tempted toward them) for half-assedness, etc. It is hard to say which led in their mutual loathing: anger-and-pride-driven Carmichael or sloth-ridden colleagues.

Why did Carmichael stay? He had nowhere to go. No other place would have him, not after querying his Bovingham tutors. Why did Siwash keep him? He had no choice, not when Carmichael published three papers in his first year, more than the entire department's output. Siwash resolved instead to make him quit, scheduled him for nothing but freshman classes, swamped him with students, appointed him to serve on senseless committees, and marshaled all the expertise of nit-picking he'd gained in thirty years as an administrator to waste his time and make his existence unbearable. Carmichael responded with granite stubbornness and iron contempt.

He also accumulated more devils: five of anger, two of envy, and one of pride during his first year at Sunburst. The numbers are worth a gloss. They reflect a change in the bedevilment process. Carmichael was no longer making pacts in an effort, however unconscious or inexact, to balance the forces of hell quartered inside him but *in response to those forces' disbalancing desires.*

Modulation of this sort invariably occurs when your collection of devils reaches two dozen or a demon of high grade is on the scene. That is, once sufficient demon power is present, it directly controls the *purport* of pacts. This was now occurring in Carmichael. The government of occupation that met in his forehead was deciding the sort of devil he admitted. The anger bunch arranged their faction's increase, began delivering on their deal with Mingo, and tossed a sop to their nominal allies, the pride delegation. Observe the incipient realignment of forces toward the rule of wrath and envy:

	Sept. 1959	Aug. 1960
Pride	9	10
Envy	1	3
Wrath	4	9
Sloth	1	1
Avarice	5	5
Gluttony	2	2
Lust	2	2
TOTAL	24	32

Such rule would have produced a much different Carmichael. Whether or not a more miserable one is hard to say, but almost certainly not an accomplished novelist. In demoniacs, artistic accomplishment usually demands the rule of pride. That the trend seen above was arrested was due to Carmichael's knack of converting pain into fantasy and the attraction it exercised over two very different beings, Nicole Stark and the Viscount Orcis.

4 ʺ The Knack
—

The knack is hard-wired into human beings, like the knacks of converting pain into wailing and cruelty. Its capacity varies genetically from person to person but tends to expand with exercise and shrink with disuse.

Pain is the lowest order of reality. The point of converting it into wailing or cruelty is to transfer it to another being. No increase in order is achieved. At best one starts with pain here and ends with pain elsewhere. The transfer is never complete. The overall quantum of pain is always augmented.

Converting pain into fantasy, however, involves transmuting it into something higher, now and then into highest reality, beauty / truth. The quantum of pain in the world is thereby reduced.

Pain is always personal and physical (even when labeled "mental" or "emotional"). Beauty / truth is universal and metaphysical. The knack's converting power is, thus, gauged on two scales. How widely can its productions be shared? How fully are they refined from perishing matter? I have some exhibits.

Here is Wickersham, by Carmichael out of loneliness. Notice his hawkish nose, his watery blue eyes, his gleaming pate with fringe of wispy white duck down, his stooped shoulders (which, in the master's presence, he braces), his long-fingered hands the color and texture of parchment, his boiled shirt, brushed tailcoat, striped trousers, and patent-leather pumps. Remark his upper-class Mother Anglian accent, his impeccable syntax, his commonplace views, his social deference to the gentry, his sense of moral superiority to the whole world. In a bit we shall hear him and Carmichael chatting together. For the present, recall how Carmichael trotted him out for Nicole's and Davy's and his own solace.

Wickersham, we agree, is elaborately worked out, to the point where he enjoys significant reality. He is something near perfection of his type. He exists yet is impervious to deterioration. In his instance, physical pain has been quite thoroughly transformed into metaphysical benefit: companionship, amusement, sense of worth. On the other hand,

Wickersham is and remains highly personal, exclusive to the Carmichael ménage, and largely appreciated only by Carmichael. How powerfully, then, was the knack that made Wickersham working? Five point two degrees of refinement, only a shade above zero in universality.

Now let us have a look at this twist of wire whose image forms in the mind of an unknown clerk—whom we may, if we wish, imagine perched on a stool in a stuffy or drafty outer office, wearing sleeve garters, celluloid cuff shields, and a green eyeshade. The wire is bent into a U at each end. Next the U's are brought to overlap in a now-familiar configuration.

What we have here is the transmuted pain our unknown has so many times experienced on stabbing the ink-stained ball of an index finger with the pin that holds a sheaf of papers together. Little refinement has occurred. Physical pain to physical convenience. On the other hand, consider the distance in space-time this fantasy is destined to travel reaching clans of clerks (and others) around the world and forests of fingers as yet unprotoplasmed. Compute, if you can, its curtailment of mankind's pain quantum. Here the knack, as exercised by an anonymous master, has converted the pain of a stabbed finger (a finger serially stabbed day after day, week upon weary week, year in year out), and the agonizing sense of personal worthlessness attendant on being prey to such merciless stabbings, into a benefaction of humanity! Less than a single degree of refinement, but many measures of universality.

Finally, some samples chosen at random from the superdreams of science and art. The harmonic mean of Pythagoras. Euclid's geometry. Any opera by Gnazzo. (*I Attore Erranti* is my personal favorite.) Speckshaft's *King Edgar the Second.* Speckshaft's *Launcelot and Guinevere.* These and like creations define the outer limits of the knack's power: human pain converted to truth and beauty; near-total universality and refinement.

Well, then, to Carmichael. In him a knack of greater than average capacity received extensive exercise in boyhood on greater than average consignments of pain. As a child he conversed with animals, in particular a burly, mustard-hued tomcat by the name of Lothar who boarded in the butcher shop downstairs. Later he built imaginary worlds. His knack grew powerful and hardy.

Still later he acquired the knack of converting pain into ambition, a program originally devised in ancient Hellas but perennially updated, the Ultranian version of which is advertised by saturation and distributed free in most parts of the Associated Sovereignties. He stopped converting pain into fantasy. Not entirely, but some atrophy resulted. Still, the dropoff took place from a high degree of robustness. Knack circuits remained intact and capacity considerable. When the effects of demonic possession both thwarted his ambition and furnished him bumper supplies of pain, the knack reasserted itself spontaneously. In Sunburst he resumed its exercise in a serious fashion.

We need not concern ourselves with his systematic revival of long-unused fantasies (such as being a craft and its crew and its captain), or with his prolific creation of new ones—insomniac unmaskings of Dr. Siwash; a serial daydream involving his finding a suitcase full of money—except to note his compulsion to refine them. Exactly how much money? In which denominations, and what sort of case? Left where, by whom, and why, and when did he find it? Every detail etched to maximum clarity. What I mainly mean by "serious fashion" was his lengthy chats with literary masters during wolfings and rewolfings of their works. Through them he learned to see fantasy as a science. And his similar converse with long-dead mathematicians. They taught him that science is fantasy rigorously refined. And his adaptation of the knack for use in the classroom.

Let's watch this last. Room 312, Julia Ebberly Hall, March or April 1960. He and sixty freshmen are doing Bio 101b. We have seen his jacket, considerably aged and equipped with elbow patches, in our snoop of his meeting with Everson Tordle. His chinos are not the same pair but of similar type. He is not yet balding. His hair, in fact, is both copious and unkempt, some years before such coiffures will be modish on campuses. His jowls are still firm, his eyes as yet unbaggy. Late reading, however, has tinged the latter with crimson. He is, as usual, in evil temper. Nonetheless, he is enjoying himself (though he'd never admit it), to the point where some students are enjoying him also. Others, to be sure, are actively loathing him. Few, on the other hand, are tuning him out. Nor do those who listen suffer atrophy in their circuits for converting pain into fantasy. He is passing them knowledge of biology by encouraging them to imagine out-of-world life.

"If the atmosphere is propane, what are birds' lungs like? Would there, do you think, be birds in the first place?"

Or, "What might be the design of a sentient plant, a photosynthetic organism with a nervous system and a glom of neurons? Is it likely to have roots and live on land? Is feeling compatible with immobility?"

He bowls the questions, needles for responses, then needles for refinement of the answers. Failure to refine elicits an "Aggh!" Success, a "You see, you're not as dumb as you look." When the class has been poked to its limit, he holds up his hand.

"Okay, don't rupture your brains, here's what I think. But if what I think doesn't fit, if it's inconsistent with what we know of biology or the circumstances we've proposed as givens, show me no mercy, give me a Pohuncus bravo. A Pohuncus bravo, you will recall, is produced by pursing the lips, inserting the tongue between them till it protrudes, puffing the cheeks, and blowing forcibly."

During his exposition he glances about, like a lion tamer in a crowded cage. Does he spread his attention in equal rations? Not so. That girl midway back is getting more than her share.

5 ″ Nicole Stark

Nicole Stark had shoulder-length dark hair, and wide blue eyes that did not flash but sparkled. Fore and aft her figure was adorable. She was prettier than her cousin Ruth Ann Tomlinson (who had already won the love of dashing "Runaway") but not the least stuck-up about it. She might have had the hero of her choice, or any rich man's son on campus. Nicole, however, was highly evolved, hence not interested in such fellows.

In humankind, the female determines the pairings—most cases of rape aside, yet even there sometimes. Genetics programs the male to heed her come-hithers. She emits these on the basis of male strength. Strength's manifestations are various, however, grading upward from the physical-material. Your less evolved female is moved by physical prowess. Wealth excites the somewhat more advanced.

Nicole, though, went for potency of mind, the highest sort of which is imagination, and the extra helpings she got of Carmichael's attention came in response to invitations she sent—a toss of dark hair, a sparkle of blue eyes, a wiggle of snugly jeaned buns in his direction.

I don't mean she was blatant. It was Ruth Ann's trick to mince up and ask little questions, to gasp about how thrilling the lecture had been—classic technique impeccably executed, through which she siphoned an A from Grimes in World History, in the process poaching the poor man's mind like a haddock. Nicole didn't operate that way, it wasn't her style, and wouldn't have tried it with Carmichael if it had been. She noted his classroom integrity (founded on pride), warned Ruth Ann to take it easy, and later allowed herself an I-told-you-so. On Ruth Ann's third postclass mince to the lectern, Carmichael interrupted her gasp as follows: "Save the Delilah act for your primate boyfriend; all I grade on is how well you do the work."

Besides, Nicole didn't need such tactics. She was already earning an A in biology. What she wanted was Carmichael's energy inside her. She blushed when Ruth Ann confronted her with this desire. She even achieved a flash of authentic anger. But that was at Ruth Ann's manner, not her matter. "Don't play Miss Priss with me, honey. What you want is his pushy, smart-ass, big-city cock!" Nicole took exception to Ruth Ann's vulgarity, but her blush proved the insight was right on the button.

Poor Carmichael, meantime, realized nothing. He thought that in humans the male initiates romance—a deplorable flaw in his knowledge of biology. He responded to the signals without guessing them such and was boobified with love by midterm.

6 ''Love Twinged in Carmichael First

—

Love twinged in Carmichael first at age three and a half, apropos of a doll in the form of a bunny. This object was six inches tall exclusive of ears, upholstered in porridge-hued plush, and stuffed with minced kapok, a gift from his godmother on his saint day. When Carmichael saw it, his spirit leaped like a salmon, though he didn't really know how much he loved it till his pie-eyed old man almost sat on it one morning and squashed it flat.

And that, darlings, is love: spontaneous joy in another's existence, a salmon-leap of the spirit at the mere circumstance of its being in the same world, and an equal, opposite pang in reversed circumstance. An emotion not to be scrounged for: it's there or it isn't. The spirit leaps (or plummets) or does not. If yes, it can't be suppressed; if no, it's unfakable.

I've never felt it myself, but that doesn't mean I'm not qualified to define it. I've felt its effects often enough. We know what makes your sort repugnant to us.

Carmichael loved his bunny though its button eyes fell out, though its ears became flaccid, though its red felt blob of a tongue got pulled off somehow. He loved it though its coat grew slick with grease and its pom-pom tail threadbare, though a fistula opened in its throat from which stuffing leaked. Carmichael and his bunny were inseparable. And then—there is no record why—he loved it no longer.

Recovered is how I'd put it. Came to his senses. Why get all worked up over a stuffed bunny? Or anything else, for that matter. But I shouldn't apply demonic standards.

We look on love as a disease, but it's a sign of health in human beings.

In any case, the episode was over. The next took place seven years later.

Why the long wait? There is no record. But while love is hard-wired into human beings (along with that other human attribute, speech), its circuits (like those of speech) rarely work well unless the possessor is taught their use by example. No one in Carmichael's ambit did much loving. His father was riddled with demons, his mother worn out. The only examples he had were from books and movies.

At age ten he worked after school for the butcher downstairs. One day a big Wembley pulled up out front. A lady and a little girl came in. While the former was asking Mr. Fleischmann if, as she'd heard, it was true he made real Almein blutwurst, the latter tossed young Carmichael's heart like a flapjack. Without wanting to, certainly without trying (though not without knowing she'd done it, precocious minx!), merely by displaying the conventional attributes of a fairy-tale princess: blond hair, blue eyes, pretty features, good manners, and money. Outside movies and books, Carmichael had met no one like her. He went deaf and dumb with joy at the mere circumstance that such a creature should be in the same world with him.

Which of course wasn't so, which was nothing but an illusion. He and Erica Dienst were not in the same world. Realizing this, having his snout rubbed in it, may have accounted for the appeal certain concepts later had for him: wormholes in space linking opposite poles of the universe and time warps connecting vastly separate epochs. It certainly accounted for ambition's sprouting in him. But all that was afterward. First came a lozenge of joy and a cargo of anguish.

Joy in discovering her name and repeating it mutely—as at filching a jewel, then fondling it in one's pocket. Erica Dienst. His deafness subsided before she left the shop, in time to hear her mother speak to her. Discovering her first name, therefore, was easy. But for her surname (and address) he had to go into the register for the check her mother wrote to pay for their order—a feat worthy of the hero in any story, or as played in a movie by Egan Foyle. Joy in looking up her address—237 Briar Prospect, Southwerk—and charting a course to it in *Kingman's Pocket Guide to Greater Powhatten* (filched in matter not metaphor from Robbins the stationer). Joy in planning his raid, and in working up the courage to undertake it.

He set out Sunday morning aboard the huge, unwieldy delivery tricycle. This conveyance had two front wheels flanking a basket (with FLEISCHMANN'S MEAT in large letters on each side) and a single drive wheel behind. In the basket, so as not to get creased, was an enveloped greeting card ("To My Sweetheart," unsigned), another unwitting gift from Mr. Robbins. In his pea jacket pockets were a cheese sandwich and *Kingman*. Up Harbor Street to Mealey, with his breath plumed out before him in the gray winter forenoon. Along the canal, a peasant lad on a plow horse (though actually he pretended the trike was an airplane). Out Conklin Boulevard all the way to the end of it, by which time he was farther from home than he'd been in his life, except for when his Uncle Eddy (killed three months back in action against the Moscovians) took him to see the Powhatten Clippers play Claybrook. Yet he pressed on, stopping at Southwerk Circle to consult *Kingman*, then

striking off on the long climb up Endicott Avenue, standing on the pedals, swaying left and right, because the rich
always make sure to take the high ground—twenty-three
blocks uphill backward through the alphabet, Escarole,
Dogwood, Cubeb, and finally Briar.

He glided past the house once for reconnaissance, then
glided past again simply to gape. All the houses in Southwerk were large by his standards, but the Diensts' house
was huge. He went woozy with amazement that he knew
someone who lived in such a house. Which he didn't, of
course, which was not even an illusion, although in his
daydream (running nonstop for five days) he and Erica were
already secretly married—eight or ten years having zipped
obligingly by—and about to consummate, before he and
his squadron flew off to fight the Moscovians. On his third
pass he swung into the drive, dismounted by the door,
plucked the card from the basket, poked it through the
letter drop, remounted, and fled. His heart was still pounding
halfway back to Pohuncus.

This went on three Sundays in succession. On the second he made several slow passes in hope that Erica might
show herself and was rewarded with a glimpse of her as
she, her parents, and two bundled-up younger siblings
boarded the Wembley and set off for a spin. Two days later
he saw her again, for what turned out to be the last time
and for what may have been the high point of his love life.
She and her mother came into the shop. He stood strangling his broom trying not to stare. And Erica, the minx!
floated a smile to him—the way Pignatelli floats the pian-
issimo at the end of "Grazia, cuore mio, per tanto amare"
up to the garlic-breathed fans in the top gallery. I'll bet
anything she knew who sent those cards!

On Sunday number three he never got to drop one. As he stepped to the door, it swung open. There loomed Dienst, a lot more sternly than the occasion called for.

"Who are you and why are you bothering my daughter?"

"I love her."

"—!" Then he glanced toward the trike. "Ah! The butcher boy! Is that what he pays you for, delivering mash notes? I'll call him tomorrow. If you come out here again, I'll call the police."

So Carmichael lost his job, and got in return a fine set of lumps from his father. Which he scarcely felt, loss of Erica having numbed him to ordinary pain.

There you are! Isn't that amazing? She was never in his world, not for an instant, yet he agonized for months because he'd "lost" her, and in fact carried the scar all his life! What incredible beings! Many of you refuse to believe in devils, but the wonder is we can believe in you!

6 ⋅ The Force of Love's Boobification

The force of love's boobification was constant in Carmichael. The professor was more adept at dissembling but no less addled than the butcher boy. He looked forward to the days he taught Nicole's section, grew apprehensive on days when she arrived late, exulted when the class seemed to amuse her, ached with shame whenever she looked bored. Meanwhile, but only through great efforts of will, he managed not to aim his whole lecture to her, not to show her preference over others, not to do more than nod when they met in the hall, and not to ask her out while she was his student. All of which left Nicole deeply dejected. She thought her charms insufficient to the occasion. These smart-ass, big-city men were spoiled, evidently. Too bad he'd never know what he was missing.

Carmichael called her the day the term ended, as soon as he had filed his grades. Nicole, her mother said, had gone to Nezona to spend her summer working at a dude ranch.

Carmichael spent his summer tutoring dunces and polishing a scientific paper, as well as being tormented by his tenants. Mingo and the newcomers from Envy furnished him tooth-grinding wide-screen depictions of Nicole at starlight boff with muscular cowboys or frolicking on silk sheets with affluent dudes. His anger devils drew on this material to make him enraged at both her and himself. His drink devils undertook to help him forget her, his lust fiends to help him find a substitute. His pride demons harped on her provincial background to make him think he was too good for her, while his greed imps stressed the money he'd save by not dating her. Even the humble Odvart put his oar in. On the theme of "Why care? Nicole Stark doesn't matter." We knew exactly what we were doing. Love is your sovereign exorcist. It isn't my style to hog credit, but I happen to think that my part was decisive. Carmichael didn't phone Nicole in the fall.

But, nonetheless, he ran into her by chance, at which all our work counted for nothing. This was a few weeks into the fall term, in the Anglian Lit section of the library. Robin Speckshaft was the go-between. Carmichael was conversing with him by means of a scholarly text of *Allhallows Eve* when Nicole came in looking for *Queen Agnes*. He put his book down at once. She never found hers. They ended up walking all night around the campus.

Most of it, anyway. Speckshaft remained on duty. Nicole came to feel exactly like Queen Agnes, although she never got round to opening the play. She knew what her parents would think of her companion, and of what she hoped to be doing with him shortly, but would have renounced a crown had she possessed one in order to have Carmichael's love in its stead. As for Carmichael, he might have stepped from the work he'd been reading—except that Lord Randy only pretends to be a raised spirit halloweened to life from dusk till dawn. Carmichael sang Nicole show songs! Or talked them to her at least, since he couldn't sing a note and knew it. Putting me and his other lodgers through proper torment, and the even more unpleasant terror of even greater torment to come. A bit before midnight he began to speak of Pohuncus—the rotting piers, the blocks of gin mills beside them, the tunbledown human antheaps, the cruel streets. He undercut it all with grins and wisecracks, nodding like this film gangster, chuckling out of the side of his mouth like that, pointing with his finger like the other, so that a less sensitive woman would merely have been entertained, but pain informed each sentence (as it had every hour of his childhood), and when he saw that Nicole, even while laughing freely with him, pitied and wondered at the life he'd had (for to her those streets were exotic as well as cruel), his heart melted and a wave of love surged through him that left us demolished. Not dead, for we cannot die, but too weakened even to flee his person and save ourselves from the waves that followed.

An hour or so before dawn they went to his apartment. Twelve weeks later they were married in Otranto. Without best man or bridesmaid. Carmichael was friendless. Nicole and Ruth Ann weren't speaking. Davy, however, attended *in utero*.

During the year that followed, Carmichael's love for Nicole made his person unlivable for thirteen of the thirty-two demons camped in him. There is nothing on earth so noxious to devils as authentic love infecting a host. Mingo and his colleagues cleared out at once. The lust demons followed, then the five recent anger arrivals, then the two specialists in drink. Finally, the latecomer pride fiend departed, went over the transom of Carmichael's ear without so much as a glance behind him. The influence of the rest of us was neutered. We had all we could do not to be poisoned. Fumes of love were floating all around us. Everyone but yours truly considered bolting.

Love did not flower long, however, in Carmichael. In the first place, it was an unfamiliar growth, like a palm on the tundra. As for love in marriage, that went against all his training. In all the models he'd seen—his parents, the neighbors—married folk weren't meant to love each other. They were supposed to feel resentment and self-pity, and express them in abuse and nagging. Besides, there was the strain of eking, the fear of slipping back into poverty. Fatherhood deepened these anxieties. They balked fatherhood's fertilizing effect. And Carmichael's love required a great deal of tending, which diminished after Davy arrived. All this blighted Carmichael's love very thoroughly.

Love didn't disappear from him entirely. The bloom went off it, though, it started to wilt. By Davy's fifth birthday it had dwindled to an unprepossessing shrub that gave off very little odor, nothing to cause a devil to seek a new home. By the time the dog entered Carmichael's life, his love was no more than a patch of withered lichen, but that is getting events out of right order.

On the stimulus of Nicole's attraction to it, Carmichael's imagination asserted itself boldly—but inappropriately, as things turned out—in a study that sponged his free time and halved his sleep and then all but smashed his academic career. For rejecting a deal of biological dogma, the resulting work was rejected by six learned presses and became the cause of doubt being cast on Carmichael's professional fitness, and on his sanity, by the influential editor of a seventh. This in a letter to Siwash. Who read it with glee and issued the following edict. Carmichael could not pollute the department's regular course offering. As a charity he might teach night school on campus, and at the extension in Spring Glades. If this was beneath him, of course, he could move on.

At a certain point in the study's preparation, Carmichael decided he had greatness in him. Its serial rejection confirmed that opinion. The editor's attack he took as praise. Siwash's ultimatum did not surprise him. But, having mouths to feed, he could not laugh at it. That he could not tell Siwash where to put his offer, and fetch him a shoehorn, and help him shove, pitched him into a state of unconscious willingness to make a compact with whatever power would promise to salve his scalded pride.

7 ″ Orcis

—

Orcis liked to croak, "My name is Legion!" and give out that he had been in command of the devils cast out by Jesus of Nazareth, in Person, from the mad demoniac of

Gadara. He liked to say he'd possessed Empress Messalina, and taken part in the temptations of Saint Anthony. He liked to drop names of popes he had infested, and introduce disquisitions on humanology with hors d'ouevre tidbits from their private lives. He liked to recall his terms in two tsars of Moscovia, Igor the Small and Pavel the Embittered.

He liked to yarn of crossing the Atlantic in the turgid spleen of Dámaso da Silva, and to doubt da Silva ever would have made it had he not been on hand to goad him along. He liked to describe Cécile Rondine's famous tantrums as witnessed from inside the actress, and the Battle of Vunagrad as experienced by its victor, Manfred von Toplitz, for he liked to suggest he had bedeviled them both. He liked to tell how he had driven Mogulov crazy and inspired Soulbury's assassin, Violet O'Shea.

Well, no one puts much over on his batman. Not a word of his vaunting was actually true, though I think he sometimes came to believe a good bit of it through the autohypnotic effects of repetition. Details varied, however, from telling to telling. That was a tip-off. Nothing a sometime confidant would pick up on, but I had to listen to him day in and day out. In the Gadarene business, for instance, sometimes his account tallied with the Gospels—the demons' plea to enter the herd of swine, the herd's downslope stampede to destruction by drowning—though Orcis ascribed this unseemly bolting to the panic of an overawed subordinate, and held that a court of inquiry had absolved him of blame. At other times he denied the herd's existence— "Now, what would Hebrews be keeping swine for, I ask you?"—and insisted he had withdrawn his force in good order.

Sometimes he confirmed La Rondine as Henri IX's mistress. At other times he maintained she had turned the king down. Not out of love for the playwright Jules Vaugirard, but from Orcis-inspired pride in her beauty and talent. Besides this, he sometimes told me hard-luck stories to impress me with his fortitude in adversity, and most of these contradicted his vaunts. And the ass has never grasped that I wasn't spawned yesterday. Lack of rank doesn't always mean lack of intelligence. In my branch it usually means quite the reverse. I'd heard of him, I'd served with fiends who'd served under him. He couldn't put much over on me.

He'd never commanded a legion. His largest charge was two cohorts—in Midori, a Nipponese courtesan of the twelfth century. Nor was he in Palestine in Jesus's lifetime. He'd possessed Roman senators' wives but not an empress, had bothered a number of anchorites but never a saint, had inhabited dozens of churchmen but none above cardinal. He had never had a ruler, never been within six leagues of da Silva, never actually boarded Cécile Rondine. His view of Vunagrad was through the eyes of a losing-side janissary. His only connection with Violet O'Shea came when his host of the moment attended her hanging. As for Mogulov's madness, it was none of his doing. Carmichael was his first writer.

Still and all, Orcis was a considerable demon. His lies didn't really overstate his powers. They merely redressed some unfair slights of fate—Orcis's way of giving himself his due. That his true achievements remained unrecognized, that none of his actual landlords was as illustrious as those whom he made pretense of befiending, was chiefly a matter of bad fortune.

He went a bit far, perhaps, in suggesting that only Jesus Himself could cast him out, yet he had resisted several top-drawer exoricists. Is it wrong for a pride fiend to show a little chutzpah? At least two of the patrician ladies he lived in were every bit as depraved as Messalina. Was it Orcis's fault neither's husband was ever enpurpled, and neither's depravities properly written up? His anchorites were as crazed as anyone else's. Ought he be blamed for the vague and slovenly way the early Church handed out sanctification, passing over many who were worthy and canonizing some who didn't exist? As for rulers, would not the Tsarevitch Oleg (whom Orcis entered when he was a toddler) have likely proved more evil and tormented than Igor the Small and Pavel the Embittered together, had his mother not reached precisely that conclusion and caused him to be strangled before he was crowned?

Rigoberto Cardinal Vibroso was as lowly born as anyone in Iberia, and as empty of ostensible potential. Orcis glimpsed his hidden gift of hypocrisy and picked him as a comer when he was a novice. Orcis supplied the prodding that he needed, helped him become the indulgence peddler of his day. He would surely have been pope in 1460 had plague not carried him off on his way to the conclave, and at the rate he was going when he expired the rascal might have collected two legions of devils, had he lived to his rightful threescore and ten.

Ambrosio Piccione, whom Orcis hounded through many a terrible gale, reached Ultrania three years before da Silva—the mainland, too, not some wretched island!— but what did it count for, what good was it in the end? Ill winds shoved him south on his homeward voyage. Foul seas belched him up on the African coast. Cannibals ate him and every man in his crew. No one ever learned of his discovery.

With Cécile Rondine, Orcis blundered, but had bad luck too. He spotted her depth and play of imagination. He guessed she'd go far and hovered around her for years, angling for a way to get inside her. He worked on her day and night without the least respite, till he loathed her pallid prepubescent body and retched on her insipid girlish dreams. Meanwhile he had to drag through every dull provincial town in Francterre with the troupe of mimers she belonged to, and catch their stupid act a thousand times.

In Loviers, when she was twelve, he broke his vigil, crossed the river to have a look at the convent in case there might be a better prospect at hand. Failure of will, cowardice of conviction, but (dash it all!) it was the seventeenth century! Every second nun in Western Europe was getting herself possessed in those merry days, and some were getting famous in the process. Could Orcis really be blamed for being tempted? He was only gone an hour and a quarter, and in that time Cécile admitted six devils who just happened to be passing through. Not by any special skill on *their* part. It was Orcis who had done the softening-up. His long efforts had at last borne fruit. Just bad luck the fruit was plucked by others. The jewel of the classic Frankish theater, joint mistress of a genius and a king, perhaps the greatest tragedienne of all time. Blast!

His janissary might have proved a greater captain than von Toplitz. The impromptu flanking maneuver he thought up and led would have won the day at Vunagrad, but he was deballed by grapeshot in the midst of it. Orcis's Byednian anarchist Ivar Szmata would have assassinated the kaiser of Almeiny—bigger game than Violet O'Shea's mere prime minister—but the idiot blew himself up with his own bomb. And Mogulov's talent was meager, his lunacy mild, compared to those of a poet Orcis inhabited.

This was in super-refined, decadent Wiesefurt at the waning of the Mikelsbachs and the last century. The poet was just an adolescent dreamer till Orcis got inside him and made him work. Made him loony too, but not before he'd composed incomparable verses. Then Orcis solved the problem of getting them published by arranging a connection with Sigmund Traurig through the help of a quartet of lust devils Traurig was boarding. Traurig was forty-two and placidly married, yet the boy seduced him. As for the boy's work, one reading convinced Traurig that it was better than anything he could write. He insisted on showing it to his own publisher—thirty-seven lyrics, twelve to twenty lines each, the least of which was stamped with genius.

That same night Orcis's hand slipped, pressed a little harder than it should have, jostled his poet over the edge. Sent him scampering, buff-naked, along the rim of the dress circle at the state opera house, then down in a dragonish pounce among the performers during the immolation scene of *Der Zwerghelm*, then into an endless, mindless raving. No matter, he would be famous—except that Traurig was boarding gluttony fiends too. On the way to the publishers he stopped off at a café for a piece of *schnecken* and left the packet of poems on the streetcar.

The poet raved on for decades, while Orcis tried and failed to drive him sane. No point in dropping his name. No one cares about madmen who haven't published, or murdered someone important, or misruled a country.

In the wake of this disappointment Orcis made his way to the New World, his first visit since his voyage with Piccione. Almost at once his luck turned, his insight was rewarded. He was drawn to a young football coach, not much of a strategist or tactician, but with an utterly fiendish imagination for making husky fellows doubt their manhood and thus goading them to play beyond their skills, as well as for intimidating officials and taunting opponents into indiscretions. Orcis got on board him and drove him to the top of his profession: Bascomb Bucephalus Thigpen, "Old Bu," head coach of Rameses Sovereign, first citizen of Kennesippi, a reputable address for any demon. By the end Bu was harboring nearly five hundred, over which Orcis exercised full command.

The end came in Sunburst Stadium, abruptly, out of the blue, without the least warning, leaving Orcis no time to prospect for a new residence, or even make a farewell address to his troops. Rameses Sovereign was on the Sunburst ten-yard line, leading 17–13 with thirty-eight seconds to play, when the tailback cracked off tackle, danced into the open, and, inexplicably, let go of the ball! It fled along the turf like a terrified hedgehog, wriggled out the grasp of three Rameses players, climbed the wingback's leg, clung to his thigh pad, then leaped capriciously toward the Sunburst safety. Meanwhile, the vessels in Old Bu's brain engorged. By the time the safety clasped the ball to his bosom, all Coach Thigpen's gauges were showing an overload, and some were niggling toward the last limit of tolerance. When the safety broke into the clear on the fifteen-yard line and headed, uncatchable, toward the Rameses goal, every capillary in Bu's head let go at once. He was stone dead before Sunburst scored.

Rameses Sovereign took the subsequent kick-off with nine seconds left, ran it back for a touchdown, and won the game 23–20, but that was no consolation for Orcis. Orcis was suddenly minus both home and command. He flitted disconsolately out of the stadium with the equally disconsolate Sunburst crowd. He moped across the campus with a pair of gentlemen—biology professors, as it happened—who were mourning the cruel reversal sustained by their Ocelots. He was hovering above them, wondering where to go next, when a younger man approached them grinning—the only glad face to be seen, since the Rameses State team and fans were mourning Bu.

"Ha!" the fellow gloated. "I hear our noble cretins blew the ball game!"

That was how Orcis met Carmichael.

Carmichael's glee over the pain of his colleagues was, of itself, only mildly attractive. That it was brought on by a loss at football, however, marked Carmichael as an outsider (if not an outcast) and caused Orcis to look at him more closely and notice the cargo of pain he was trucking around—all the early pain he'd converted to ambition and that now had been converted back, for it was the season of his study's rejection, a little before the Siwash ultimatum. Also of note was Carmichael's sense of greatness. Put alongside his virtual lack of achievement and total obscurity, this made him somewhat an interesting case. As a type your megalo's a great collector of devils, as prolific now and again as your paranoid. That Carmichael had already gathered some was another point, though his nondescript crew was neither numerous nor energetic enough to offer much in the way of a new command. That he was cancered with love was an obvious drawback, but not overwhelming. The disease was no longer acute and perhaps in remission. Having nothing better to do, Orcis followed

Carmichael to the library and sat in on a conversation he had with Lobonsky via a translation of *Eva Morosova*. He followed Carmichael home when the place closed, browsed a few of his fantasies, and sat in on his insomnia. On observing Carmichael's knack, he decided to stay.

Orcis hadn't been demoning all those millennia for nothing. He'd become an excellent judge of human character. Carmichael had arrogance enough to outfit nine Tuscan magnificos, six Anglian duchesses, four Ibero-Ultranian military despots, or two TV network heads, yet he had nothing to be proud of. A good mind, a fine education, a decent profession, a loving wife, a healthy child—these might do for some. To Carmichael they were feebly insufficient. He'd made pacts before, he'd be making them again, and would be in the market for a pride devil.

As for being worthy of Orcis, the quality of his knack argued he would be. He had turned it to science with negative effect. He was now about to turn it to fiction, a trajectory Orcis glimpsed before Carmichael did, the direction those library conversations were leading. Pain plus imagination yields achievement, no matter what field, provided imagination is aimed correctly. The literary and scientific imaginations differ only in their degree of objectivity. Carmichael's knack was quirkishly subjective, and would work best when applied to telling stories. With Orcis to supply the push, he could be made into an excellent residence—not so flashy, perhaps, as Bu Thigpen in a country where sport is a sacrament, but quite respectable. Money, too, was sacred in Ultrania, and Ultranians lost their native contempt for writers in the case of those who managed to get rich.

Finally, the chap had a strong constitution. He might

live long enough for Orcis to get his legion. All in all, he was worth hanging around for.

Orcis only had to wait till the end of the term. Carmichael welcomed him in right in Siwash's office. He took over Carmichael's right frontal lobe as his quarters and stayed in seclusion there a number of days, considering the merits and demerits of the devils who had preceded him in residence and thereby seeding us with apprehension as to what his being with us might signify. Then he assembled us and took command.

THREE

1. "The External Semblance of the Demon
—

The external semblance of the demon is a minor matter, since it may be arranged and altered at whim. In essence we are non-substantial/dimensionless, massless, weightless, volumeless, and timeless. In practice we take what shape we feel at home in—animal, vegetable, mineral, human or bestial, male or female, solid, liquid, or gas, homogeneous-simple or combo-composite—or the form we find convenient to the moment's purpose (seduction, say, or solace or stonification, fright or flight, lulling or lurking in wait), or simply remain unformed, void, and invisible, for we have no need to manifest materially in order to attest that we exist. Orcis, though, was by character picky with details, and by temperament given to gaudy displays. He judged that we could do with some pomp and circumstance (as encouraging to discipline and morale) and ordered us to fig out in demonic traditionals—antlered beast head, humanoid body and arms, goat shanks and cloven hooves, supple tail with barbed stinger, leathery hide and bat wings in branch coloration: purple for pride, crimson for anger, black for avarice, and off-white for me. He arranged himself likewise, with fallen cherub's silver horn tips affixed, and had us materialize at microscopicity, so that the council site became a vast antre through which his voice resonated, rebounding in echo. He spoke, besides—or, rather, bellowed hoarsely—in a babble of ancient, rude, guttural tongues, beaming out baleful glares, brandishing his stinger, and mantling his wings for emphasis—the perfect picture of your old-time archfiend.

He began by reciting his thirty-seven titles, most of them dreamed up for the occasion, then ran a highlight reel of his career. It opened with Bu Thigpen and then traced backward, through actual and confabulated hosts, and closed with the bellowed croak "MY NAME IS LEGION!" Then he assured us that before he and we were done with Carmichael the space around us would be packed with devils. Rank on serried rank, I think he said. At which I had an anxiety attack, but all the others cheered like the fools they were.

But not for debate, Orcis went on. Those days were over. Henceforth, he would command! We and all who joined us would obey! That brought another cheer from my imbecile lodgemates.

Here Orcis gianted, so that his horn tips brushed the vault above him. For the present our orders were to celebrate his coming, in any way we wished so long as it was noisy and chaotic. He reached up and clawed off a chunk of Carmichael's brain, crumbled it, and strewed it for us to gobble. Then he turned himself into a sulfurous smoke and wisped up into his apartments, leaving disembodied laughter booming behind him.

These theatrics roused my fellows to great excitement and gave Carmichael a raging headache. This the ensuing festivities intensified and complicated with a queasy malaise, a disorientation, a tormenting restlessness, as the general hubbub vibrated through his system and special rancidities fouled his unconscious mind. I recall a slow quadrille of coupling roaches and a screeching contest among toucans and macaws. A lizard banquet was held on the losing contestant, who took the squirming likeness of four-year-old Davy. There followed a set of mixed doubles played by a duck-billed rat and a feather duster against a blue orangutan and an ostrich, with other devils forming the court and equipment, where the same point was repeated over and over while the foursome railed at each other and hollered "Let," while the lines developed sudden bends and bulges, while the net hoisted and dropped pitilessly, while the rackets turned to frying pans, fritters, and palm fronds, and their handles became ejaculating dongs, and the ball abandoned all pretense of sphericality to moth and kangaroo in absurd directions.

What we had was the first essay at Mode "A." Carmichael's reaction is instructive. Pain snuffed the rush he'd felt on Orcis's entry and kindled up a craving for the rush's return. It was pact-making time again in a few hours. But Orcis posted a sentry at each orifice, and meanwhile flogged the celebration on, till the craving flamed to desperate intensity. Then he recalled the guards at Carmichael's nostrils and let the devils mustered there troop in.

These were Onglebarth, Vadis, Bogomul, and Nenk, officers of his on board Bu Thigpen. He'd collected them while awaiting his own admission and asked them to stand by and do some recruiting. Each brought about a dozen lesser ranks. Fifty-odds devils' simultaneous entry jazzed Carmichael to the vestibule of mania and was a contributing factor (if not the whole story) in his turnpike contretemps with Sheriff Quease. The commotion that occurred in getting them billeted, the stampede for choice regions of Carmichael's anatomy, the altercations between old hands and newcomers, the howled commands, the threats, the gripes, the curses, the incidents of insubordination, the summary punishments imposed thereon, the brawl in Carmichael's pancreas between Bogomul's and Onglebarth's detachments, the marshaling of a section to drag a mutinous anger fiend from Carmichael's prostate so that a pair of lust devils might be installed there, the assault on Vadis by two of Nenk's recruits when the former claimed his bunk in Carmichael's left earlobe, their headlong flight when they realized his rank, the search for them through Carmichael's extremeties, their capture and gang emprongment by the whole force—all this bashed Carmichael into a thorough depression during his night in the Elmore County jailhouse.

Fortunately for him, it exhausted the devils, so that they left him in relative peace for a time. Fortunately too for Orcis's plans. Carmichael had nearly gone sailing into full lunacy, past the ridge of creative madness Orcis meant to lodge him on.

2 ″ Humans Board and Lodge Devils

—

Humans board and lodge devils in hope of advantage, the false hope that they will dispose of demonic power. It enters them all right, but they don't possess it. On the contrary, it possesses them. They get only the intermittent illusion they wield it.

This has its uses. The possessed attempt things healthy

folk prudently shy from, and get appropriate plaudits if they succeed. The illusion, though, is basically destructive. Most such attempts finish very badly.

Possession disbalances personality, balks its expression here and boosts it there. This may produce the appearance of advantage. People infested by greed demons often get money. Those harboring lust fiends tend to get plenty of sex. And so on. But not because special powers have been conferred on them, of business acumen, say, or sexual attraction. Their energy is blocked from broad lanes of expression and stuffed into this or that narrow channel, along which it squirts with exceptional force.

Besides the concentration brought by disbalancement, the only contribution of devils to human achievement, public or private, criminal or socially approved, is in the provision of pain, augmenting normal life-supplied consignments, to goad built-in or acquired knacks. And while where we block and funnel varies according to our branch of service, one thing is constant: insofar as humans board devils they do not love.

Humans always lose with diabolic possession. What one has, after all, is a master-slave setup. The host's energy is at the demon's disposal. And enmity has been put between our kind and humans.

Not that it makes any difference what I advise. People, and animals too, will keep on inviting us. We'll keep on possessing host after host. There's no end to it, not as things are presently arranged. But if you feel you must have devils, I strongly recommend you choose from Sloth. We don't go in for pain and goading. We make a contribution to human ease. Temporary ease, but you mustn't be piggish. After all, in human life nothing lasts forever. Deadening of the senses works every time, and there's not a single problem that can't be solved, can't be made to vanish entirely, practically speaking, by the simple strategem of not caring about it, by accepting that, after all, nothing really matters.

Well, to return, unless curtailed by death or exorcism, demonic possession always causes madness. There are various sorts. Creative madness is a state (not necessarily induced by the presence of devils) in which humans with the right knack in good working order find it stung to intense activity and fed with an adequate flow of pain, so that their entire being is concentrated on emitting fantasy at significant levels of refinement and universality. Creative insofar as these levels are high. Madness because one is lopped of all other capacity.

This state is precarious both in attainment and maintenance. No knack is of infinite tolerance as to the volume of pain it can gulp at one swallow or the length of time it can keep gobbling flat out. As overload nears, the knack may shut down for a while, or seize up entirely, or jolt off into hyperactivity. The last is by far the most serious outcome. Unprocessed pain will at length stuff the sufferer down into depressive dementia of the numb, dumb, muddled, fuddled sort, but your runaway knack brings immediate, total disaster. Emissions proceed at accelerated tempo with catastrophic loss of refinement and shareability. What you have is full, gibbering lunacy, audiovisual-tactile hallucination, delusion, delirium, raving, and the like.

Orcis's goal was to lord over numerous devils in a high-status host. His strategy was to induce a creative madness. He was overly zealous, however, in execution, and underly wary of what might go awry. His draft of new recruits was excessively heavy. Their billeting was blundersome in the extreme. Overload very nearly resulted.

Subsequent maneuvers were less clumsy. Carmichael managed to adapt. That the madness he entered was creative, however, was due more to his personal resiliency than to any artistry on Orcis's part.

Nor should one suppose the near miss uncharacteristic. My branch aside, devils are, at best, pitiful creatures, possessed of power but sadly inept in its use. As for your pride fiends, their capacity for mucking up is exceeded only by their blind self-assurance. Oftentimes the fools seem almost human.

3 ʺ Carmichael Entered a State of Creative Insanity

—

Carmichael entered a state of creative insanity three weeks after Orcis entered his person. He stayed in it for thirteen years, eight months, and five days. A good part of this time he spent celled in a room with a typewriter. When loose he got by, more or less, as a functioning human, the way title pages get by as toilet paper. He even looked sane from a distance or from certain angles, the way a movie mock-up looks real on film. But mad as a goat he certainly was.

His knack churned at full blast, night and day, without letup, milling his private distress into shareable dreaming. This he coded in words and loaded on paper. Nothing else had much existence for him. His brain was aswarm with figments. Imaginary stars and dependent planets, imaginary oceans and continents, imaginary beings sub-, super-, and human, imaginary crimes, vendettas, and loves, imaginary societies and institutions, imaginary histories and dreams, imaginary words of imagined languages, imaginary saints of imagined faiths, the battles of imaginary conflicts, the fanglings of imaginary technologies. These he saw as real; they received his attention. He took infinite pains to understand their natures, to tell the truth about them, to do them justice. Meanwhile, the actual people and things around him, though visible, audible, tangible, and so forth, had the moral consistency of annoying mirages that weren't there but wouldn't go away, that made demands upon his wearied perceptions yet couldn't be wholeheartedly believed in. His interactions with these were perpetual bungle. They bruised his head, he bruised their heels. Much of the time, however, he managed to avoid them and dwell in the reality of Vama.

Carmichael was asleep when his higher reality was first revealed to him, splayed next to Nicole in a secondhand brass double bed in the one-story, wooden-frame, four-room East Nelson Street bungalow they had been renting since Davy was two, while Central Verdura heaved dawnward, stabbed by starlight, in the January of his lunacy's onset. Six pops of Balalaika the previous evening had knocked his dreaming faculty down for a nine count, but it came up swinging just before daybreak. The result was a space scape of Vama gleaming in the glance of its major sun, with its triplet moons in echelon beside it, as envisioned in death's stare by Tarn ent Vukuri.

Carmichael users will probably remember, whether they free-based the books or snorted the movies, that Tarn ent Vukuri flourished (earth) eons ago and was the first great Vamian space explorer. Marooned in the glower and blast of combustion tempests, on the methane-shrouded wastes of Kiri-Dûm, short of oxygen, unable to contact his base, he spent his last hours composing a tribute to his native planet in the terse and classic *lorghë* form. The poem was found in his smashed thruster twenty (Vama) years later and gained the stature of a planetary anthem. It figured the homebound view denied Tarn in life.

Vama came to Carmichael, thus, in a double dream vision. Dreaming in Sunburst, Verdura, he dreamed of Tarn, who shipwrecked on Kiri-Dûm dreamed of Vama.

On walking, however, Carmichael couldn't recall it. It shimmered at the bottom of his consciousness. He lay surfaced in sleep's trough trying to raise it.

Maybe you've seen a bum at a subway grating trying to raise what looks to him like a half-thaler by means of a lump of gum on the end of a stick. He squats in the flow of pedestrians, peering hopefully, probing carefully, and if he's lucky, hope and care are rewarded. But the way his luck runs a cop struts by instead, sneers, snorts, stabs grimed neck with shined nightstick: "Geddoudah heah, ya bum, ya blockina sidewalk!" And, sure enough, as Carmichael lay groping, the seventy-odd devils inside him rousted him from bed and bemusement.

In the middle of tying a shoelace he sat up abruptly. A phrase butted into his brain and he said it aloud, before he was conscious of having thought it: *"Pranotu, oracî, Omati kyr."* He had no clue what it meant or where it came from. He blinked twice, trying to guess, then fled to the bathroom, bayed by a leash of demons.

Confirmed Carmichael users will recognize, of course, the last line of Tarn's *lorghë,* "Trilunate, iridescent, Omë's jewel." It took Carmichael eight months to bring it to consciousness.

Even while the poor madman brushed and gargled, figments were attempting to form in his brain. Or, rather,
already formed, they attempted to slough the folds of pla-
cental thought tissue, provoking a peristaltic urge to code
and load. This he bore for three days in burgeoning urgency
while he prepared a place in which to ease it, for he'd lost
his Bio Department cubicle and had nowhere to work in
except the garage.

The garage was an afterthought of the bungalow's owner's, a low structure shacked against the side wall, com-
municating with the kitchen via a doorway carved from
what had once been a window. In Carmichael's time it had
never had a car in it but had instead become jumbled with
disparate junk. Day one, till he left for Spring Glades, he
spent removing things to the town dump and heaping others into two corners. On day two he made himself shelves
from unsanded planks and cement blocks, then unpacked
his books onto them from their cartons. On day three he
built a table from similar planks and sturdy three-by-four
posts. A powerful bulb completed the renovation. That was
Carmichael's bookyard for the first four years.

During this time he said nothing of his intentions, partly
because he scarcely knew them himself and partly because
he couldn't bear conversation, what with the demons'
cavortings, the figments' kicks, and the peristaltic impulse's
insistence. On the morning of day four, which was a Fri-
day, a day when he had no class, he confronted Nicole.
This was in the kitchen, when she returned from taking
Davy to kindergarten. Carmichael had just got up and was
drinking his coffee. Under his pate the fiends queued up
for breakfast.

"I'm going to work."

He instantly held a hand up to stop her from speaking, although she had given no sign that she might do so.

"Don't ask me on what, I don't know. Don't ask me anything. From now on, you take Davy to school."

"I take him most days. I just got finished taking him."

"Don't argue with me, Nicole. Just listen." He was already exhausted by so much communication. "You take Davy to school. After that, do whatever you want. Just don't call me or bother me. If somebody's dying, all right, if the house is on fire. Otherwise no. I won't be making a bomb or planning a holdup. I won't bother you. Don't bother me."

"Will you come out for lunch?"

He groaned and hauled around to face her again. Clumsily. Without his understanding what had happened, or being aware of anything but the effect, the huge, invisible hulk of his first novel had cabled itself firmly to his stern. It operated as a massive sea anchor.

"Didn't you hear me before? Don't ask me anything! I don't know when I'll be out! If you keep asking questions, I'll never get in! I'm not bothering you! Stop bothering me!"

He hauled around into the wind and drove for the bookyard.

That day Carmichael wrote a page and a half. Maybe you've seen a soldier filling sandbags and loading them onto a waiting truck, one soldier doing disciplinary extra duty while the rest of his outfit is off the post on pass and a lone sergeant sits in the shade eying him warily, making sure he keeps busy. He grabs one lip of a sack and stands on the other, worries sand into it with an entrenching spade. He pauses, ties the mouth shut, scowls at the product. He grabs two corners, drags the sack to the truck. He grabs two sides, then pauses, scowls again. Hoists the sack to his chest, turns with it slowly. Hefts the sack to his shoulder, then onto the truck bed. Pauses, turns back, scowls, goes for another. So Carmichael, coding figments into words, loading words onto paper. But though he didn't understand what was happening, and wasn't aware of anything but the effect, so long as his pauses weren't excessive, the devils inside him left him in peace.

He wrote the same page and a half for seven weeks. Often enough he got washed out of his anchorage and bucketed about the bungalow and its environs, during which time his devils tormented him mercilessly, but much of the time he spent actually writing, writing the same three paragraphs over and over. By mid-February he had them pretty well polished. He'd bullied the words till they sat on the page very primly. He'd held tryouts to let other words show how they would look. He'd whistled words off without the least sentimentality, no matter how eager they were to please him, or how welcome they had seemed at first appearance, the minute others proved they would fit better. By the end of three weeks those particular three paragraphs were as perfectly fashioned as mortal mind could make them, yet Carmichael kept writing them over and over, in order (so he believed) to maintain momentum until he could figure out what to write next. But no one figures out alternative universes, no matter what Carmichael supposed. Alternative worlds reveal themselves when they feel like it, as Carmichael, much later, clearly suspected. What, then, was Carmichael actually doing during those seven weeks, and in similar periods that occurred afterward?

1. He was teaching Anglian words who was master—a thing they need to be taught again and again—by teaching himself to treat them with absolute sternness, and never

let on how much he enjoyed fondling them, much less go gaga when this or that piecey word flounced by.

2. He was showing the world he had glimpsed in dream vision that he would wait on its pleasure, attend it faithfully and with flattering patience, for however long it pleased to keep him dangling, until its modesty should relax a little and it decide to let him possess a bit more of it, for while one has to treat words like the trollops they are, available on call to virtually anyone but truly pliant alone to the unsentimental with the sternness to turn them out and put them to work, imaginary worlds and alternative universes give themselves but once, to one person only, and thus require the stance of the courtly lover.

3. He was bashing himself toward a trance state by the method of repeated incantation.

4. He was calming the devils inside him, since so long as he remained face to face with his typewriter, they remained blessedly placid, making up for this restraint before and after, and especially when his attention flagged.

One day he wrote his page and a half again, for the two or maybe the three hundredth time, and then instead of stopping and starting over, continued on with a fourth paragraph. The next thing he knew Nicole was banging the door. Did he know that it was six-thirty? Didn't he have to teach a class that night? Eighteen pages of visible bulk lay piled on the table, and though Carmichael didn't understand what had happened, wasn't aware of anything but the effect, the devils inside (instead of just staying placid) had transformed themselves into adorable succubi and were laving his person with unearthly bliss.

Which delight persisted the rest of the evening, subsiding gently in echoing reverberations. Nothing he'd ever known was half so sweet. Meanwhile, three fifths of his wits kept coding while the other two fifths drove his car and gave his lecture, so that all he had to do the next day was load, and the succubi resumed their ministrations.

True enough, after three or four days the trance state crumbled and he spent a month reworking what he'd done during it, slapping the words around, firing lazy ones, hustling fresh prospects, breaking them in, and generally playing the cold-hearted pimp to keep his stable in line and productive. Then, with rewriting completed, he might spend another month in patient and submissive vigil, awaiting his mistress universe's pleasure. The devils bayed him to work each morning, were lurking in wait whenever he dared to relax, and did no more than keep still while he was busy. He remembered the delight however. And prayed it might come again, and at length it did. So he continued for thirteen years, etc. And when the words rebelled (as they did sometimes), when his mistress grew impossibly coy or angry, when the devils inside him grew unbearably swinish, when actual people and things bruised him too painfully, he welcomed in additional demons for the momentary relief their entry brought.

He'd been conditioned in youth to a certain toughness. His chromosomes, besides, were oddly mixed. He scarcely dwelled on his most-of-the-time misery and thought instead of his now-and-then joy. Everyone who saw him close up knew he was tormented, but once he glimpsed Vama he believed himself happy. He was crazy, of course, by demonic possession, but we would be crazier still to pity him much.

The trances themselves were not demon-induced. Carmichael beat himself into them. His devils encouraged, however, with stick and carrot. As time passed these states came with greater ease and frequency, and lasted longer. During them he composed till fatigue overtook him, sometimes in midsentence, sometimes in midword, then let the tide wash him from his bookyard. At such times only his body was in this world, drifting vacantly, emblemed with a wispy smile, or simply parked somewhere, like a car whose owner is out of town. His mind was in an alternative universe, maybe on one of the planets he had invented, or in a region it found unfamiliar and wouldn't recall when it returned. Nicole might come on him before sleeping, when she went to check the doors and the stove burners, and if he liked fix him a drink or a sandwich, or simply lead him to their bedroom, while he smiled wispily at her and nodded agreement at whatever she happened to be saying. Later, when he had stopped teaching and they lived on Marston, he sometimes wandered into Davy's room to stand in silence while Davy did his homework or browse the baseball game Davy was watching. Once during the summer before the dog came, Davy returned from a date to find his father parked on the corner of Marston and Wilde, swaying slowly, gazing at the night sky. He blinked when Davy took his shoulder, kept blinking during his mind's return voyage, then smiled and let Davy guide him home. At such times Carmichael was always docile. Why shouldn't he be? No Indic fakir visioning nirvana was ever so enveloped in bliss.

There was, besides, the conscious joy of creation, of begetting worlds, of bearing them, bringing them light— and of bringing light to them, of beholding and finding it good. Carmichael's mind teemed with stars and beings. He rejoiced in the power to breathe life to them. We would be crazy to pity him at all.

4 ⎯ Artists and Parasites

Artists and parasites have at least one thing in common. Both may be classed as either efficient or not. How does this sort out with Carmichael and Orcis?

Artistry, broadly defined, is high-grade order. Its characteristics are elegance and economy. Its instigator, or muse, is pain. Recurring pangs of emptiness in the lower abdomen due to insufficient intake of love, praise, or notice. Alternating vertigo and heaviness induced by the boundless promise of life and the limitations of practical existence. A choking sensation in the upper thorax brought on by awareness of one's mortality. The nip of shame or guilt, the gnaw of worry, the nag of doubt, the natter of confusion, or (to crib from the Gloomy Duke's lengthy catalogue),

> The tweaks and pinches of a low estate,
> The chafe of want, the rack and wheel of passion.

The efficiency of artists is a function of their service to the muse and is computed by means of this equation:

$$E = \frac{O}{P}$$

where P represents the pain applied to the system and O the order it emits, always allowing that, where order's concerned, quality counts to quantity thirty to one. The more order discharged in relation to pain encountered, the more efficient the artist.

Moscovian critics insist that artists must suffer and flourish the lives of their principal writers as proof. This concept, while true to a point, is deeply misleading. No discomfort, no artistry; no argument there. Unirritated oysters do no pearling. But pain to the level of suffering is not strictly required, not do creative peaks imply chasms of misery. A twinge of loneliness may yield a sonata. A throb of angst may do for an altarpiece—or a comedy act, or a seven-figure swindle. A poke-prod of annoyance at a datum left untucked by accepted theory—persistent, unremitting, implacable if you like, but no nearer agony than the press of a morsel lodged between one's cuspids, or the itch of a fleabite in the small of one's back—may generate a scientific advance.

Pain is something everyone gets some of. You humans, creative or un-, often lead lives of appalling stupidity, and in consequence, therefore, of exquisite distress. You conceive yourselves above the laws of probability and end up paying dearly for your imprudence. Or, obeying all the signs, taking the slow lane, stopping at corners, looking left and right, you nonetheless get head-on'd by private disaster or sideswiped by historical events. Some people, however, escape serious suffering, and there have existed artists so efficient as to spin abundances of order from no more pain than what life doles the lucky, without dipping a toe (much less having to wallow) in Mogoluv's demon-driven frenzies, or Garrulevsky's automutilations, or Krissloff's fits, or Nitsky's melancholy, or Grotkin's drinking, or Lobonsky's lusts, without getting tombed in debt like

Odorenko, or eternally cuckolded like Payosovich, or sentenced to forced labor in the arctic like some of those named here and many others.

Carmichael, alas, has no place in this category. His books are good, his artistry is beyond question. On a creativity scale of zero to ten, balancing grade and bulk, with Speckshaft the measure, Carmichael's work rates a solid three, as high as any living Ultranian writer's, though below that of leading scientists and tax accountants. But it does not at all reflect the muse's bounty. While more or less slighted by unprovoked misfortune, neglected by deformity and major illness, disfiguring mishap and shattering grief, ignored by fire, flood, tornado, and earthquake, and cut off from all share in his century's rich legacy of war, Carmichael as a self-made, fiend-ridden madman disposed of lavish tracts of pain—enough, had they only been farmed with decent efficiency, to have yielded one or two certifiable masterpieces or an entire shelf of lesser productions. Far from being thriftily invested, Carmichael's treasure of pain was largely wasted, allowed to slosh over the rim of his artistry, so as to slop his life and lives of those near him. In fact, we'd have to go to Golconda, or to an all-day, multigroup Pump 'n' Pull concert, to gather a representative sample of less efficient artists that he.

The efficiency of us parasites, in contrast, has to do with the hosts we exploit and is a function of the benefit we siphon in relation to the length of time we enjoy it.

Cholera bacilli are inefficient. They prosper dramatically, but very soon put their hosts and themselves out of business. Metastatic cancers and military juntas are only very slightly more adroit. Spirochetes and courtier classes do better. They live well yet suffer their hosts to provide for them lengthily. Bedbugs and bureaucrats make more modest demands, but for practical purposes are assured of them permanently.

The hardiness of the host is always a factor, along with the degree of external stress. The old regime in Francterre, for example, supported a useless nobility for centuries before the cost of doing so proved fatal. The A.S.U. is unlikely to be as lucky with regard to its similar plague of lawyers and lobbyists. One can, however, distinguish two broad categories. Inefficient parasites pillage their hosts in short order and then either move on or perish with them. Efficient parasites take a longer view and settle in more or less like rentiers.

Orcis deserves to be classed with the latter, early impatience not withstanding. He prospered according to his lights without destroying Carmichael in the process.

I don't suggest efficiency after my fashion. He had to have a celebrated host and a cloud of underlings to do his bidding. Fulfilling these needs inflicted unneeded damage. But give him his due, he behaved pretty well and was lucky.

After his nearly disastrous early maneuvers he restrained himself from excessive recruitment, swore off the deliberate incitement of pact-making binges, and posted sentries to curb those brought on by slips. As to new fiends sought by Carmichael on his own hook, Orcis established a policy of prudence and broke it only once or twice a quarter: no more than half a dozen new fiends at a throw, and none passed inside till billets had been provided. And when his lieutenants carped about being short-handed, he admonished them with a spurious quote from Pope Adamant: *"In spaghettibus non cacare est!"*

Mass excretion in Carmichael's bloodstream he naturally countenanced, along with all manner of roughhouse and cacophony. He gave a commander's cup for vexatious nightmares and lent the prestige of his person to camel-racing meets in Carmichael's medulla. But not while the man was composing. No disturbance was permitted then. As soon as Carmichael stationed himself at his typewriter, directly he left off putzing around—fiddling with the stapler, making paper-clip chains, stacking and restacking the visible bulk—the moment he actually got down to business and began beating himself into his book, all demonic turbulence ceased completely, or at least was supposed to on Orcis's firm order, and usually did, since infringers were dealt with severely. And whenever Carmichael entered a trance state, achieved perfect concentration and departed this world for the higher reality of Vama, the whole command converted to Mode "C," Solace, on cue from whichever officer had the watch. Maybe not as smoothly as it sounds here, or without some idiot's failing to get the message, but nineteen times out of twenty in less than three minutes, pliant fiendettes, soothing light shows, the works. Then Orcis would tip-toe round on inspection, trailed by an entourage and his (and your) servant, with everything soft and calm and headily fragrant, while Carmichael's knack weaved braids of beauty/truth.

Mode "C" wasn't Orcis's scheme, but let's give him credit for trying it when it was put to him, and for grasping its worth the moment he saw it in action. The author, Gonwe, was a lust devil, the last of Bogomul's recruits and the first of some lucky accidents for Orcis. She had better bona fides than he did when it came to world-class diabolic possessions.

"She" because Gonwe preferred to take feminine gender

when materializing in beastly or humanoid form. Her practice had been mainly in West Africa, a great center of demonic influence, and had brought her roles in many spectacular befiendings of the sort arranged by voodoo conjuration. Her chief credential, however, was New World and recent. In 1811, when her slave-dealing witch-doctor host tried to swindle a trader and ended up part of the merchandise, Gonwe crossed the Atlantic to the Frankish colony of Abattage, soon to become an independent republic. Her sojourn there culminated in responsible office in the bedevilment of Achille Déjeuner, president and dictator of the country: a twenty-nine-legion enterprise commanded by Furcas, a grand duke of hell, in a host of global renown and repugnance.

Under Déjeuner's guidance the Republic of Abattage achieved the world's highest per capita index of misery and widest distribution of despair. Some of the credit was due to a program of Furcas's for heightening the joy Déjeuner found in senseless cruelty. Gonwe was its director of special effects.

She might still have been at them but for Déjeuner's hemorrhoids and his decision to have them removed at the Napley Clinic in Otranto, Verdura. In strict secrecy, *naturellement*, under an alias, but one of the orderlies was an exiled compatriot with numerous relatives among Déjeuner's victims, including an uncle impaled, a first cousin garotted, a twin sister fed alive to zoo panthers, and an infant son eaten stewed by the statesman himself.

"Dieu est grand!" the fellow avowed silently, when he entered Déjeuner's room to empty the wastebasket and recognized the bed's incumbent. Wreathed in beatific smiles, breathing praises to heaven, he read the chart and backed

into the corridor, but returned that evening to tidy the bathroom and substitute a pint of insecticide for the fluid in Déjeuner's preoperative enema. The nurse who administered it was a gristly old yak, a former major in the Royal Ultranian Army. She wasn't put off by the squeals and appeals of civilians. By the time she supposed that her patient might not be exaggerating, Gonwe was homeless.

Along with thirty-five thousand other devils of all ranks and branches. Central Verdura was saturated with them, and when Furcas led the main body south to Tamami, even that sump had trouble absorbing them all. Gonwe went west. She drifted into Sunburst just as Carmichael entered his pact-making frenzy and persuaded Bogomul to take her on by enlisting at the bottom of the ladder and promising not to seek above that station. She broke her promise, of course, at the first opportunity and in three months was special assistant to the commander with private quarters in Carmichael's pituitary.

This after the first trials of Mode "C," the value of which Orcis was quick to appreciate. The trance state, after all, is where artistry lives. Reinforcing Carmichael's ability to attain it was as useful to his artistic development, hence to his fame, as bullying him to the typewriter each morning and giving him peace (Mode "B") while he was working. It was Gonwe's genius for flattery that let to the institution of Mode "D," Rut, during which all our resident lust fiends came temporarily under her command and she herself took the con of Carmichael's person. This too furthered Orcis's aims and his efficiency. The release produced by Mode "D" refreshed Carmichael for labor, and as shagging was his only physical exercise, it may also have forestalled premature infarction.

Orcis's next lucky break was me as his batman, lucky because he chose me for the wrong reasons. He found me of small appeal as a personal servant but entirely useless for everything else. Picking me freed a better hand for line duty. That's what he reasoned—and told me to my face!—in the aftermath of the billeting balls-up when he was getting his crew shaken down. He has never recognized my value, or appreciated the good I did him. My influence, insinuated below the plane of awareness in the course of our continuing close contact, furnished him a measure of prophylaxis against reinfections of untoward zeal. Observe:

Orcis's rooms in Carmichael's forebrain, ten or so days after I took up my duties. From without the muffled uproar of Mode "A." Orcis sits at ease judging its quality while reflecting on a meeting he's just had with Nenk. He retains the semblance in which he received him—spare and muscular male humanoid body in the tunic of a Roman proconsul on campaign, surmounted by a sleek gray wolf's head. I putter behind him, formed as an upright hippo with mittenish paws. Orcis sniffs, then rises and wheels on me.

"Haven't I told you to find new quarters?"

I pretend not to hear, continue my puttering.

"You! Offal! I'm speaking to you!"

I go into a scrape. "Pardons, Your Honor. What was it you said?"

Two inches of wolf tongue flick toward my left ear, which becomes a Nipponese fan, then bursts into flame. "You heard well enough. Answer!"

"Yes, Your Worship," whimpering, rubbing my injury. "That's so. That's what you told me."

"But you haven't done it, have you? Why not?"

"I've been busy, Your Masterdom."

"You used that excuse last week, and the day before yesterday. Do you think I'm a fool?

"Of course not, Your Perfection."

"Then why have you not carried out my order?"

"I'm happy where I am, Your Excellency."

"Simpering turd!" The roar knocks me sprawling. "Do you think my purpose here is your happiness?" His tone carves me into irregular thirds. "Speak up, filth! And come to attention! Is whether you're happy or not of any importance?"

I recompose into a cringe. "No, Your Mightiness."

"Correct. Thus you have no excuse. Thus you must be punished."

"Confinement, Your Graciousness?"

"Ha! In the bowel, I suppose. Wouldn't you love that! No, my dear. I said punishment, not comfort. For defying me I'll have you buggered. I'll have you buggered by electric eels."

"Please, Your Supremacy, no, I don't deserve that! I wasn't defying! I was only thinking of you, Your Serenity! Please!"

"Ha! Were you indeed? I don't believe you."

"It's true, Your Benevolence! I swear it!" This and the rest in a nauseating whine, combined with a contemptible grovel. "It's because I'm the senior spirit. In point of residence, that is to say. I don't expect you to check things like that, Your Potency. You've too many more important things on your mind. But all the lower ranks know I was here first. Nine years, Your Exaltedness, come this July. Lower-rank billeting goes by seniority in residence. If I'm ordered out, Your Splendor, that would break custom, and that might weaken Your Glory's authority. So you see, Your—"

Orcis kicks me through the wall of Carmichael's frontal lobe and up against his skull bone beside the temple. "Pahh! Ordure! Bunk where you please!"

Notice my influence in operation. In his disgust, Orcis ends up *not caring*.

And now listen to this. In response to my subliminal influence, Orcis adapted a *laissez-faire* attitude toward the designation of devil that joined his command. Meddling in pact purport is standard practice. Favoring his own branch would have been normal. But whatever sort Carmichael wanted was all right with Orcis. And this helped Carmichael write his books.

In fiction, imagination does the steering. Reason sits in the back and keeps its mouth shut—though now and then, if it notices something important, it may make respectful comment or suggestion. But what's under the hood? The writer's emotions. Without them his book won't make it around the block.

For vigor and health, emotions need stimulation. Carmichael's got most of theirs from his contact with devils. He had little contact with anything else except figments. So he made a lot of his pacts for professional reasons. When a book required a jolt of this or that feeling, beyond what figmentine stimulation afforded, or his fugitive contact with actual people and things, he signed up an appropriate power of devils from the appropriate branch of infernal service. They stimulated negative feelings directly, and positive ones by revulsive reaction. Carmichael came to depend on this procedure. If his pacts had been interfered with, his books would have suffered.

Orcis had no call to meddle in the first place, but certainly would have, if not for my influence. The pacts Carmichael made for personal reasons, for coping with his life as opposed to his art, kept pride devils in the clear majority. This too favored his writing. The sway of pride demons fosters an urge to be God, and the intermittent delusion you've actually made it. No one would even sit down to write a novel who isn't prey to nuttiness of this sort.

5 ″ A Better Class of Devil

—

A better class of devil began to join us. Not your celebrity fiends; they seek out the glamorous, and small glamour accrues to a person who's celled in a room. Your great princes like Furcas waste no time in beauty/truth mongers but abide instead with those who make the world's messes. But a higher grade of demon than we'd been used to. After *Vama* was published they came in some numbers—ex-thrones, ex-cherubs, even an ex-seraph. By the time the dog showed up, Carmichael housed sixty-odd notable devils of the sort your neighborhood exorcist trembles to tangle with and prayer-slingers sent out from Rome confront with respect. A few merit "mention in dispatches."

An early arrival was Hifni. Her branch was envy. She specialized in recent Ultranian writers, the way a professor might, or a biographer. She'd possessed Henry Whitlow until he took the gas pipe, and Sidney Baumholtz until he hanged himself, and Mabel Grace Davenport until she decided to jump from a bridge in Lutèce but grew impatient during a slow crossing and jumped instead from the bridge of the *Étoile due Nord*. Hifni had infested Miles Finnegan till he drank himself to death (the most boring suicide of her collection), and Richard Courlan till he jumped from a barnstormer's biplane flying over the Asgaard Centennial Exposition (the most colorful), and James Cod Wales till he jumped from the Emery Building into a pushcart full of casaba melons (the most touching if also the funniest, since what Wales couldn't bear any longer was being a humorist). She'd resided in Edward H. Carr till he cut his wrists, and in Paula Siltdown till she took sleeping pills, but her prize domicile was Arnold Manley.

Manley was still alive when Hifni left him, being driven north by his new wife on the Pecan Tree Turnpike from the beach house in Playa Almeja to the hunting lodge in Pebblefoot, Avalon. As they crossed the Sunburst overpass, a battered green Knauser shot up the ramp alongside them with Carmichael at the helm growling, "Flank speed ahead!" Seven tenths of his wits were still in the bungalow, or in the garage beside it more exactly, struggling with Chapter Fifteen of *Vama*. Two tenths were drafting a pact with the powers of envy, as required for a character he was making. One tenth was contriving to drive his car. He was just shy of a year into his madness. His first novel was still less than half built. Yet as the Knauser whooshed by a giant *YIELD* sign and passed the Manleys' Springbok on the inside, Hifni leaped from the laureate's nostril and flung herself between Carmichael's bared incisors.

Orcis was enchanted to have her with him but couldn't understand why she had come. Why leave the most celebrated living author in the Anglian language for an unproved unknown?

"Manley's finished," she told him

"Cancer?"

"His body's healthy enough, it's his will that's corroded. I know the signs, I've seen them often enough. I give him two months."

And Manley blew his brains out five weeks later.

Hifni helped Carmichael make his favorite character, Abë ent Anuri, the harp dancer who became High Queen of unified Vama. He gorged himself on envy devils till revulsive reaction aroused some feelings of love, enough at least to give Abë her salient trait. Hifni was the most potent of these spirits. But her great contribution came in her effect on Orcis. Having Hifni on hand relaxed him immensely. Her arrival direct from Manley gave him a sense of being in the big time and ratified his guess at Carmichael's potential. Her expertise of writers made him feel secure. None of her previous picks had been losers.

None had died of old age either. That aspect troubled him. The gist of Hifni's response: too late to worry.

"If you can't bear risk, stay out of writers. In countries where they're taken seriously the governments tend to kill the good ones. In countries like this, they tend to kill themselves. The only low risks in literature are critics. They always know which side the butter's on, and a suicidal critic is rarer than a buzzard with heartburn. I won't live in one, though. I like to mix with spirits from other branches. All you find in critics are low-grade envy imps."

Lugo, a gluttony demon (and a marquis), distinguished himself as a logistician of emotional stimulus in the regions of fear, terror, and dread. In Carmichael the vigor of such feelings was generally adequate, even to the demands of science fiction, thanks to their rigorous exercise during his childhood on attentions from his father and neighborhood bullies. Without additional prodding, however, he could not have written *Outcasts of Vama*—could not, that is, have drawn Danor ent Ronad, paranoid biologist and despot, who fled to Earth after his Vamian downfall and created the human race in his own image by recombining monkey DNA. Lugo provided. His forte was horrific manifestation.

Devils and humans have in common that they can transform themselves. We do so directly. You use costumes, instruments, makeup, props. On the other hand, you humans are much more inventive. We devils have to take our forms from nature, or crib them from some human's imagining. In Lugo your high-grade fiend's native malice was joined with outstanding mimetic ability and centuries of experience in dyspeptics and drunks. Their indigestion nightmares and *deliria trementia* furnished the models from which Lugo composed his repertoire. The best of it he auditioned in Carmichael's dreaming.

Carmichael got many recurring shudders from Lugo's murdered baby with maggot swarm and nose-gnawing brown rat, but what frightened him most was Lugo's giant cockroach. This apparition was the size of a stretch limo, with feelers like sport-fishing outriggers and a fuselage gleaming with slime. Lugo reproduced it in detail from an original hallucinated in Chilpanzango by an expatriate Anglian dipsomane named Berkham whose family paid him a stipend not to come home. Orcis had to ask him not to display it, lest it take Carmichael out with cardiac arrest, but authorized a showing one midafternoon when Carmichael dozed off on the couch in his study. The effect was exemplary. Carmichael had the couch moved out the next morning and never dared lie down on the job again.

A trio of ex-throne lust devils arrived before dawn on Carmichael's thirty-eighth birthday and set up a ménage in his left big toe. This was at the Sheldrake in Powhatten, where he'd gone to deal the reprint rights of *Outcasts*. At 3:00 A.M. he woke in profound depression. Part Two of *Lightbringers* was no good.

No zest, no life, no spark, no kick, no thrill. No punch, no excitement, no point kidding himself. Everything from Emror's mission to Gomorrah, up to the city's (and Sodom's) destruction by blast ray, was utterly dead, not worth a cup of warm cat shit. Eighty closely worked pages, four months of toil, every syllable, would have to go. The worst part was he doubted he could improve them, doubted he had what it took to get them right. He rolled from one side of the bed to the other, wondering if the whole book shouldn't be junked, while unconsciously drafting a pact with the powers of lechery as purveyors of the emotions Part Two required.

Twenty feet away, in the next suite, the great Nipponese actor Yomamo Itiro was dealing in the fashion of his ancestors with a depression of similar profundity. Four days before, while resting between takes in Kotaka, he'd had a vision. He saw, as in a movie, a street in Powhatten, and walking along that street the perfect boy, the one boy on earth who could ease the desire that flailed him. He dressed and went directly to the airport. In Powhatten he hired a car and had himself driven about the city. When he found the street in his vision, he waited. Two days later, at dusk, the boy appeared.

Seduction was superfluous. All the boy required was some money. But Itiro had too much samurai self-containment to hurry the long-awaited denouement. He kept the clerks at Fenice an hour past closing time to give his Ganymede a new wardrobe. He fed him at Le Lévrier, left his own food untouched, and gazed at him all evening long. He took him to hear guitars at El Retiro—as if whetting anticipation were needed or possible. But when they reached the Sheldrake, when Itiro had rented the grandest suite in the building and brought the boy up there and given him champagne, when he'd led him to the bedroom and kissed his lips and gently removed his new clothing, he found himself, of a sudden, void of desire, limp as the boy's wrist, totally impotent. After two hours, seeing that nothing availed, he sent the boy home with a rich present. Then he ordered a steak from room service, and when it came took the steak knife into the bathroom, and sat down in the tub and carved out his intestines.

No devil need be homeless long in Powhatten. Of the six hundred evicted on Itiro's demise, the greater part found new hosts by sunup. Their chief, a movie-star groupie, went crosstown to the Pimloco and joined Miss Claire Cartwright. The trio in question popped through the wall into Carmichael. With their help he vitalized his drooping chapters.

One we've already met, the able Enyeh, at the controls when Carmichael skewered Adele Ainsley. Each, besides, was an accomplished succubus. Their talents greatly enhanced the effects of Mode "C." And their triad romps enhanced Carmichael's fourth novel, inspired the tri-sexed ruling species of Jarp. Not much, perhaps, given Carmichael's scope of inventiveness, but the inspiration occurred at an opportune moment. Carmichael's knack never slacked from maximum effort, but during his fourth book it began to labor and needed every boost that it could get.

Finally, there was the wrath fiend Duke Agla. This ex-seraph had been condemned to a thousand years in obscure, lower-class hosts (one of them, oddly enough, Carmichael's father) for offenses against infernal authority. His sentence ran out in the tenth year of Carmichael's madness, along with his current host's stay of execution at Verdura Penitentiary, eighteen miles from Sunburst. Orcis welcomed him on board with full honors and made him his second in command. It gladdened Agla's heart to see the rages he had inspired in Carmichael *père* perpetuated in a new generation. Quality had declined, though, and Agla deplored that. Carmichael's wraths were commendably intense but depressingly liable to verbalization. His father never wasted good anger in words.

Agla helped Carmichael with a number of passages and fueled his famous wrangle with "Genghis" Kuhn. Agla also had notable contact with Carmichael's dog, but that is getting events out of right order.

6 ″ Orcis Got His Legion
—

Orcis got his legion the day Carmichael finished his book. This was under the revised table of organization instituted during the seventeenth century. The ten-cohort, three-to-six-thousand-fiend structure was junked as unwieldy and replaced with a trimmer, standardized formation: three cohorts of four hundred each plus a headquarters establishment. As Carmichael was struggling to destroy Vama, he called on the powers of anger to furnish him some extra resolution. Six ordinary wrath devils entered his person, filling up the last rank in Nenk's Third Cohort.

No action of any sort marked the event. The infestation was in Mode "B," Tranquillity. But when Carmichael laid the last page on the visible bulk and with nothing in tow attempted to sail from his study, word went around of a full-dress review at midnight.

It was held on the spot where Orcis had taken command, with size and semblance as of that occasion. The looming space was not exactly packed, but—give Orcis his due— there were plenty of devils. His original prediction no longer held the slightest whiff of chutzpah.

The three cohorts were drawn up behind their pennants in phalanxes twenty fiends across and deep. Onglebarth, Vadis, and Nenk stood front and center, wearing the triple pips of cohort leaders, two paces behind Troop Commander Bogomul. Facing them at a distance was Agla. Behind him the headquarters staff was formed in two ranks. A stirring display, if you're stirred by martial pomposity, and Gonwe had charged two dozen of her department to show up with oliphants and bagpipes. They were assembled to the left of the headquarters, tooting stridently in the Dorian mode.

Orcis kept everyone waiting for twenty minutes, sat in his private office vaunting to me—Saint Anthony, the herd of swine, like treacle. Then he whooshed down in the form of a purple mist and materialized to the right front of Agla, two and a half times everyone else's size, with his wings outspread and his stinger raised and quivering. He surveyed the complement, scowling haughtily. Then Agla began the shout that was taken up at once by the whole legion:

"OR-CIS! OR-CIS! OR-CIS!"

The vault above us echoed back the din. In the depths of his drink-sodden sleep Carmichael shuddered.

Orcis's scowl dissolved to a slavering grin. At length he raised his taloned hands for silence. Demonic laughter broke from his bristled throat, followed by a reverberating croak:

"MY. NAME. IS. LEGION!"

A great shout went up from all the assembled devils. In the depths of his drink-sodden sleep Carmichael mewled.

Orcis nodded to Agla, who gestured to Bogomul. Who raised a fist in salute, then wheeled about.

"Legion!"

"Cohort!" "Cohort!" "Cohort!" from their leaders.

"Pass in review!"

Onglebarth, Vadis, and Nenk stepped off to their units. The band took up "Vexilla Regis Prodeunt Inferni." The phalanxes wheeled and paraded past Orcis and his headquarters, under a fly-by of elements of the First and Third Cohorts.

When all had regained their original positions, Agla invested Orcis with the eagled baton of a legion commander. Then Orcis held forth. On his generalship, its meager and unpromising beginnings, its spectacular success, its unquestionably splendid future. Then he beamed and bellowed: "Tonight I have only one order. Amuse yourselves! Until further notice, this command is in Mode 'A'! Legion, dismiss!"

Hullabaloo and confusion. In the depths of his drink-sodden sleep Carmichael cringed.

Later on Orcis received his chief officers in his apartments. For boasts and self-congratulations, toasts in spinal fluid and snacks of gray matter. And vaunting by Orcis, as you may imagine. He recounted scenes from ersatz former possessions. How Pavel the Embittered had strangled the Metropolitan Evgeny with his own beard. How Cécile Rondine earned three of the Frankish crown jewels by pretending to be scandalized and shame-stricken when Henri IX requested a deviant caress. But also twitted Agla about his imprisonment, and Hifni for a supposed secret yen that Carmichael blow his brains out, so that she could keep her streak alive. And recalled events that from present vantage seemed humorous. Bogomul's fit of pique over Gonwe's promotion. His own worries when Carmichael insulted Everson Tordle and seemingly wrecked all hope of his book's being published. And so on, with Lugo joining in to play all the parts, drawing hoots and cackles from the whole gathering.

In this jocund mood, with the muffled din of lower ranks at rampage, no one remarked a low crunch around four in the morning, followed by a clear diminishment in the customary flashing of Carmichael's synapses. No one, that is, except me, trudging around with the trays. And Hifni, who'd been expecting it. After nearly fourteen years running at full power, Carmichael's knack had shut down.

It had borne up under incredible stress. It had turned deserts of pain into high-grade order. It might have quit in midsentence. Who would have blamed it? Instead it hung on to finish Carmichael's tetralogy, but not a day longer.

His madness continued, of course. It simply ceased to be creative.

The devils' games raged on. The higher fiends laughed and applauded in Carmichael's forebrain. In the depths of his drink-sodden sleep, Carmichael wept.

FOUR

1 " *Carmichael's Redeemer Was at Hand*

Carmichael's redeemer was at hand, was under his very roof at that very moment. No one realized, of course, least of all Carmichael. He didn't even know he needed redeeming. He didn't know he was possessed by demons, or that his sole means of calming them was smashed. All that occurred to him the next morning, when he crossed the living room and saw his wife cuddling a small dog, was that he hadn't authorized its presence. He brought this to Nicole's attention at once, and to that of such near neighbors as weren't stone-deaf, and when she reminded him that he'd been consulted, and asked how she was to know what his grunts meant, he answered at length. His mood was choleric, his mien severe. His accent was that of his birthplace, Pohuncus, New Guernsey. His lexicon often reflected that city's slum streets, and his tone the rampage of demons proceeding inside him.

"You knew goddam well what I meant, I've said it enough! Don't bother me with foolishness while I'm working! What do I have to do, walk around with a sign? Buy a fucking parrot and train him to squawk it?

"And don't tell me I was walking through the living room!

That's what any moron would say who'd never met me, who hadn't been married to me for nineteen years! Forty-three percent of my life! I've been here, where have you been? Don't you have any idea what I do?

"Of course I write books! Every idiot knows that! That's *how* I do it, it's not what I *do!* I make worlds, Nicole. Alternative universes! Any asshole can write a book. Jesus knows there's enough of them out there doing it! But can they make worlds? Hunh? That's a different story! That's not so fucking easy, try it some time.

"For years I've been making the world of Vama. The planet, its suns and moons, its four continents and seven archipelagoes. And all kinds of other planets in and out of that system. Rivinar, Jarp, Kiri-Dûm, a whole bunch of others. Including Earth as it was a million years back, with the continent Plato called Atlantis, when Danor ent Ronad created human beings. And Earth as it was ten or so thousand years ago when the Lightbringers of Vama brought humankind all manner of useful shit—agriculture, metallurgy, whatever. Till the Darkers took over on Vama and stopped the program, and whacked Atlantis out with a meteor. Remember what our Earth is known as on Vama? 3-16-Tansë, the third planet of the sixteenth-brightest star in a constellation named for a species of vermin, a cowardly, treacherous semi-aquatic rodent.

"I made the *tansë*. I made the *danga* that swims and the *lurë* that flies and the *nurna* that scampers around like a super-iguana. I made the *aesnir* of Vama and their three-million-year civilization, their language, their science, their myths, their traditions, their gods. I made the seasons of their year and the stations of their day. Ompharë, Disavi, Bisorghë, Harna, Litana, Norghë, Omturi. Birth, Growth,

Transformation, Triumph, Fall, Penance, Death. I made Mornur, No-day, for fasting and meditation, and Toranur, Urge-day, when all restraints and laws are lifted, a day for letting go and getting even. I made the Vamian year two hundred four point one four days long, so Toranur could be added every seventh year between Harna and Litana. The phrase *Avarni net Toranur*—'May we meet during Urge-day'—can have all kinds of meanings. If we had an Urge-day, this world might be less fucked up.

"I made *aesnir* education: direct spool-to-brain input of data done with a casque that fits over the head like a hair dryer. I made their art. The harp dance. The *lorghë*. The art of the *antorgha*, where the artist sits casqued at a thousand-key console, sending impulses to different parts of his brain, punching up the simulacra of experience, images of sound, textures of fragrance, chords of taste and color, emotions, events. Fantasies, memories, whatever, and when they're worked out, he edits the spoolings for playback so what he's felt is punched up in the brains of his public. I made Abë ent Anuri. She began as a harp dancer in a whorehouse on the farthest archipelago and ended up Karnt Gargh of the unified planet. I made Danor ent Ronad. He began us.

"I made the *qarn* of Kiri-Dûm, thinking plants who breathe methane and converse by telepathy. The *wumi* of Jarp I just got through making. They come—the pun's accidental—in three changeable sexes and reproduce by triangular cluster-fuck. Try imagining what that does for their social life. What it does for their morals and politics and drama. I had to work all that crap out in order to make them.

"Making worlds takes concentration, and not the kind you turn on and off like a light. I have to be in a world to

make it. I can't fotze with it at long range, that wouldn't
work. So for years, and years I've been commuting to Vama.
That's where I was when you *thought* I was here in the
living room. Six point seven parsecs, twenty-two light-years,
a hundred and twenty-nine trillion miles from here! And
you expect me to trot back just for some foolishness! Just
like that! Aggh! You don't have the flimsiest fucking con-
ception!

"You *thought* I was walking around! Know what I was
doing? That week, all last miserable month, if it makes
any difference? I'll tell you what I was doing, I was destroying
it. I was shoving the planet Vama out of its orbit, till the
pull of its suns split it fucking in two, and the chunks went
hurtling back into Omë and Narga, the thermonuclear fire-
balls they came from!

"Worlds end, Nicole. Ending them's part of making them.
Don't believe me, ask God. I'm sick of Vama, Nicole, I'm
fucking fed up with it. I never want to think about it again.
I love it too, of course, but I want to forget it, and destroying it's the only way to be free of it. So I did, I wiped it
out, I wrecked it forever. That's what I was in the middle
of doing.

"To an idiot, destroying things sounds easy, but nothing's easy if you want to do it right. It took me years to
make the world correctly. Destroying it correctly required
care. Look, put it this way. Two million people have read
the books. Twenty million have seen the fucking movies!
I've been running guided tours of Vama, and twenty million poor shits have been glad to sign up, to get out of this
half-assed world they normally live in. I do a crummy job
of wiping it out, and some of them will figure Vama's still
up there, and start hounding me to take them there again,

to make some more of it and show that to them, and maybe con or bribe me into doing it. Or I won't convince myself, that's the real danger. In a weak moment I'll think, What the fuck, it's still there. And before I know what I'm doing I'll go back there. I don't want that to happen, Nicole! I don't want that world on my mind, I'm too fucking sick of it! I'd rather put a bullet through my head!

"So I couldn't just bungle along any which way, even if I were in the habit of doing things half-assed. I had to take care and wipe it out correctly, so that not even I could ever reconstruct it. I make them right, I wreck them right, that's that!

"Think it's easy? Even if you're having fun, it takes concentration. No, that's not right! There's no word for what it takes to beam your mind twenty-nine trillion miles! And what about if you're dying? What about if you love the thing you're wrecking, but have to wipe it out or never be free? Hunh? Hunh? And you come with some blah-blah-blah right in the middle, and expect me to give a shit what you're blahing about! Aggh!

"It's a good break for us all that I'm not a brain surgeon! You'd be blahing around the OR while I'm trying to saw a tumor out of some poor fuck's head. There'd be corpses lying around all over. And brain surgery's easy compared to what I do. What's a brain surgeon got to watch out for? Three or four things. And he's got a team of trained people to help him. Me, I'm all alone! And I'm responsible for a whole universe!

"Would you blah-blah at God while He's parting the Red Sea, or blasting the piss out of Sodom and Gomorrah? You bet your ass you wouldn't, you wouldn't dare! All the Hebes might get drowned! God might miss His shot and whack out Athens, and there wouldn't be any Parthenon or Plato. You don't want awful shit like that on your conscience. SO DO NOT FUCKING BOTHER ME WHILE I'M WORKING! AND WHEN I GRUNT, THAT'S WHAT I FUCKING MEAN!

2 ″ *Carmichael Didn't Stop There*
—

Carmichael didn't stop there. He didn't even stop to get his breath. His harangue bowled on, in fact it gained momentum. I've decided, though, to present it in two parts with an intermission.

The decision was touchy. I like a good piece of ranting (as long as it's not aimed as me) and am loath to interrupt this one lest I mar its burst-dam/escaped-gorilla effect. However, I've been thinking about Nicole, sitting there on the couch, holding the puppy that started this whole business. Her knitting was by her left hip. Her dress was tucked under her legs, which were crossed at the ankles. Her eyes rested calmly on her husband, blinking only at his louder detonations. What did she see?

An *egomaniac* like the one you and I see. I list him first, though, only because we can connect to him. From Nicole's vantage he was off to one side.

More centrally she saw a *man in torment*. What, exactly, tormented him she didn't know. Nothing she did or failed to do, that she was sure of. Much of the time—right now, for instance—it was as if he had sat down in a nest of fire ants. In that state everything is an annoyance, even a puppy dog. Now and then, for no clear reason, the stings subsided. Now and then they were worse. She was drawn to him by an urge to give him comfort, although there was no effective balm for his pain, and although he resisted the gesture the way a wounded animal resists petting. At the same time she was repelled. If one gets too close to a person who suffers, one's own compassion becomes a torment. After years of diminishing oscillations her position toward this aspect of her husband reached equilibrium at a certain emotional distance, though less than arm's length.

A *nurturer* and a *destroyer;* a combination builder and wrecking crew.

How he fussed over his creations! What passion and interest he showed, what tenderness even! And he could be that way with Davy and her.

He'd walked Davy. Up and down in that little house on East Nelson. For hours some nights, when the child was cutting his teeth. He wouldn't let her do it, so he was nurturing both Davy and her, putting him to sleep, letting her get hers.

"Nah!" he said. "I can do this. I couldn't have him or nurse him, but this I can do."

Tough, of course, with a grin at male limitations. And gruff, ashamed to be caught being tender. And competitive, not wanting to be in her debt. All the same . . .

And the course he taught Davy a few months back. In religion, of all things, would you believe it? The man never went near a church, much less inside one, yet he spent all spring teaching his son religion.

"No special religion," Davy explained. "What he calls the core themes and some variations."

"Does he scare you?" Nicole asked. "He always scared us, his students, I mean, or at least made us nervous."

"A little. He gets very caught up in what he's saying, and you get caught up in him."

Nicole nodded.

"But he doesn't yell at me, and he's very patient, though sometimes I think he's going to bust."

"Why religion?" she asked her husband a few evenings later. They'd made love, but her body had stayed in the room.

"Basis of everything," blowing smoke at the ceiling. "I realize belatedly, in middle age. Of art and science, anyway, but what else is there? Trouble is, it's retailed mainly by morons and shits."

"It's sweet of you to teach Davy."

"Wait a minute! Teaching Davy is fun! Keeps me on my toes. Other day I'm exposing the dual character of the sacred. You know, helpful and harmful, blessed and cursed. Going real slow, Greek myths and the Old Testament, old Yahweh's obsession with vengeful justice. Because, you know, it's a difficult concept. Primitive, not really present in Christianity. And I say that, and Davy says, 'What about Mary?' And I say, 'What about her?' And he right away compares her to Zeus's girlfriends—Leda, you know, and Europa and Semele. 'No one asked her,' he says. If she wanted to be the Lord's handmaiden, is what he meant. 'And she suffered a lot, though she earned grace too.' And I say, 'That's it! And Jesus died for Yahweh's obsession, to free Him from it so He could be a loving father.' And Davy says, 'Like Job, so God would win his bet with Satan.' And we're off, I mean, there we go, discussing the thing, this incredible paradox where what you depend on for life and salvation is also what's constantly bashing you around.

You know, it's in Isaiah. 'I make peace, and create evil: I the Lord do all these things.' Imagine discussing a thing like that with your own kid! He's smart as hell!"

"In this house you have to be smart just for survival."

"Sure, I know, Carmichael the Cruel. But I'm having fun teaching him. And besides, the best way to learn a thing is to teach it."

"It think it's sweet of you to do it."

"Yeah," dragging smoke in. "It won't hurt him any. Teach him to hit a curveball, that would be something, but sacrality and such won't do any harm. Only thing I learned from *my* old man was how to duck."

But now a blast shattered Nicole's reflection. Her husband, as his present mood asserted, was also adept at smashing things up, beginning with the peace and security his nurturing side engendered. Irrational wrath, intolerant fits, insane demands for perfection placed on himself and others, and now an incoherent act that disturbed Nicole deeply. He had destroyed Vama. He'd grown weary of it and wrecked it beyond fixing.

Yes, no doubt of it, he'd turned middle-aged. That was cause for worry. The middle-aged, Nicole knew, were older by far in spirit than the aged. They felt sorry for themselves, as if everyone else on earth had stayed twenty or thirty. They spoke of laying down burdens and meant not accepting challenge, much less seeking new worlds. Did her husband have a new world to build? Nicole hoped so.

A *dedicated worker* and a *self-enslaved fool*.

I don't mean a *provider* or a *money-maker*, both of whom she saw also, but in the background. The money-maker had made the provider much less important. He was distinct because he made money for its own sake, and made much more than his family needed. Nonetheless, while Nicole liked money, she accorded no great importance to making a lot of it, no more than she did to being somebody's heir.

Work was another thing. She was old-fashioned enough to think a man ought to, and ought to go at it with integrity. Her husband worked hard. She respected him for it, and would have even if his books had sold poorly. But not if they'd had no more depth than *Soignée* and *Môde*. She would have tried to respect him for something else, for, say, making money, though that would have cost her a good deal of effort. As things were, she could respect him for seeking perfection.

On the other hand, his work had the status and character of a mistress, of a pair of them actually: a slut he mostly despised yet was gaga over, whom he trotted off to every single morning and spent the whole day with doing God knows what, then woke up in the night and scribbled notes to, and a snow queen whom he was pledged to in selfless devotion, whom he'd never even seen, much less possessed, but whose rumored grace and beauty were unearthly, whose acceptance of him as her slave he took on faith and then scourged himself doubting, whose commands he had to invent before fulfilling, in whose name he confronted horrible monsters on terrifying descents into himself, and for whose smile—a smile he would never see but which might perhaps someday be reported to him—he would sacrifice anything.

Nicole was not an especially jealous woman, but she found it hard to put up with these rivals. The hurt of his squandering attention on them, of his seeking beyond her, of his neglect—all this she tried and more or less managed to live with by reminding herself how much he needed her. She kept him in touch with the earth. Planet Earth, not one of his dream worlds! Without her he would float away and never come back. It didn't matter whether or not he knew this. Nicole did. But why couldn't he show a little discretion? Why did he have to rub her face in it always? Why demand that *she* defer to *them?* And why wasn't he man enough to keep them in line? It was disgusting the way they made a fool of her husband. No, the way he made a fool of himself!

Three children: a child her husband had been, a child he became, and a child he had never stopped being.

Nicole saw the child at the kernel of everyone, the child one had been at five or six. This useful approach to personal relations increases insight, lessens insecurity. It's not hard to do, the hard part is wanting to do it. If one likes children—and Nicole did—the effect is to make almost everyone more or less likable, or at least forgivable, in the sense of *tout comprendre*, etc. There are child-monsters, of course, but her husband hadn't been one of them. The child he had been was afraid for its life, and correspondingly eager to please, but too tense to be very effective at it.

The child he became was a petty tyrant of the sort most children start out as in the cradle but are usually trained to stop being. Her husband had had no chance to be one while young and had taken to becoming one in his late thirties, once he was successful, to make up for years on short rations of respect. He was no great trial for an experienced mother. The thing to do was let him have his tantrum, without showing any indulgence of his self-pity, or guilt at his ridiculous accusations, or apprehension when he went blue in the face. He'd be properly ashamed when it was over (though couldn't be expected to admit it), and on his best behavior for a while.

The child he had never stopped being practiced the trick of transformation. Most children do. Most people, however, stop being those children. Not Nicole's husband. What had he said one time about being a boat? This child was terribly lonely but didn't know it. He was the first draft of a man Nicole loved.

The man differed from the child mainly in power. He could flesh his transformations to the senses of others and insert them into alien lives. This power had drawn Nicole to him. Some people found it tiresome, or at best no substitute for many qualities that Nicole's husband lacked. It attracted Nicole, though. Once she had been its chief, almost sole, beneficiary. Now the best of it was exported to strangers, and came to Nicole as if she too were a stranger, through his books. That didn't matter. She loved him for what he was, not for what he gave her. Still, she liked observing his transformations firsthand, without having to share them with crowds of readers, even when they were packaged in self-centered shouting. A brain surgeon! God the Father! How wonderful! Absurd and appropriate at the same time.

Nicole didn't sort out these aspects of her husband the way language has obliged me to do. She perceived them as one does a ballet troupe or chamber orchestra: as an integrated ensemble with some differentiation of component performers. Those that, from her unique vantage, were most distinct might not have been noticed at all by another person. Some that another might focus on were to her so shadowy-faint as to miss attention. One or two she didn't note now would appear later: a father or a lover, for example. That was what Nicole saw that particular morning, during the early party of his lament.

3 ⫶ *"And Why Bring It Up?"*
—

"And why bring it up when you know I hate dogs to begin with. We've had maybe fifty dogs, have I ever varied? Okay, I admit I almost reconsidered when Brunhilde bit the old hag next door. There was a dog I figured was on my side. Felt like biting her myself plenty of times. But then came the doctor bills, the goddam wonder drugs, and her shyster son-in-law threatening to sue us. Turned out I'd been right all along, dogs are no good.

"And what about Spark, the one that ate Davy's hamster? Busted the cage and killed the little fucker. Not that I gave a shit, I can live without hamsters. But Davy loved it, remember how he cried? The trouble was he loved the scruffy mutt too. All I did was raise my hand, and Davy got mad at me. I know how he felt, it's a miserable feeling. Remember in *Lightbringers* when Karn ent Ortavi kills his brother Kor? Grief and anger all mixed up, and you don't know what to do with the one that's guilty. Justice or mercy, that's a terrible bind. A little kid shouldn't have to go through it. And all because of a goddam mutt!

"And the one that ate my sandwich! There was the prize! Bowser! I'll never forget that mutt. What a dumb fucking name! I'm teaching a class in the fucking night-school extension, all the way over to hell in fucking Spring Glades. Seven-thirty to nine every Tuesday and Thursday, with a wonderful hour and a half on the turnpike each way. Forty-

two benighted fucking morons, dragging their asses to night
school to get a degree. Not for education, nobody wants
that! Just a piece of paper so they can get promoted and
maybe keep up with the fucking inflation. The college
requires biology, they've got to take it. I have to feed my
family, I've got to teach. Not exactly what I dreamed of
when I was in grad school, but what can you expect in this
half-assed world?

"So there I am in Spring Glades, night after night, peel-
ing back the foreskin of ignorance. A thankless fucking
task if there ever was one, and also impossible with that
herd of dolts! Not that I blame them. They didn't make this
world either. Know who made this world? A sadistic
humorist! Who else would set things up so that dolts who
belong in college like a moose on a bicycle have to get a
degree or fucking starve? And the poor bastards worked all
day long and were all crapped out by the time I got them.
I'm bushed too, but that doesn't matter. I've got to keep
staggering on from chapter to chapter. Someone in the room's
got to stay awake, or the fucking dean might come by and
think he's made a wrong turn and walked into a flophouse.
One thing keeps me going. If I can make it through class
without murdering someone, without killing two or three of
the wall-eyed stiffs, and if I can make it home on the fucking turnpike without falling asleep at the wheel and killing
myself, I'm going to fix myself a Siberian Sunset out of a
whole can of juice and six or seven shots of Balalaika—
cheap domestic shit, no fancy footwork; all I can afford,
but at least it can punch. And then, when I'm three-quar-
ters zonked, I'm going to have dinner. Not what even my
stiffs call a regular dinner. A sandwich I make myself, but
at least it's all mine.

"Everyone thinks I'm a prick. Do I give a fuck? No, not me, they can think whatever they like. But if I was a prick, would I have to make my own dinner? You bet your ass I wouldn't! I'd have my wife waiting up to make dinner for me. But my wife, my wife, she likes to go to bed early. And what the fuck, why should both of us suffer? Besides, the mood I'm in, she makes the wrong face, or passes a remark, we're all in trouble, and I don't want this wonderful night to end in violence, because, whatever they say, I'm not a prick. So I make my own sandwich, because if there's one thing I hate it's warmed-over shit, or a sandwich that's been sitting around all day in the icebox, with the bread all cold and soggy instead of toasted.

"So there I am in class, dreaming of dinner, like a martyr in the fucking Colosseum, dreaming of harps while a lion chews on his balls. And there I am on the turnpike, staying awake, keeping clear of the abutments, by thinking about how good my sandwich's going to taste.

"—What's in the larder, Wickersham?

"—Cold cuts, milord.

"—Of course, fellow. I've given Cook firm instructions to keep cold cuts in stock. But what sort has she put by for this evening?

"—Milord, I believe half a pound of smoked ham.

"—Don't taunt me, Wickersham. I shouldn't be able to bear the disillusionment. Salami will do very nicely. Smoked ham is beyond my wildest expectation.

"—With respect, milord, I think your lordship has always found me a serious person, not given to idle jest on questions of weight. The twelfth earl, your father, always said . . .

"—Quite so. Quite so, old fellow. But nonetheless, I don't want to put my hopes up. What else is on hand?

"—Helvetian cheese, milord, and I believe coleslaw. And mustard, of course, and I think some Moscovian dressing.

"—Capital! But tell me now, old chap, is there really smoked ham?

"—Milord, I do believe so, half a pound.

"—By Jove, Wickersham! Now I remember me, I think you're right! I distinctly recall Cook's mentioning smoked ham, that it was (as they say) on 'special' at Wingate's. Ah, Wickersham, old friend, what a feast I shall have, if I don't go off the fucking road thinking about it!

"So I'm salivating for seventy fucking miles!

"And there I am, at last, safe and sound in my house, with my wife and little kid tucked away in dreamland. Just me and Wickersham, putzing around between the icebox and the table. I've made my drink and maybe gulped about half of it, and what the fuck, I don't feel so bad anymore. There we go, laying the stuff out. Coleslaw, dressing, cheese, here comes the ham. Not the whole half pound, someone's pinched a little. Somebody's moused off a couple slices! But why get my balls in an uproar? They didn't take much. If I were a prick like they say, I'd break someone's arm. Stealing my fucking food while I'm out slaving! But no, live and let live, that's what I say.

"So there's the ham, laid out all nice on waxed paper, and all I've got to do now is get the toast. My back is turned for maybe twenty seconds. Ten to get the bread out of the toaster, another ten to put it on a plate. And when I look around, what do I see? I'll tell you what I see! I see that goddam fucking shitheel Bowser, with his fucking paws up on the fucking table, polishing off the last of my fucking smoked ham! Cocksucker's come from nowhere like a rocket! I take two fucking seconds longer, and he's gone, and I'm going to have to think the place is bewitched, or that I've finally gone off my fucking rocker! And when I come out of my paralysis, when the scope of the disaster prints out on my cortex, when I link up the shit-eating grin on the scumbag's face with the fact that all I eat tonight is cheese, and I give him the kick in the gut that he's got coming— not the kick in the balls I was going to give him, because, whatever they say, I'm not a prick, even to a treacherous, thieving mutt—he gives a yelp would wake the fucking dead and shoots off to my loving wife for sympathy!

"And what about me? Whose fucking dinner is gone? Hunh? Hunh? That doesn't matter! What's the reaction I get from my loving wife, that I get from my own kid when he hears about it? Do they care that I've got to go hungry after busting my nuts all night providing for them? No! I'm a monster, that's what! I'm an inhuman beast! I'm I don't know what the fuck kind of horrible fiend! And the fucking dog, everyone's sorry for him! Poor Bowser this! Poor Bowser fucking that! Poor Bowser, did the mean man hurt your tummy! Aggh!

"So why bring it up in the first place? You know goddam well I don't want any more goddam dogs! I've got enough on my mind! My break for sending Davy to Cawdor is I don't have to have any more fucking dogs around! But what's my opinion count for? Since when does what I say cut any ice? You wanted a dog, you got one, what the fuck can I do? BUT DO NOT FUCKING EXPECT ME TO LIKE IT! AND IF *YOU* LIKE IT, KEEP IT OUT OF MY WAY!"

4 " The Dog Whose Advent Provoked This Amazing Tirade

—

The dog whose advent provoked this amazing tirade was unequal to it alike in size and ferocity, barely a month old, a pellet of fur, and nothing in its ancestry, base or noble, would cause it to grow very large or become very menacing. It was, besides, unsteady on its thin legs, incontinent at both ends of its runtish body, disoriented by its new surroundings, and hysterical at the roars that had suddenly filled them. Most of these traits warmed Nicole's maternal instinct. None would have bothered a healthy, dog-neutral man. But given the volume of fiendshit in Carmichael's system, and his record of strife with *Canis familiaris,* no dog could have wangled a friendly welcome from him. He might, however, have been a little less vehement had he seen this one's horoscope.

Orcis ordered it cast as soon as he came to realize the threat the dog posed. The work was done by one of Nenk's subalterns who'd possessed Bardesanes of Syria back in the third century and had hobbied in astrology ever since, boarding with a number of sound practitioners. He established moment of birth on info from Iscilblost and did a very competent job in short order, including comparisons with Carmichael's chart and with charts of our enfiendment, one based on my time and place of entry, the other on Orcis's. All the poor devil got for his pains was abuse. Orcis wanted to know the dog's weak points. It turned out there were few. Which Orcis wouldn't accept, couldn't face up to, so he made Nenk's subaltern eat the charts he'd drawn. The upshot of the whole business was to worsen

Orcis's flaws as a combat commander, overconfidence in himself and underestimation of the enemy.

But this is getting events out of right order. Carmichael didn't consult the dog's stars, but not because he thought astrology worthless. He was prejudiced only against people and animals and oddly open-minded toward systems of thought. Oddly, because he had had scientific training, which in its common dispensing seals the mind airtight. His training, however, had been uncommonly good. It immunized him against scientism and related disorders. That is, he viewed science as useful in dealing with certain aspects of reality but not to be puffed up into a religion. His antagonistic nature did the rest. Whenever science-worshipers, lay or ordained, took to fulminating bulls and proclaiming dogma, anathematizing heresies and execrating heathenish creeds, his middle finger achieved instant erection, and his lips emitted a flatulent buzz. He was tolerant of whatever the faithful shunned or couldn't account for, including creationism, the heritibility of acquired traits, clairvoyance, faith healing, and astrology.

The last had received the least of his scrutiny, and yet a few scraps of astrological reference lay on an important shelf in his mind. His mind, by the way, is worth moseying through. I used to take my ease there in the lovely days when I had him all to myself, and later on in the aftermath of lust seizures, or when he was drunk, when not too much activity went on.

Carmichael's mind has the look of a spacious attic into which a compulsive acquirer has for years and years been trucking disparate junk. Items newfangled and ancient, thirdhand and brand-new. Happened-on, scavenged, ungarbaged. Dumped here and there without any method or plan, though in our posited pack rat's bustlings among them he will have picked up this, disinterred that, rummaged in a corner for the other, blown off the dust, polished a bit with his shirtail, and set certain articles, so, up on a shelf.

To begin with, everywhere are piles of text. No form or subject is unrepresented. No indexing relieves the total jumble. Lithe passages from Speckshaft drape on lumps of theory. A sentence of dry argument by Weatherstone sops up a page of Festung's liquid prose. The bawdy parts of Petronius sprawl among anecdotes out of the lives of saints. Loose rhetorical figures are strewn all over. So too taxonomical terms and word derivations and aphorisms orphaned from their sources.

All about, besides, are human beings. Mostly from books. Mogulov's Lieutenant Champignonsky. Emperors out of Mandrill's *Rise and Magnificence*. A great herd of others, along with characters from movies merged with the artists who portrayed them. There's Egan Foyle arrayed as Captain Dastard. Cutlass, baldric, plumes, quiff-eating grin. This lovely woman is Lara Lamont playing Lady Heather in *After Strange Gods*. Why has she nothing on but black elbow-length gloves? That's how she looked on the screen of Carmichael's fancy during a memorably explosive wet dream.

People from Carmichael's life are present also. Most are shadowy compared to those from books or movies, but a few stand out clearly. That hulk in the back is no troll from a Skandian folk tale but Carmichael's longshoreman father, memory-bulged six- or seventeen feet tall. There he goes reeling about in high drunken dudgeon aiming swipes at that terrified child, six-year-old Carmichael. Whose mother is represented by an effluvium of cabbage and alkali soap and a disembodied expression of peace in adversity cribbed from the face of the Virgin in Piccolomini's *The Flight into Egypt* from a 1940 religious products calendar. Nicole is on hand in multiple incarnations. Here's Carmichael's favorite: a pair of snugly jeaned buns wiggling delectably out of Room 312, Julia Ebberly Hall, spring semester, 1959.

This gravelly voice belonged to a dockside saloon-keeper. It was reexposed to the ear of consciousness some time back when Carmichael went arummage for features from which to compose a renegade space bandit and came up with the man's rheumy eyes and richly veined schnozzle. They went on a shelf. The voice was attached, but Carmichael peeled it off and dropped it. The bandit's voice, he judged, had to be squeaky. And here's an interesting item: the texture of Frances Toomey's fourteen-year-old tit as recorded by Carmichael's left middle and index fingers during a feel copped in the Signet Theater balcony one afternoon in 1948. Three decades binned in here and scarcely wilted!

Mixed throughout are clots of emotion, some loose, most stuck to this or that, and the entire mess is goo'd with imaginings. Imagined triumphs, imagined slights, imagined martyrdoms. Imagined punches thrown in lost one-punch fights. Imagined retorts, imagined apologies. Imagined feuds and reconciliations. Imagined clevernesses never uttered. Imagined humps thrown girls never approached. Imagined kindnesses, imagined sacrifices. Imagined terrors, guilts, and exaltations.

And over here, on shelves above the clutter, are the imaginary worlds Carmichael has fashioned. The submarine world he visits most nights before sleeping. The world

of toy planes and micromidget pilots he built between ages
eight and eleven and still takes trips to every now and
then. No part of these and others has ever been shown
outside Carmichael's mind. But here, on this special shelf,
in the world of Vama.

Notice the scraps of astrological reference. Two. Three.
That's about it. Acquired like makeup smudges on the collar, or silky hairs on the lapel, in the promiscuity of Carmichael's reading, later on culled up and put to use.
Minuscule use, but every scrap counts. They help substan-
tiate the *aesnir* of Vama and their relationship with humankind on Earth.

Carmichael users will certainly remember that his Vama
dream presents the human race as the creation of a Vamian
criminal madman, and human civilization as largely the
gift of Vamian lightbringers attempting to make amends for
the madman's mistake, One of their gifts is the scheme of
the zodiac, an educational toy and metaphor-model showing opposing forces in balance, wholeness compounded from
contradiction, to help the predatory meta-monkeys get along
better with nature and each other. The scraps of reference
provide a few strands of detail. The strands are part of a
huge web. The web snares the Carmichael user in an illusion of authenticity. The illusion induces him to share Carmichael's dream. The dream, in the manner of dreams,
takes him out of this world, into an alternative reality.

Well, that's enough of Carmichael's mind. Astrology got
us into it. Astrology can now get us out, and into the luminous order of the dog's horoscope, a casting of which is
displayed on the bedsheet-sized chart that the boys in the
booth—thanks, boys—are lowering.

What strikes the interpreter first—here, and here—is

the triple trine of paired planets. Sun and Mercury at the Ascendant in Virgo. Moon and Jupiter just past Midheaven. Mars and Venus Capricorning in the Fifth House. Male-female planet pairings are benefic. Trine, a separation of one hundred and twenty, is a favorable aspect. The overall impression is of balance and strength.

The eye steers next to where nine would be on a clock, to the Ascendant, the degree of the zodiac rising at the eastern horizon of the birthplace (Sunburst, Verdura) at the moment of birth (eleven hours, fifty-two minutes, Stonehenge Mean Time, September 2, 1978). This is usually the most sensitive point on a chart, and here the first of the mentioned conjunctions is celebrated. The Sun is straddling the Ascendant, since the Native (that is, the dog) was born at dawn. Mercury is just below it, rising. Both are in the Native's sign, Virgo, the Maiden, of which Mercury is the ruling planet.

The Sun at the Ascendant confers power or influence, though its placement here in the Twelfth House suggests the exercise of this quality mainly behind-scenes. This last is reinforced by the Sun in Virgo, announcing service and humility—Christian virtues, worthy in all who possess them, but especially so in a junior associate. Mercury is the planet of intelligence. Those born under it are clever and fond of activity, gifted with dexterity and communicative skills. With the planet, as here, in the First House, the House of the Self, these traits are emphasized to indicate persuasiveness or salesmanship, which in turn reinforces the quality of influence supplied by the Sun at the Ascendant.

A planet's impact is strengthened when it is transiting the sign it rules. Virgo, an earth sign, gives solid grounding, common sense. Add in a strengthened measure of mental quickness and the product is practical intelligence, precisely what Carmichael has least of, hence what would be of most use to him in a companion. And had Carmichael had more than those few scraps of reference . . . Suppose that, like me, he'd spent twenty-six years in Guido Ponsigleone, in Maestro Guido's left kidney, to be exact. Suppose that, like me, Carmichael had bathed in the knowledge by which "Il Dottore" foretold the Biscay earthquake of 1740, by which he made Danzig a power in Europe during his stay at the court of the Grand Duchess Sonia. How poignantly Carmichael might have responded to the dog's Sun and Mercury conjoined in Virgo! The effect is vision plus discipline, as shown by the same conjuction's prominence in the chart of Elsbeth of Erleidheim (1157–1222), minnesinger, nun, abbess, and finally pope (1217–1222), the model for Carmichael's own favorite creation, Abë ent Anuri!

We now swing our attention to just past the top of the chart, where the Moon and Jupiter are paired in Taurus. The Moon, which governs emotion, is the loftiest planet in the Native's chart, a clear indication of powerful feelings. Which might be a cause for concern were they not balanced by intellect and common sense. In Taurus, too, the Moon is exalted. That is to say, its influence is purified. The inconstancy associated with Luna is purged, as are anger, hatred, jealousy, and spite, to produce a loving, loyal, forgiving nature. The Moon in Taurus suggests showmanship too, the power to improvise and entertain. The planet is so placed in the charts of Robin Speckshaft and dancer-impresario Serge Bolokovsky.

Jupiter in Taurus signals materialism, its elevation the will to dominate. But balance is the fruit of male-female pairings, and here the tendencies of the power planet are softened by those of the sentimental Moon. Power plus feeling yields philanthropy, the means plus the desire to help others. These planets in the Ninth House show religious temperament and spiritual development. This is no thievish Bowser or murderous Spark.

Similarly, when Venus and Mars are joined, as we see here, Martian aggression is curbed without loss of energy, Venutian affection is given constancy. Mars in Capricorn shows self-control and good timing. Mars in the Fifth House, here, creative force. And Venus so placed reinforces the already signified traits of loyalty and artistry.

Saturn in the Seventh House—here, near three o'clock— sounds the theme of loyalty yet again. Saturn in Aquarius amplifies it with devotion and self-sacrifice. A most interesting feature is the ringed planet's sixty-degree, or sextile, aspect to Jupiter. The tendency of Jupiter is to expand, that of Saturn to devalue or limit. These planets opposed would likely produce a boom-and-bust nature, jerking their native through manic-depressive fits. Well-aspected, however, as they are here, they signify political ability. Sextile aspectings of Saturn and Jupiter occur in the charts of Baldur von Ockstein, unifier of Almeiny, and Ultrania's own King Stephen II, the Liberator, who managed to abolish slavery without precipitating civil war.

We have left till last what pop star-mongers start with: consideration of the Native's sign. Virgo is a halfway house of the zodiac, midpoint in the cycle from spirit to matter and back to spirit, from intuition or faith to reason and back. Its element is earth, its quality mutable. In it, common sense and flexibility combine with mercurian intellect to yield a reasonable nature oriented toward service. Since, in the Native's chart, Virgo is rising, since it is almost entirely in the First House, and since it is hosting the Sun and its own ruling planet, these characteristics are powerfully reinforced.

To sum up, we have here a rational, practical individual who is also deeply emotive and spiritually inclined. A critic, if you will, with feelings, and respect for those of others. An *homme*, excuse me, a *chien du monde*, but no *boulevardier*. Gifted for politics yet free of your pol's lust for power. Talented as a performer yet unnarcissistic. Affectionate yet loyal, even-tempered yet lively, persuasive and nonetheless self-effacing, with a marked urge-cum-capacity to serve and aid others, putting up with their moods, as a buddy/counselor/cheerer-up/helpmeet/companion.

Now, as to the dog's getting along with Carmichael, one needs no help from the stars to figure out that the personality I have just described is uniquely well suited to accomplishing that nearly unaccomplishable feet. The stars, however, bear it out clearly. I shall not turn your stomachs by exposing Carmichael's chart. Venus and Mars opposed. Four other major planets in square to each other. Moon and Mercury mismatched in his sign, Pisces. Carmichael's horoscope is a disaster, in the root sense of the word. Nonetheless, comparison with the dog's reveals a strong tendency toward friendship between them, and of benefit in Carmichael's direction. Carmichael's Sun is conjoined with the dog's Mercury, showing ease of communication and mutual mental stimulation. That their signs are at opposite points of the zodiac suggests tension between them, but even stronger attraction. And the dog's planets are aspected healingly to Carmichael's afflicted Moon and Ascendant.

Yes, indeed! Carmichael might have ranted less fiercely.

5 "Good timing?

Good timing? What about in arriving at Carmichael's? The dog shows up just as Carmichael goes bookless and his talent shuts down, as the force of fiends inside him reaches legion strength and reels off on a more or less permanent rampage. Not a propitious moment, no question there. Before the dog had been on the scene twelve hours, Carmichael's brain wasn't fit for decent impulses. They couldn't walk the streets of his mind in broad daylight for fear of being abused or murdered. Not for years had he been so hopelessly evil of humor, and then he'd had students and colleagues to dump his spite on. Now Nicole's little dog got the full brunt of it.

The welcome he received, for instance. Verbalized wrath but, in passages, worthy of Agla. And when Carmichael was done, he flung to his study and slung the oak door shut with a thundering fwap. The dog was still trembling an hour later.

The business of the alarm clock, for another. It included a basilisk stare and a dragonish pounce, a snatching of the clock that shook the box seismically. It put the dog in fear for its life.

And what of the howl emitted, the blood-chilling shriek, when Carmichael found the dog chewing one of his sneakers? What of the assault that followed, the wrenching of the sneaker from those terrified jaws, the hurling of it at those scuttling hindquarters?

And what of the murder attempted and almost committed? Lurching one afternoon into the kitchen, en route to a fourth or fifth Siberian Sunset—made these days with imported Pervaya Lyubov, smooth as a teenager's bube, but it could punch too—Carmichael slipped in a puddle of puppy piss and fell heavily, nearly destroying his coccyx. Snarling, he got to his feet and went stalking the culprit. Cornered the dog in Nicole's room, bellowed and lunged. Missed by a hair as his quarry shot under the bed, and was down on his belly, groping in fury, when Nicole at last came to the poor thing's rescue.

And even when no spite was directed dogwards, when its objects were Nicole, or Flora the maid, or some hapless delivery boy or repairman, even when the man was outwardly calm, shut in his study despondant, or vodka'd to near coma in his bed, his pain reverberated through the house, and his gloom shrouded every corner and hallway.

No, not on the face of things very good timing. I don't mean merely for the dog's peace of mind. The dog's actual existence was in hazard. A time of greater peril cannot be imagined.

On the other hand, that may have been the point. When does the slender stranger destage in Dry Gulch, gunless, asking for soda pop at the saloon, except when the place is packed with desperadoes? Or, in an earlier variant, doesn't the sackclothed youth astride a plow horse show up at Camelot on New Year's Day, when the court is in most sumptuous array (of Tharsian tapestries and crimson pennants), and the deadliest quest, the one with the dragon, is portioned? Seen from that point of view it was good timing.

6 ″ *The Hero*

The hero need not know he's needed. Or that he's a hero. He may think himself the son of the churl who reared him, Swink the woodcutter or Gnof the herdsman, not of Count Reneval and the Princess of Faeryland. He may think he's come to court to see the tourney. He may even have been headed elsewhere, till a dying knight, unhorsed and run through at a crossroads, begs him to bear word of his fate to the Queen. The King, gulled by a traitor, or angered by the suppliant maiden's haughtiness, will have promised the quest to the next rider passing the gate. Or his knights, to a man, will be daunted by its deadliness, leaving none but the youthful newcomer to undertake it. No matter. Nothing the hero does is accidental. Every move he makes is full of purpose, as though he were acting on knowledge he wasn't aware of.

You humans compose such tales. You humans demand them. No reasonable lad would take on a dragon, but then no reasonable ape would leave the ease and safety of the trees to lurch about exposed on the savannah. Forced to? Diddly squat! Most apes stayed in the trees where they belong, and are still there, jabbering happily, picking their lice. Reason can't explain beings like you.

On the other hand, you find it depressing to think the universe and your career in it products of chance. Ten to the whatever mindless collisions of particles, and if one of them hadn't lucked out, the whole thing would be different. That doesn't satisfy either.

The point is you want meaning. No one else craves it. We imps, for example, couldn't care less whether things make sense or not. So, among other techniques, you make up stories that suppose a different sort of operator, neither reason nor chance.

Well, are they just stories, fantasies cobbled to give an illusion of meaning? Or do they refer to something that really exists? Personally, I don't care one way or the other, but I've had extensive contact with your sort of being, and efficient parasites understand their hosts. I've learned how to ask such questions and how to answer them. If I were human and cared what the world is about, I'd have to say that the kind of guidance system at work in the genre of fiction referred to above exists and operates in actual life. On animals, for example. On humans at one stage in your career. Elsewhere for all I know. I can't be bothered to think the thing out completely. Consider:

The Craigs (or the Crofts, or the Criswells) resolve to relocate—from Zeeland, Aquitaine, say, to Abbeyville, Zion. They decide (why isn't important) not to take Fido. They give him to neighbors or relatives, grab a jet west. Fido isn't himself. Acute anguish, morbid melancholia. Trots restlessly about, whimpers, and so forth. Mopes in a corner, takes no food. Then disappears. Fourteen months later, three thousand miles away, Ken (or Kay, or Karen) hears scratching at the door. *Ecce* Fido!—emaciated, bedraggled, missing part of an ear, but wild with delight to be rejoined with his humans.

How has he done it? Not by accident. Not by conscious plan either. The idea of a happenstance Fido trotting hither and yon, and by blind luck crossing the continent to the family's new home, is as goofy as that of a reasoning Uberhund who recalls his abandoners' mentioning where they were moving to, consults a road atlas, and plots his itinerary: Shoreline Turnpike to Racebury; Passroute A-7 to Moulting, Ponsonby, and Asgaard; A-5 to Las Nubes, etc. Fido can't know his goal, yet his action is purposeful. He acts on knowledge, information acquired through a sense humans have lost and processed by a faculty you have let atrophy.

Don't ask me to say what they are. We reasonable fiends have never had either. Reason supplants Fido's method, but does not necessarily surpass it. He and the hero have at least this much in common: something guides them, and they trust it.

So with Nicole's dog. His name, by the way, was Furfante, after the pet dwarf of the madman protagonist in Speckshaft's *Malaspina, Duke of Ancona*. Davy supplied it, supplanting Scamp, which was what Nicole had been using. I don't think he was being either ironic or prescient. I don't think Davy was aware his father was crazy, or guessed whose dog Furfante was destined to be, though perhaps Davy was acting on unconscious knowledge. The dog was still Nicole's at Christmastide when Davy came home on vacation, met, and renamed him. Nicole's, that is, in the eyes of human observers. The dog had his own ideas on the subject.

The consciousness of dogs is oddly tranquil. Oh, yes, dogs are conscious. The point is they don't know it. They're aware of themselves but unaware they're aware. If that sounds paradoxical, I'm sorry. You humans were much the same once, not so long ago either. As a species. In early life each of you is much the same now.

Tranquil, as I say, and oddly so, because their minds are really quite active. By temperament, however, dogs are religious. That gives their consciousness a peaceful aspect.

Cats, of course, are skeptics. Rats believe in nothing, just like us devils. As for other beasts, I can't expound. My vast acquaintanceship with demons includes infesters of just about all the fauna, including one who lived briefly in a pigeon that behaviorists at Bork had taught to play Ping-Pong, but I'm loath to speak except on firsthand knowledge. I know something of dogs. I sat out six years of plague some centuries back in the belly of a hound who lived near Uxbridge. Colleagues of mine who stuck with human beings found themselves host-hunting over and again, but dogs were immune to the illness and had plenty to eat, there being no way to bury or burn all the corpses. I'd possessed dogs before and have stopped in them since. That Hellenic for "dog" gave rise to the word "cynic" is something I have never been able to fathom. Dogs, as most humans intuit, are believers, a crucial aspect of their consciousness.

The knowledge of dogs resists communication. I can't explain what Furfante knew in his terms. He had no terms. I can't construe it in yours. Unreasoned thought deals with things whole without linear order. Putting a thing into words involves mincing it up, and then arranging the bits in Indian file. The best I can do is approximate what he knew by pretending he reasoned. Having clearly printed this warning on the bottle, here are his conclusions:

1. Carmichael was the most powerful being in the universe.
   a. His physical strength was unrivaled, now that "Runaway" Sledge had left Furfante's world.
   b. His psychic force was immense: only Nicole could contest it, and that only fitfully.
   c. His moral might was without bound: never for an instant did he so much as consider he might be wrong.
2. Carmichael's wrath was upon him, Furfante. Hence, his (Furfante's) life was in mortal peril and scarcely worth living.
3. If only Carmichael were to look kindly upon him, Furfante, Furfante would be in Paradise. He would fear not, neither would he want.
4. But Carmichael, alas, was infested by demons. They balked the benevolence he was capable of. (Furfante could smell us clearly, could hear our hoots, could make out the blotchings we left on Carmichael's aura. He also divined Carmichael's loving-kindness—what Nicole saw as his nurturing side—a poor shoot below the stony soil of the desert, that few human beings believed existed, and fewer thought might respond to cultivation.)
5. This demonic pollution might, nonetheless, be viewed dually: as obstacle, but as opportunity also. It made Carmichael suffer. Whosoever should, thus, divert his mind from his torment, or somehow ease it, or actually purge the demons from him, might be worthy in Carmichael's eyes of continued existence, and deserving for Carmichael's countenance to shine upon him.

6. Fear of Carmichael was the beginning of wisdom, but love of Carmichael was the middle and end.

7. All other beings—Nicole, Flora the maid, Mrs. Sned, everyone—were essentially powerless. There was no Carmichael but Carmichael, and Furfante was his dog.

Such was Furfante's knowledge, as closely as it may be tramped and trumped into language. I've put numbers in to make it clearer, but in form it was perfectly spherical and seamless. When did he gain it? Perhaps at the moment Nicole entered his life, bearing the scent of Carmichael with her. It may have motivated his glance. Surely he had it by the turning of the year, when he had been three months in Carmichael's presence, when Davy returned to Cawdor and an ever thickening shroud of gloom descended.

This knowledge compelled and guided Furfante's guest. His goal, unconscious yet clear, was as follows: to be Carmichael's jester, physician, and champion, to free him of the demons that possessed him, to transform him from a being of wrath to a merciful savior, thenceforth forever to dwell in Carmichael's glory, yelping Carmichael's praise.

FIVE

1 " *Carmichael's Dog Entered the Practice of Exorcism*
—

Carmichael's dog entered the practice of exorcism through a back door that some call art and others call show business. The navel of the world then was still Nicole's room, where an ensemble of canned fragrances—Comme Tu Veux, Tempête, dusting and face powder, *huile d'Anvers*, lip rouge, beauty and body cream—played behind the cool scent of Nicole's serenity and brass echoes of her and Carmichael's eventide coupling. The box had given way to sheets of newspaper. These, in turn, became superfluous. He slept on the wide bed and retreated beneath it when he craved solitude.

On waking he transited the hall briskly, drawn by enticements beyond it and hustled on by prudent trepidation not to meet the lord in maneuverless narrows, resisting the urge to pause by the sill of his door to gather seeped emanations of his person. His first stop was the kitchen, to be fussed over and given some milk by Flora. Then he was let out into the back.

There a number of ritual duties awaited, delightful in themselves and morally fulfilling as affirmations of faith and his place in the world. Chief among these was maintaining the emblems of sovereignty in the lord's name. Performed with pomp of preened ruff, flourish of tail fur, stateliness of gravely hiked hind leg. Beginning at the flower bed by Nicole's window, working east along the fence that bordered the Wimples, then south along the fence that bordered la Sned, freshening yesterday's blazons and erecting a cairn, usually at the apex of the perimeter, near the live oak with its drapery of long moss. Invariably Mrs. Sned's paunched amber catess had first to be snarled off one of the lawn chairs, or blared from mincy sipping at the birdbath, for no amount of clearly posted notice dissuaded her obscene, infidel trespassing. The birds, too, had to be harangued (not that the insolent snips paid much attention), and now and then a bullfrog hassled, and if possible cornered, captured, and dispatched.

Blessed are the believers! They can feel important and selfless at once. What's happiness if not that combination? The sincere among them make uncomfortable hosts, supposing one can manage to possess them, but the other sort are adorable, religious in temperament yet too poor in spirit to manage any sustained devotion. My Uxbridge hound, for example, who dined on his late master after convincing himself he was taking communion.

His type is much more common among humans, people who think they believe but don't really, who concern themselves with obliging others to pray, or to liberate mankind, or to serve their country. That's an elaborate and tricky way of not caring, but they too can feel important and selfless at once.

The whole idea of faith is senseless, of course. The dog's belief in Carmichael, for instance. As ridiculous as any other form of love, and yet one can envy the benefits some derive from it. Happiness, peace of mind, a sense of purpose, as expressed in sincere performance of ritual duties.

Gathering intelligence was one of them. This was mainly a case of updating the commonplace in a lengthy procession of shrugging sniffs, but now and then Furfante turned up something exciting. As, say, the pungent spoor of an outland night visitor, vagabond raccoon or touring polecat, garter snake or terrapin or land crab. Such received exhaustive analysis. He made historical-critical inquiries too. An ancient, fading relic of long-dead Brunhilda—that is, of one of her heats—left under the magnolia at the back wall of Flora's room was bottomlessly rewarding of consultation. He also studied shafts of autumn sunlight driven through the fronding of Mrs. Sned's gum tree to pierce obliquely into the lord's domain, and breeze-borne children's voices glottering in the bus that picked up the young Wimples. And on December days, when mist hung in the crown of the live oak and an enforced lethargy overtook plants and insects, he surveilled the moribund beetle as it limped beneath the sleeping orange and rose bushes, and nosed through the small rain to watch its droplets assemble on ragged cobwebs.

He gave these observances the care they deserved without ceasing for an instant to delight in them. Thus he rejoiced in Carmichael's existence. Carmichael lived! Every act and thought celebrated this truth. Ears were pricked for news of his arising, glances taken through the glass door that gave on the dining room. And if the dog failed to notice the event, rapt in research of some alien droppings or enraged by the idiot flit of wintering swallows, or drawn off yelping to a distant fence by snout-curling presentiment of feline incursion, he was properly penitent. The idea was to be in the kitchen doorway when Carmichael made his crossing to the study, to catch a scent and sight of him up close and pay him panting reverence.

In those days the order of the world did not yet permit Furfante's taking station outside the study. That would have been presumption of favor unearned, of grace unaccorded, and therefore impious, and therefore unthinkable. One might, however, trail Flora to the bedchamber to gather emanations of the lord's person. From the air, which was thick with them. From yesterday's socks, though these were not to be swiped for lengthy perusal. From sneakers, though these were absolutely not to be chewed. Then, when the bed was made and the laundry collected, when Flora called him out and closed the door, he withdrew beneath Nicole's bed for his meditations.

These were performed facing the study, head between paws, ears laid back, neck ruff flattened. Their theme was Carmichael's nature and attributes. His majesty, his power, his dominion, his unassailable justice, his terrible voice, his gashed tranquillity, his balked loving-kindness, his as-yet-unborn mercy, his demon-bred pain, his mortal need of a rescuing champion. At such times the world was sotted with Carmichael's presence, and the scent of his pain resounded like breakers on a headland, sometimes a low and slow-recurring crunch, sometimes an impatient, pitiless pounding. Till on a day Furfante went forth and calmed it. Then his reverie sought the theme of favor earned.

2 *Dead Calm*
—

Dead calm and glare of midday. Expanse of torpid sea, vast and horizonless, sky and water bleached to the same hue. Only Carmichael is afloat on it.

He slouches thirty feet up on the flying bridge, a recent structure storked above the wheelhouse, functional and ugly, like the rest of his tug. Four posts, canted inward like a squat oil rig, support a catwalk, a chair, and a slab of dashboard, twin throttles, twin tachs, and a spoked wheel; then they rise another few feet to support a stretched awning. Its postage stamp of shade slides port and starboard, one edge nudging Carmichael's butt, then the other creeping toward his left shoulder, as the ocean swell humps gently beneath the keel. The screws are turning just enough to give steerage. The wheel is held by a knee crotched between two spokes. Carmichael slouches down, barefoot and barechested, in sunglasses and ragged green shorts, squinting out into the distance.

Off where the horizon might be if there were a horizon, phantom books materialize and fade. Every few minutes he spots one to port or starboard. Each looks real, but he's learned to be circumspect. He notes its position, then looks away with pretended nonchalance.

Think of a man alone, gloomy in solitude, who spots an apparently pretty woman giving him an apparent come-on— in the lobby of a concert hall during intermission, or on the terrace of a café, or several pictures down at an exhibition. He hesitates, contrives to keep his shirt on, allows the situation to clarify, lest she turn out to have an escort or a harelip, lest her smile be directed at someone behind him, lest the incident, so seemingly full of promise, end by deepening his loneliness instead of relieving it. So Carmichael. He hums a few bars, keeps track with discreet glances, crosses his mind's fingers, bides his time. At last he looks back. And yes, by God! It's a book! A two-hundred-thousand-worder! Powerful as a dreadnaught, graceful as a racing yawl!

He resists the impulse to stand up and seize the wheel, to haul it around and ram the throttles forward, to bellow, "All hands on deck! Swing out the dory! Man the winch! Stand by to tow!" Already he can feel the drag astern, the bustle of the bookyard as it gets back in business, the joy and pain and fear and peace of book-building, yet he rushes nothing. He moves his knee gingerly, puts the helm over. He taps the throttles with the heel of his hand. The prow comes around and lifts, the fantail drops. A broad wake boils behind it.

Carmichael moves his knee, puts the helm amidships, steadying his course on the book's bearing. Sits up and peers ahead, sees the book's shape grow clearer, considers some approaches to construction. Begin at the beginning? Do the end first and work back? Build several sections at once, then weld them together? A smile crosses his face. He closes his eyes the better to savor the moment.

When he opens them, the book's aspect is altered. Ungainly, squalid, pocked with disgusting defects! On every side gross and irreparable flaws that make building it both senseless and impossible! Carmichael's smile curdles to revulsion—as if our solitary gentleman, convinced of a romance in store, were to make his approach and find himself face to face with a whore or a drag queen.

The book fades, it was never real anyway. Carmichael

throttles back, resumes his slouch, snarls an obscenity. And within him the demons, momentarily stilled, resume their headsplitting uproar and swinish romping.

What's that, a waterspout? Nicole's little dog comes whirling past Carmichael's bow. His sea, after all, is the living room, his bridge the sofa. Spinning clockwise, the dog bursts from the hall to the kitchen, like an acrobat crossing a stage, like a trio of Bokhara dancers, satin blouses and flaring skirts, flinging themselves along in a mad reel. Pause for applause, and now he bursts back from the kitchen, spinning in the opposite direction.

Carmichael seizes a cushion and wings it at him, but at the last instant takes some zip off the toss. Cushion pelts harmlessly by as dog exits hallward.

Carmichael's scowl softens briefly. What the fuck, at least *somebody's* happy.

3 ‖ *Furfante Attended Nicole*

Furfante attended Nicole much of the day. Cheerfully if looked at, joyfully if addressed, respectfully if her attention was elsewhere. Patiently when it came to baths and combing, playfully whenever play was her pleasure, ecstatically when she felt like scratching his throat. On walks when she could be persuaded. About the house if she knitted or entertained visitors. On excursions if she fancied his company.

Visitors and excursions more often than not involved Nicole's relations: one grandparent, three siblings, four uncles, five aunts, a sextet of siblings and siblings-in-law, a dozen first cousins, and an uncertain, burgeoning quantum of nieces and nephews. And though Tomlinsons were populous they were prominent also, deriving original prestige from Nicole's grandfather, Colonel Noel "Tommy" Tomlinson, hero of the Balmosas War and speaker of the Verdura Chamber of Deputies, and from her grandmother, the reigning matriarch, Edna Dawes Tomlinson (daughter of the Right Reverend C. Merrimam Dawes), then consolidating it through exogamic unions with notable families of the region, the Pucketts of Avalon, the Clydes of Fentacky, the Creels of Gloriana, the Starks of Jamesland. As a girl Nicole flapped happily in this flock. Then, abruptly, she was pecked from it. The occasion, of course, was her marriage. To everyone but Nicole it was disastrous.

Its haste and stealth argued shameful necessity. Those who bothered to count were surprised that Davy was born very nearly nine months after the wedding. Its presentation as a *fait accompli* offended the clan's old women of both sexes, who claimed the right of approval of prospective members. And if ever one might be turned down, Carmichael was he.

To begin with, he was a foreigner. Greater Powhatten was as alien to the Tomlinsons as Cathay or Hindustan, and in lower repute. He had no social background whatsoever. Financially his prospects were poor. And as for his morals . . .

Here two misapprehensions flourished: first, that Carmichael was thirty years Nicole's senior, a twenty-four-year error grounded in his having been her teacher that clung in Tomlinson minds long after truth should have expelled it; and second, that he had perverted his tutorial authority, to seduce poor Cynthia Stark's baby, an error propagated by cousin Ruth Ann:

"He came on to me, and I turned him down, and he flunked me." So Ruth Ann took to mewing. After which, a pause for effect, then: "Nicole got an A."

Half the family dropped Nicole at once, led by Dawes J. and Amy Clyde Tomlinson, Ruth Ann's parents, who displayed a revulsion that would have been excessive had Nicole joined herself to an orangutan. The other half, preening their magnanimity, suspended judgment on the moral question, allowed it just possible that a big-city northener of obscure lineage might not be a total savage, and agreed to give Carmichael a chance. They soon repented. Carmichael did not respond well to being patronized.

The doors of Nicole's own home remained open to her, but barely. There was a reason why she and Carmichael eloped.

The sole thing of consequence most humans do is rear offspring, yet most contrive to botch the job very badly. From among the many ways of achieving this outcome Nicole's parents chose that of doling affection in dribbles and in return requiring their children to live so as to minimize parental anxiety. In the case this meant, above all, to keep up appearances, and never, ever to risk respectability in quest of passion, excitement, fervor, or fun.

This program was wildly successful with Nicole's brother and sisters. From puberty on they were middle-aged in outlook, kept their little lives neatly tucked in, and furnished no distress to Daddy and Mommy. Nicole, however, was the family rebel. Despite all persuasion to the contrary, she thought the thing to do with life was live it, and that no one else could do that for her. She was, besides, the last child. Her parents proved too weary to crush her spirit. Yet, though Nicole was brave, she was nowhere foolhardy. Carmichael was for confronting her parents openly. Nicole knew better. Her mother had mastered all forms of emotional blackmail. Her father played his mild heart condition the way Misha Klepfiscz played the fiddle. So lest her and Carmichael's romance be crimped or frustrated, they married first and told her parents later.

The telling came at 10:30 A.M. on Sunday, October 18, 1959, the morning after the elopement. Carmichael met with Mr. Stark in the latter's study. As they faced each other, screeched phrases seeped in from the living room, where Mrs. Stark was having a nervous breakdown. Not an actual breakdown. Its symptoms vanished completely the moment she was convinced that Nicole could not be blackmailed into annulment. Few specialists, though, would have doubted its authenticity. "You'll be poor all your life!" she wailed. "And the two of you come from entirely different cultures!"

Carmichael had promised Nicole and himself that the meeting would end in reconciliation. He would comport himself so sweetly and tactfully that even a wild lion would be charmed. Nicole didn't put her hopes up, which was as well. Her father's first phrase made estrangement inevitable.

"Why pick on my daughter?"

Nineteen years later, poised before his typewriter in his own study and seeking within himself for a portion of rage with which to fuel the close of *The Twilight of Vama*, Carmichael suddenly realized why Mr. Elton Stark enraged him so fiercely: his approach was that of Dienst, fair Erica's father, that long-ago Sunday morning in Southwerk, New Guersney.

Carmichael, though, was no longer a butcher's boy. He

made the connection to Dienst, albeit unconsciously, and shook his head, smiling. "Not your daughter, my wife."

Nicole loved him for those words, but they did not bring him and her father together. Davy's birth somewhat restored her in her mother's affections, but no visit between them passed without her mother's imparting, one way or another, that while divorce had never smirched their good name, in Nicole's case it would be the lesser evil. Only her aunt Betsy Puckett remained truly friendly. No other family member would pay her a visit, or receive her with more warmth than one shows a leper. Each pretended great sorrow that poor Cynthia's youngest had thrown herself away on northern trash, and was now doomed to poverty, squalor, and shame. All delighted in secret. No clan of humans or devils can do without scapegoats. How else can the majority feel virtuous?

So Nicole lived seven years an outcast.

Her status changed, however, when *Vama* was published. These Tomlinsons were Ultranians, after all, and so were the Pucketts and Clydes and Creels and Starks. Literary merit left them unmoved, but money and celebrity went a long way with them toward redeeming people socially. Mr. Stark wasn't fully converted till his son-in-law's face appeared on the cover of *Now*, but long before that Edna Dawes Tomlinson had signaled Nicole's return to favor by inviting her and her husband to the annual matriarchal New Year's Day brunch.

Carmichael didn't go, and Nicole was glad of it. By then two cohorts of demons were quartered in him, and though Nicole didn't know that, she knew the effect. There wasn't a hope of his being sweet and tactful, and despite her relations' shabby treatment of her—because of that shabby treatment, in fact—she didn't want them insulted. That would only convince them they'd been right all along. What Nicole wanted was their respect and repentance.

In the next years she got them. Nicole was gifted, as things turned out, for the savage arena of family politics. So adroitly, in fact, did she manage her assets—her snubbers' guilt, her husband's success, her own good judgment, along with her good nature and concern for others—that she soon was a force to be reckoned with in the tribe, a counterweight to the rule of the decrepit in spirit.

She was no revolutionist, however. She made no move to depose the Empress Edna. But by the time the dog entered her life, her grandmother was past ninety, and Nicole was preparing, when the old lady passed on, to install Aunt Betsy as the new matriarch and succeed peaceably to power as her prime minister. So she was at home to well-wishers and respects-payers, to allegiance-pledgers, petitioners, and the like, and on the move among her constituents-to-be. Furfante attended her during these visits and excursions.

Furfante lay sphinxed beside Nicole on the chaise longue and let his auburn ruff be ruffled idly, while Alma Creel Tomlinson, unspeakably snobbish wife of Nicole's Uncle Arthur (and a prime mover of Nicole's ostracism two decades earlier), perched gingerly on the edge of the sofa opposite and gingerly probed what the new regime might mean for her—what penance she might receive, what reprieve she might hope for, what demotion in status she might have to bear.

Furfante sat at attention next to Nicole's handbag (which sat at attention next to Nicole's chair) in the impeccable parlor of Gloria Nance Stark, Nicole's sister-in-law, whose fetish it was to live in the previous century among overstuffed chairs with antimacassars and ottomans, loveseats with bolsters, sideboards with candle slides—as well as figurines, bric-a-brac, and doilies that she had constantly to realign, to leap from her chair and pounce and reposition, in the thrall of an overly rigid toilet training.

Furfante fetched sticks and tennis balls for Nicole's nephews, nipped cookie shards from the fingers of her nieces, and allowed his tail to be pulled by their grinning toddlers.

All without forgetting Carmichael for an instant. Wherever Nicole's whim took him, whatever her pleasure required him to do, and whether the lord was in his study, or lunging from room to room about the house, or pacing in the backyard, or stomping with lowering scowl around the neighborhood, or off in his car, Furfante continued to celebrate his existence. Carmichael lived!

At night, though, Carmichael's estrangement was heavy, his pain a weight on the dog's heart. Adream beside Nicole on the wide bed, Furfante composed olfactory nocturnes that figured Carmichael's pain and his demons' foulness. Sometimes the dog woke from such, heart thumping, coat bristled, to find the truth more horrid than the specter, to lie trembling in presentiment of Carmichael's ruin, in terror of emptiness and worldsend. Till on a night he went out and fought Carmichael's misery. Then his dreaming found the theme of grace accorded.

4 ” The Kitchen
—

The kitchen, 11:00 P.M., maybe closer to midnight. Carmichael is fixing his dinner. At 8:00 and again at 9:00

Nicole thought of fixing it, but the closed study door published a mute bellow: "DON'T BOTHER ME WHILE I'M WORKING!"

Carmichael, however, wasn't working. He had nothing to work on. That was clear from a day spent staring at his typewriter, now and then placing a sheet and pecking a title page, instantly tearing it out, jamming it in the trash. From dusk on all he did was read his own books.

He browsed *Outcasts* and the *Vama* for an hour, then settled down with *Lightbringers*, his favorite. He went slowly and carefully, recalling the effort of driving the sentences forward, phrase by phrase, often one word at a time, with phrases getting mangled, being cured or abandoned, and ideas proving unfit and being relieved, and the sentences themselves, what was left of them, having to be pulled out, regrouped, refitted, and then flogged forward across the page again—a day's struggle to advance one or two pages, much of which, too, would have to be retaken, since the next day always revealed shaky paragraphs that couldn't be reorganized without being withdrawn. He also recalled the ease with which the story sometimes rolled ahead after a line of resistance had finally broken, passages (sometimes whole chapters) flinging themselves onward unopposed, while he, as it were, sat and watched, scarcely involved, perhaps noting a bypassed pocket to mop up later, until the advance encountered a natural barrier or (what was most often the case) slackened to a halt from sheer fatigue, and the book had time to collect itself and dig in, and the slogging began again. He came on portions—a section, a phrase—that reflected his life. He relived the lived incident, marveling at how he'd transformed the original matter, pointless or ugly or trite, into something that had freshness, beauty, and meaning. He watched people and events teem from the pages, and wondered first at his former fecundity, then that now he had nothing to say, no more people or events inside him. He read and reread the end of Part One, twelve pages he had spent twelve weeks composing—the best pages he'd composed ever, the last weeks before *Vama* was published and he became in a week or two wealthy and famous. He heard the mournful horns, the hopeful strains of clarinet and oboe. Falsely hopeful, so the horns insisted. Then their prediction of doom, for all its being true, was engulfed in joy, as the strings, then all his orchestra, horns warmly joining, came on in pulsating crescendo. Carmichael's eyes were moist when he stopped reading.

Not for long; he threw the book in a corner.

"Moron!" he hissed. "Reading your own fucking book! Let someone else read the shit! Your job is to write it!"

Then he spent an hour staring at his typewriter. Then he got up and went to fix his dinner.

Where we now find him. He has chopped up an onion, three celery stalks, and two peppers, and has put the choppings to fry in an olive-oiled pan. He has added a teaspoon of capers, a handful of parsley, and lacings of this and that condiment. He has trimmed the fat from a gigantic T-bone and pressed peppercorns into the bloody meat. Between these maneuvers he has administered himself slugs of vodka, half-filling a shot glass from a bottle he keeps in the freezer and whacking the chilled, viscous stuff back onto his tonsils. By slug three he had become somewhat anesthetized to the roughhouse, gnawing, and howls of his resident devils, though (as may be imagined) the day he has passed has left them especially rambunctious, to the point where no

quantity of booze can bring much relief. Since slug five he
has been conversing idly with Wickersham, who stands
(attentive if invisible) by the sink. Now he prongs the steak
with a large meat fork, and (spatuling the vegetables aside)
flops it into the pan.

"Nothing like this in the old days, eh, Wickersham? In
the old days I ate for a week on what this thing costs."

"Quite so, milord. May I say that you've come a long
way."

"Hmm. I suppose," gazing into the pan. "But in what
direction?"

"I pray your lordship would take me with him. What
means your lordship?"

"In what direction, man? Forward or back?"

"I should have to say forward, sir. You've three books
selling famously in numerous editions, translated into every
civilized tongue. A fourth not yet published, yet the reprint
rights have gone for a million thalers. Two most successful
films have been based on your work, with another in production. Vama globes, Vama banners, Vama glassware.
Vama T-shirts, and what I believe are called Vama 'warm-
up jackets.' Dolls in the likenesses of your principal characters, and of extraterrestial fauna you made up. Regis-
tered Lightbringer Clubs throughout the Sovereignties and
in a number of towns in Mother Anglia. On the continent
as well, for all I know. There is even a Pump 'n' Pull group
called the Outcasts of Vama whom you are currently suing
with very good hopes. What more? A *Now* cover story.
Cascades of admiring letters. Not to mention great praise
from the critics, whose opinion I know you don't care a fig
for."

"All right, all right! Big deal! What have I done lately?"

"Milord?"

"Are you deaf? Are you simple? What have I done lately? I haven't written a fucking word in two months!" Carmichael pours out slug seven and whacks it back.

"Begging your lordship's pardon, I should say your lordship is being too stern towards himself. A few months are hardly an excessive period of inactivity between the completion of one long work and the start of another."

"Fuck inactivity! I've been busting my balls! No book wants me to write it!"

"I fear your lordship has left me behind again."

"What's the matter with you? No book wants me! I've no book to write!"

"For the moment, milord, perhaps not. But surely in time . . ."

"Aggh! In the old days I had books pleading with me to write them. Christ knows how many! I turned books away! I told them, 'Go find someone else, I'm too busy.' Or, 'Have a seat, take a number. Maybe I'll get around to you in ten, twenty years.' Know what I worried about? Living long enough for the books I'd given my word to. There was no way I'd live long enough to take care of all those I liked but couldn't promise. I felt sorry for some of them. Good books that would never get themselves written, or end up being botched together by dumbbells. Now I turn around, and no book wants me!"

"Milord!"

"I had people inside me, Wickersham. Hundreds of men and women, little kids too, hanging around in my brain begging me to invent them. Places, events, relationships. Animals, plants, machines. I could pick and choose. 'Okay,

So-and-so, you're in this book.' 'Sorry, Whatever-your-name-is, maybe next time.' Now, all at once, I'm empty! Aggh!"

He gouges the steak up and turns it, slams it down in the pan.

"Milord."

"Yes?" Carmichael sighs. "What is it, Wickersham?"

"Milord, the countess, your mother—may she rest in peace—asked me on her death bed to look after you. May I speak to your lordship without mincing my words?"

"Of course, Wickersham. There's no quibbling between us."

"Thank you, sir. May I say, then, without making light of your current predicament, that I believe you are reacting excessively to it. To begin with, the 'old days,' as you call them, were not really so pleasant."

"I could write back then, damm it!"

"You often had difficulties."

"Sure! Sure! I busted my balls! But books wanted me! I had people inside!"

"And will have again, very likely."

"I tell you, I'm empty!"

"Give yourself time, sir."

Carmichael shakes his head, whining, "You don't understand." He himself doesn't understand fully. He doesn't know why he's in torment, just that he is. He doesn't know that he's possessed by devils, just that he's never at peace save when building a book.

"Milord, self-pity scarcely becomes the acclaimed and wealthy. Your lordship has indeed come a long way forward. Very likely your lordship will go even further. But even if you should never write again . . ."

"Don't say it!"

". . . you should count yourself fortunate in your signal success . . ."

"It means nothing!"

". . . and the pleasure that your works have brought to others."

"Fuck 'em! Fuck do I care if they live or die?"

"I pray your lordship would view things in perspective. Very likely tomorrow, or next week, this, ah, 'emptiness' of your lordship's will seem but a bad dream. But if, as may be the case and had best be confronted, your lordship has in fact written all the works given your lordship to write . . ."

"Watch your step, Wickersham!"

"Greater writers, after all, than your lordship . . ."

"I'm warning you!"

"Speckshaft himself, sir, fell silent, at precisely your age, and passed the last years of his life without writing a line."

"Get the fuck out of here!"

"Milord, I merely suggest . . ."

"Out!"

". . . that your lordship need not trouble himself so."

"Get out!"

"Milord, your steak is burning."

"GET THE FUCK OUT!"

He sweeps the pan from the burner, nearly overturning it. Imbecile twit! He gaffs the T-bone out and onto a plate. Mealymouthed jackass! He shovels the vegetables on. Goddam mamby-pamby! And carries the plate to the counter in the pantry, a waist-high shelf topped with white Formica, installed especially, to Carmichael's design, for these solitary, self-made meals—about the only gift he gave himself on growing wealthy. No Bowser could poach his food now, not at this height.

He grabs a fork and steak knife from a drawer. He adjusts the cushion-topped stool and perches upon it. Still grumping to himself, he assaults his dinner.

Enter Nicole's little dog on Carmichael's left. On hind feet in tiny, mincing *bourrée* steps, nose pointed at the ceiling, blond eyes half closed, paws held daintily before its breast—like Anya Karlova or (better!) Dame Heather Ashford as the queen of the wood sprites in the bewitchment scene of *La Sorcière*. Carmichael lifts his head, chewing, and catches sight.

"Out of here, goddamm it, ya goddamm mooch!" Darts his glance about for something to throw. "Get the fuck outta here, ya fucking panhandler!"

The dog performs two slow turns left, as if Pechorin's score (not Carmichael's snorts) were on sound track.

"Bum! You get nothing from me, nothing but trouble!" Snatches a potholder and slings it dogward.

The dog takes no notice as the missile zings past his head; performs a slow turn to the right, then continues its progress *(pas de bourrée, en pointe)* toward Carmichael.

"Aggh!" His scowl softens. "What the fuck!" He grasps bone between thumb and forefinger and saws off the meat. He looks down at the dog (who now balances near his left calf) and wiggles the bone above its still-upraised snout. He flips the bone past the dog into the kitchen.

Does the dog actually bow, or does Carmichael dream it? No way to be certain. But he does make a graceful half-turn before dropping his forepaws and trotting to his prize.

Carmichael shakes his head. At least *somebody's* happy.

He chows slowly, watching the dog's concentrated work, noting inspiration balanced by thoroughness. Goes at the thing the way I used to go at a chapter. Carmichael finishes eating yet remains watching.

The dog works diligently, polishes, polishes; still working, lifts its eyes and gazes at Carmichael.

Carmichael gazes back, cheekbone braced on fist.

Carmichael's face is relaxed. He may even be smiling.

5 " *Then on a Morning*

—

Then on a morning the dog backed into the practice of exorcism.

Morning in Davy's room. Carmichael sits slumped on a wooden chair, elbows on his knees, head in his hands. He has been hove to in this bay for over an hour. Out beyond the bar the gale has dropped. In behind his frontal bone devils are howling. The book he has had in tow has gone to the bottom.

A worthless book he should never have thought of building. A book he is ashamed to have been connected with. That he couldn't stand. That he knows he's well rid of. That he nonetheless feels bereft at losing.

He'd been searching day and night, cruising in quadrants, with not so much as a speck on the horizon, not the ghost of a blip on the radar screen. Then a book floated toward him out of a fog bank. Its lines were attractive enough if one didn't look closely. Imposing bow, but not much behind it. Rakish funnel, flashy superstructure, but no weight to speak of below the waterline. A commonplace design that lent itself to cheap, prefab construction in a

new-style automated yard. A class thumped out by many
slapdash builders. Paint a name on, launch it with a splash.
Keep if afloat for a season, two if the weather held. Then
break it up for scrap to build the next one.

Carmichael despised it, yet he took it in tow, began
building it his slow way in his oldfangled bookyard. It was
the only book around, and he was desperate. He'd have
been better off, and he knew it, with a rust-pitted tramp,
grimy topside, smelly and squalid below, that at least made
no pretense of being anyone's flagship, yet not only did he
cable the thing behind him, and busy himself laying down
its keel, he told himself how wonderful it was, how (under
his touch, of course) it would turn out a beauty.

Yes, a very fine book, very distinguished. A splendid
book, remarkable, profound. Perhaps not as good as his
others, but what did that matter? Every book needn't be
truly original. And if, in the end, it wasn't quite up to his
standard, he could always bring it out under a pseudonym.
No reason to brood at this stage. It would be fine.

Even as he defended it he loathed it. By day all went
well enough. He buried himself in the details of construction—rummaging for words, welding phrases together,
hoisting sentences onto the page—and so forgot the shape
of what he was building. At night he remembered and knew
the book was worthless, and argued himself from the
knowledge, and hated it more. Like a cuntstruck duke taken
up with a carhop. No, like a castaway, who from sheer
loneliness assails a goat. No, not even a goat, a papaya, a
melon!

Having the hulk in tow brewed off-study tempests. That
was normal, all books did that at the start. But now he
boiled into them recklessly, throttles crammed forward,

driven not merely by devils but by his disgust, since only by reaching the study and getting to work could he forget for a while how loathsome his book was. Each day, on the passage across, he put it in peril, then fought like a hero to maneuver it out.

Today, though, he's bashed it into terrible seas, and driven it abeam, and let it capsize, so that he had no choice but cast off or sink with it. In mingled horror and glee he has watched it go under. Now he slumps, head in hands, grief-stricken, despairing—and despising himself for mourning such junk—while a rabble of demons riot inside him.

In comes Furfante, six months old and at his full growth. Eight inches high at the shoulder. Twenty from foxy nose to fur-puffed tail. Ten pounds in weight, though he looks to be at least twice that, due to the plentiful fluff of his reddish-blond coat. He trots to Carmichael and regards him expectantly, tongue lolling impudently from the side of his mouth.

Carmichael jacks his head slightly, lifts gaze from the floor. A foot and a half from his eyes, blond eyes twinkle at him. His arms fly up in surprise, his trunk snaps upright. The dog's entry is an affront, the dog's love of life a final, unbearable torment. Carmichael bares his teeth and swipes with his right foot—savagely in intent, but in the end feebly, out of a life of much drink and zero exercise.

The dog springs back out of range. Then he lowers his head, snarls in mock ferocity. Carmichael snarls back—nothing mock there. The dog crouches and leaps, sinks fangs into Carmichael's trouser cuff. Carmichael kicks hysterically, like an old maid with a spider on her ankle. The dog flies off, then bounds in to nip at his shoelace, then bounds backward as Carmichael swipes with his right hand. The swipe becomes a grab, pulls Carmichael forward, off the chair and off balance, in murderous grope. He lurches, trips, falls onto hands and knees.

"Aggh!"

The two quadrupeds confront each other glaring, lips alike curled back and nostrils flared. They growl. During the struggle that follows these growls continue, interrupted (in the smaller's case) by yelps and (in the larger's) by gasping. Ready? Action!

Furfante feints a snap at Carmichael's muzzle. Carmichael responds with a right-handed lunge. Furfante springs sideways and backward, then feints a bite at Carmichael's dipping left shoulder, dragging him around that way in a clumsy scuttle. Another feint to the snout, another lunge. Another sideways escape, shoulder feint, bungle leftward. And so on in a counterclockwise circle.

Now Carmichael refuses to lunge at the feint. In the first place, he's winded. More to the point, he has figured this out. When he catches his breath, he'll make a feint of his own. With his right shoulder. Then he'll sweep, upward and out, with his left hand. Once he gets fingers in fur . . . A lesson his tormentor won't forget.

Furfante has read his mind clearly. At Carmichael's feint, he springs to his left, not his right. The sweep misses clearly, and is followed too soon by a rage-convulsed right-handed grope. Carmichael flops forward onto his chest. And when he gets back on all fours and waits there blinking, immobilized by frustration and shortness of breath, Furfante plants his paws and preens his chest forward, raises the fur at his neck in a lionish ruff, rolls his head, and emits a diminutive roar: the fearless king of beasts in miniature! Next, he drops his head and glowers, paws the floor in parody of a wild bull. Then he goes into a snap-snarling, shadow-fight prance-dance, in all directions at once, all four feet in the air.

Slowly, Carmichael's face rehumans. He begins to smile. He gives a tentative chuckle. He starts to laugh.

Carmichael is laughing uncontrollably, for the first time in years. Deep-throated, healthy laughter convulses his torso. His eyes fill with tears, his mouth opens wider and wider. A devil scampers up along his tongue in the form of a tiny black tiger beetle.

The devil pauses hunched, its front legs gripping Carmichael's lower incisors. It glares out at Furfante from turretish black-and-gold eyes. It pinces rhythmically at him with pointy mandibles. Then it takes a last look back over its shoulder, spreads wing, and launches itself from Carmichael's person.

The devil grows huge and hideous, fills the small room with a dark and dragonate presence. Furfante glares up at it fearlessly, prances and snaps.

At once the devil collapses. A wisp of gray smoke hangs briefly near the ceiling, floats over Davy's bed, then filters under the sash and out the window.

6 ⁰ Art's Exorcising Function

—

Art's exorcising function works like this: in giving glimpses of (or actual trips to) worlds where order and beauty are the norm, art induces a state of internal balance that you humans find pleasant but makes you noxious to us. As when the light goes on in a roachy pantry, we parasites may feel like bugging out.

In fact, religion's approach to casting out demons—demanding we leave in the name of higher power—often owes its success (when it achieves any) to this property of artistic entertainment. Higher power rarely gets involved, has better things to do I should imagine than be at the beck of every priest with a project. On the other hand, there is usually some sort of show. Rhythmic incantation, swaying censers, spooky adjurations in dead tongues—as *"Draco nequissime," "Hoc est malorum expulsium"*—performed with appropriate histrionics in immaculate white surplice and purple stole. Not to mention the song and dance of more earthy religions, the masks, the rattles, the drums, the flutes, the cymbals. If the demoniac can forget what's supposed to be happening, he may be lifted to artistic enjoyment and thereby purged to a greater or lesser extent.

How well art fulfills this function is a question of the tenant fiend's strength of character in relation to the degree of balance induced. The latter's a function of the grace of the work and the possessed's capacity to participate in it. Music is especially effective. During a performance, say, of Bleichstein's Twelfth Symphony the ceiling of the hall (typically embellished with cloud-gamboling cherubs puffing plump-cheeked on long golden trumps) will be clustered with morose, shivering demons lately decamped from members of the audience. We hang about in dispirited homelessness like party hacks turned out by a reform wave, the sort of pasty-faced-time-servers who show up at their offices to collect their salaries and otherwise run errands for the boss (pick up the weekly bag down at the precinct, get visiting firemen drunk or laid or both) and in between swap jokes on the porch of the courthouse—not a care in the world, then bam! they're out, and one might almost feel sorry for them, except that reform never lasts long. So soon the concert will end, and former hosts lose the gift of weighing things rightly, and go back out of kilter and take us in again.

Some music, to be sure, works just the reverse. Just about all music-to-do-this-or-that-to—including, conspicuously, music to march in thromp-resounding boots to, past reviewing stands in smartly dressed ranks, tilting chins, swinging arms, tucking butts and bellies, carrying weapons and following flags. A lot of light classical. Most love songs from Powhatten musical comedies, particularly as crooned by middle-aged tenors of Sicilian descent in the supper clubs of resort hotels in Nezona. Especially the stuff whined through telephones while you're holding, and the stuff played on airplanes during takeoffs and landings. All sham infecting a host is a comfort to devils, and besides conducive to continued pact-making. This rule applies strongly to perversions of art.

Authentic literature is balance-yielding. Had Carmichael continued to consume it at the rate he established during his first years at Sunburst, he might have been less populously bedemoned. When he became a producer, however, Orcis and company kept him penned in his bookyard, and otherwise so bobbled his concentration that he read little of worth. The visual arts operate somewhat mildly, more in the way of restraining a devil's entry than in causing one already on board to bail out, though the windows, reliefs, and arches of a great cathedral can purge a considerable infestation if the possessed is properly responsive and remains exposed for any length of time. Dance is strongly exorcistic. Ditto drama and mime. Juggling and acrobatics work almost as well, especially when bisociated with comedy.

Participating in art, however, like making it, depends on a special sort of imagination (as distinguished from the common, low-octane variety that allows you to tell a duck from a derrick or compose the familiar features of your Aunt Phoebe from photons pitter-patting your retina). Carmichael's faculty for artistic sense was shut down, leaving him with but a residual thimbleful. Every healthy child is brimming with it, hence can wax ecstatic at Pop's insipid shows, but in Carmichael's state of near-total deprivation, the dog's early stunts just weren't artful enough. A little tepid peace, a little weak smiling. Nothing to cause a devil any distress.

His comedy act in Davy's room was different. He began by offering play. Carmichael refused to. He didn't know how, had forgotten play existed. What ensued was a play, a parody of nonplayful existence, aptly conceived, well cast, brilliantly acted. It transformed Carmichael from spectator to player. Then it made him laugh.

Certain kinds of laughter are devil-refreshing. Gloating and bullying laughter, for example. Cynical and sardonic. Snickering, sniggering, simpering, and smirking. The locker- or boardroom chortles of winners. The first grade's titters when Billy wets his pants. The happy hoots of Tim and Doc and Harvey as they wire the captive's dong to the field telephone, and then when they ring, see, he answers. Laughs that proceed from comfy self-engorgement, or from the discomfort of somebody else, give devils lodged in the laughers an uplift of spirit equal to that conferred on human beings by a sunny morning in the Helvetian uplands or a starry evening on a tropical beach. But to laugh without restraint at the world's absurdity, the loony fumblings of chance, fate's practical jokes, the endless slapstick of mortality, and, especially, one's own sovereign fathead-edness, or pompous ineptitude, or simple bad luck, and the personal discomfort such engenders—laughter of that sort balances the spirit and gives your squatter devils no end of bother. The effect of Carmichael's balance on us fiends inside him was roughly that of a severe earth tremor on residents of a supposedly tremor-free zone: shock and horror, sphincter-loosening angst, a general mindless streaming from quarters and stations, running in circles, squealing and staring about.

Not in my case. I mean, I didn't hurry. I suppose I was as frightened as anyone else (though not caring helps in such situations), but I strolled leisurely up through Car-michael's bowel while panicky imps rushed past me in both directions. I didn't rush because I couldn't be bothered to, and if ever you hear of some general or colonel or major strolling leisurely across a battlefield while bullets fly and shells burst all around, there's always an outside chance that he's a brave fellow, doing his duty, setting the troops an example, but the likelihood will be that he's merely lazy. Military men are especially given to indolence, which is why I've spent so much time in them.

In any case, all the others ran about madly, gibbering, squeaking, moaning, and so on. Many took the form of insects or lizards, as conducive to that sort of behavior. One, as we've seen, actually bolted, but his desertion went unnoticed in the hubbub.

Carmichael's balance subsided in a few minutes. After which we devils came to our senses, and were all, of a sudden, deeply ashamed. Except for me. I don't care how I behave, or what others think of me. I can't be bothered to feel ashamed of myself. The others, though, were ashamed of their dread and their cowardice. They didn't want to acknowledge how they'd reacted or give the event the seriousness it deserved. They all began to laugh at one another.

An incredible spectacle. Where I was, in Carmichael's stomach, at least five hundred devils were laughing their heads off, and the same thing went on wherever fiends were massed. Officers whooped and guffawed at lower ranks. Lower ranks giggled at officers. Both hopped in derision pointing talons and tails.

"Kivgu shat herself! Look at the ninny!"

"Did you hear the way Toz squeaked? You'd think he'd been buggered!"

The legion was convulsed in scornful laughter.

After a time the fit subsided. Sober fiends trailed back to quarters and stations. Each shoved the incident firmly out of mind, till none from Orcis down recalled a bit of it. Except for me. It was as if the legion were struck with collective amnesia, as if Carmichael's laughter had never occurred.

Thus Carmichael's dog preserved strategic surprise. The legion didn't know it was under attack, even though it had taken a casualty.

7 ⋅ The Casualty
—

The casualty was a low-grade envy fiendlet, the latest to arrive of some three dozen Carmichael had been admitting in dribbles for months. His pacts now reflected only spontaneous emotions, not emotions summoned for use in his work. Most of what he was feeling lately was jealous.

This was a new and deeply disgusting experience. He classed jealousy as the lowest of possible passions, the telltale emblem of inferior people, useless to themselves and the world in general. Even as a slum child he had rejected it. Nowadays he envied just about everyone.

He envied twits who didn't come up to his ankle their willingness to write the same book over and over and republish it every year with a new title, a book that didn't need writing in the first place. He envied book reviewers those republished books, and gossip columnists their fashionable dunces, and ghostwriters their imbecile clientele. *They* at least had something to write about. He envied reporters their crimes and wars and elections, their bottomless lode of topical nonsense.

He envied men he'd met in bars and on airplanes—the sort of men encountered by every writer, no matter what link he forms on the great chain of literary being—who on learning his occupation stared at him wistfully, and pursed their lips and shook their heads and said: "You're lucky, I'd love to do that, I'm full of stories. If only I knew how to write them down." Carmichael had regarded them with pity. Now he envied them, every last one. Not for their supposed stories. Those didn't exist. If anyone—Flora's boyfriend, Mrs. Sned's son-in-law!—really had a story . . . if an actual story picked anyone to compose it, that anyone would be perfectly able to put it in words. The men he'd run into didn't know what they were talking about. Carmichael envied them their illusions and ignorance.

He envied people who didn't care about writing but nonetheless seemed to have something to live for, some purpose in their lives, a thing to believe in. He envied detectives their pin-the-tail-on-the-donkey, brokers their seesaw, politicians their musical chairs. He envied slum kids their cabbage-reeking mothers. He envied the mothers their snot-nosed foul-mouthed kids. He envied drunks their booze, addicts their dope, lechers their whores, whores their pimps, pimps their garish cars and rings and outfits. He envied Davy his future and Nicole her present and himself his marvelous past full of books to be built. He envied the dog the stupid things he sniffed at, not realizing that what the dog believed in was him.

In consequence, though envy disgusted him deeply, Carmichael admitted envy demons. The latest had come in that very morning and hadn't yet been assigned to anyone's cohort when Carmichael's few minutes of balance occurred. If that was how things were going to be, the newcomer wanted no part of them. He nipped along Carmichael's trachea and went over the side.

Carmichael's dog observed the exit snarling, the dragonizing without the least hint of fear. A salute of some sort would have augured better for him, a respectful if hostile nod to an enemy bested, followed by a quaver or throb at the demonstration, if only in acknowledgment of a good *shtick*, one performer to another. He knew better than to expect benefit from devils, but it won't do to underrate us either. We're quite real and quite dangerous.

There's your young hero's weakpoint. He's *sans peur et sans reproche* but *sans* worldliness also. But did His Brilliancy notice? No! His Brilliancy wasn't even in the ball game.

The dog watched the envy demon wisp out the window, then turned his attention to Carmichael. Who now stopped laughing but remained on all fours. Whose chest heaved and whose shoulders drooped with exhaustion. Whose face was slack, whose eyes gazed back without seeing. Whose person vibrated sweetly in a chord of relief, below a human's ken, but the dog heard it clearly.

Think of a castaway on a raft in the ocean. Days without a swallow of sweet water. His lips are cracked, of course, his tongue is swollen, but those are mere outward forms of a deadly problem. His person is rancid with accumulated blood waste that his failing kidneys lack moisture to expel. But now, but now a rainsquall brushes by him. He lifts his face, he cups hands to his chin, collects one precious swallow of sweet water, enough to void a dram of poison from him. That relief is inexpressible.

But no salvation: the dram counts next to nothing. And brief. In moments he is in agony again. His short-lived relief may even worsen his misery. He looks longingly at the waves slapping his raft. Tries to lick cracked lips with swollen tongue. Fights the cramping in his back and belly. Reaches, draws his hand back, reaches, withdraws.

Well, maybe not now, but sooner or later, he'll scoop himself a handful of salt water and be more cruelly poisoned than before.

Carmichael gets to his feet. Still trembling with relief, but it is fading. Half-bends, half-waves a pat in the dog's direction, not making contact, not really looking at him. Shambles out into the living room.

The dog observes him pass in panting reverence.

Carmichael sits on the sofa, thumbs and then rethumbs an issue of *Môde*. After a while he shambles off to the study. There he sits and stares at his typewriter. By noon it will be pact-making time again.

Carmichael's dog lies sphinxlike in Davy's room, savoring grace earned and favor accorded, that chord of relief, that halfhearted gesture of gratitude. Later on he assesses his debut as a practicing exorcist, awarding some but not much self-congratulation. An artistic success but a practical failure, and not very fragrant of promise when coldly considered. The lord's pain was scarcely eased and only briefly, his ruinward rush but for a moment arrested, his poisoning nowhere in the way of a cure.

Carmichael's dog drops his head onto his paws. Not in despair. He doesn't know that such a condition exists. In meditation. Clearly a different approach is required.

SIX

1 " On the Last Day of Nationhood Week
—

On the Last Day of Nationhood Week, Mrs. Sned rested.
The fête officially marks the birth of the kingdom but
has taken on aspects of a spring bacchanal. Traditional
observances—parades, political speeches, picnics, and
pageants (of the Rising in New Mercia, the Stand at
Younker's Drift, the Swearing of the Deed of Separation,
the Signing of the Compact of Association)—have now been
joined by the running of the Avalon Stakes, the opening of
the professional baseball season, the fertility rites of vaca-
tioning college students, and the throwing of Deed Day
parties. One of these last went forward at the home of Mr.
and Mrs. Norbert Torkis, whose terrace and pool adjoined
Mrs. Sned's backyard and were viewable from her sewing-
room window. Guests began to arrive at seven-thirty. The
last did not depart till three in the morning. The moon was
full, the night unseasonably sultry, and Torkis (as usual)
generous with the booze. A number of lechers and lushes
were in attendance, plus at least two certifiable Jezebels,
Alma Wimple and Ellen Aycock. The event would, therefore, have strained the physical energies of anyone whose
vocation it was to spy on neighbors, and Mrs. Sned was no

longer a young woman. On the following day she took it easy.

I don't mean she showed sloth. She was boarding more than a cohort of devils, but only half a dozen of my branch, admitted years before during her pregnancy a means of putting up with that unwanted state. Their only current influence to speak of was in helping her forget her daughter's birthday. She did not for an instant forget her calling. She spent the afternoon sconced in a rocker on her glassed-in front porch, in repose but by no means inattentive.

Her vantage commanded one hundred degrees of the compass, from southeast nearly to west-southwest. It afforded a view of Marston Road and its sidewalks from midblock to the far corner of Wilde Street. It gave on portions of five neighboring properties:

The northwest quadrant of 3375—Dr. Wendell Firkin and his wife, Selma;

The frontages of 3373 and 3371—the Willard Raspberrys, the Claude C. Aycocks;

The northeast quadrant of 3369—Judge Jesse P. Cashew and his bitchy wife Doris;

The lawn of 3370—Nicole Carmichael and her foul-mouthed northern-trash husband.

The day was clear and Mrs. Sned farsighted. Thus, though not traipsing around, she stayed in touch.

At a little past four she observed a novel occurrence. Carmichael came out with the dog. She spotted them from the corner of her right eye as they descended the flagstones to the sidewalk. She locked on as they struck out across the street. She tracked them to the elm in front of the Raspberrys', then left around it and on, bearing due east.

The dog wore a red harness with a chromy chain extending backward therefrom. Carmichael wore a safari jacket by Wriston, fawn-colored suede Bouquetin leisure shoes, and knee-length shorts chopped from Royal Army fatigue trousers. These were ragged to the border of disintegration, patched but too far gone for patches to help, originally stone-gray but bleached to a cloudy paleness by innumerable washings. The legs flapped loosely above his chickeny shanks. The seat displayed crescent slivers of pink buttock.

The dog leaned forward, pulling fiercely, like a miniature sled husky on a desperate trek. Carmichael leaned backward, chain arm outthrust, like a neophyte on water skis. The dog's face showed earnest joy, Carmichael's anguish. Thus they proceeded, at scramble and lurch respectively, eastward out of Mrs. Sned's view.

Mrs. Sned pursed her lips in bewilderment. Not at Carmichael's getup. The jacket and shoes were new, but she'd been expecting them. They were birthday gifts from Nicole and Davy. Mrs. Sned made it her business to know what her neighbors gave each other. As for the shorts, she had never laid eyes on anything so disgusting, but they were entirely consistent with Carmichael's loutishness, mocking his wife and son for their nice presents, marring the gentility of the block like a smear of filth on a Samarkand carpet. But she couldn't make sense of what he was doing. Walking the dog argued an urge for companionship, or concern for another being, or an essay in household cooperation.

Mrs. Sned knew Carmichael. She knew all her neighbors. More, Carmichael lived right next door and had never tried to conceal or disguise his nature. He was foul-mouthed, ill-mannered, and crabby, mingy despite the gobs of money he got writing smut for degenerates in Powhatten, too good (in his own squinty eyes) for the rest of creation, concerned for no one and nothing except himself, and too big a bigshot to help out around the house. So he had been for nine years, and it was a tenet of faith with Mrs. Sned that no one ever changed, not for the better. What was Carmichael doing walking the dog?

2 ⁌ The Myth of Human Supremacy
—

The myth of human supremacy is endlessly productive of confusion. "Dominion over the fish of the sea," and so forth. Leave it to Genesis to muddle things up!

No one gave you dominion over anything. The universe is a single organism. Humans and devils are two sorts of cancers afflicting it. We at least admit it. You confuse yourselves.

Mrs. Sned's profile of Carmichael was essentially accurate, except as concerned his novels' content and readership. Her faith in the nonperfectability of humankind was not yet under test. But confused by the myth of human supremacy, she assumed that Carmichael was walking the dog. Actually, the dog was walking him.

I don't merely mean the walk was the dog's idea. On any given afternoon or evening, in any urban residential quarter, any number of dogs will beg, blandish, bait, blackmail, or browbeat human beings into walking them. Such hounds, however, seek their own self-interest in relief of renal / intestinal surfeit, of muscular tension, of emotional malaise, of loneliness, of boredom, of claustrophobia, of depression, of existential angst. Carmichael's dog had bitten off something quite different. He was walking a human, for the human's own good. It was the opening phase of a grand strategy and the culmination of an intensive effort.

The dog had been at work on the project two weeks—a lot longer to him than to you, given the relative brevity of canine life spans. During this time he received no encouragement, no indication that he would ever succeed, and multiple temptations to drop the whole business. Nonetheless, he stayed with it, as it were doggedly, but at the same time with circumspection. After all, few relationships are so tenuous-volatile as those where all the good sense is on one side, all the say-so on the other.

One thinks of Nick cold sober in the passenger seat while Vic is roaring drunk behind the wheel. And Nick hopes only to prevent something stupid. The dog was after promoting something intelligent, and few operations are so dicey-uncommon as those where a wise and loyal junior associate tries to move an empowered madman in directions he'd take on his own if he were sane.

One thinks of Scheherazade and her husband, and of many less fortunate examples. Ssu-ma Ch'ien got himself gelded for advising the Han Emperor Wu Ti to spare a guiltless general. Baldur von Ockstein landed in prison for pushing Almein unification to Rudolph IV. Cambyses killed his minister's son with an arrow when the minister hinted he had a drinking problem. Malaspina strangled his dwarf (Carmichael's dog's namesake) for making him smile. The wise rarely remain loyal to the witless. David got fed up with Saul. The loyal are usually so out of parallel nuttiness: viz., King Fordyce's crony Lord Bramblefield. To keep trying takes uncommon devotion. To survive long enough to succeed takes circumspection.

Carmichael's dog used the method of beguilement: the implanting of subliminal suggestion. By liquid lope into the lord's presence. By preen and prance in the lord's path. By lick and loll of tongue, by empassioned panting. By whimper, wink, and wag, followed by whirling. And by telepathy when not in the lord's ambit, during daytime vigils outside the study and nights asleep against the lord's bedroom door, for the order of the world now permitted such service on the bases of favor earned and grace accorded. At all times carried on with the utmost discretion. Curtailed for the duration of the lord's scowls. Closed down at once with reverential exit (as of courtier from throne room, priest from sanctum) when the lord began to curse and grope for a missile.

Meanwhile he had to cope with distractions. Not from Orcis & Co. Not yet. Orcis scarcely knew Furfante existed, and certainly didn't consider him a threat. Neither did Agla nor Hifni nor anyone else. Except your humble servant, and I took no action. Was it for me to tell His Cleverness that his command was menaced by a minuscule mongrel? He'd have kicked me through Carmichael's skull bone for my trouble. Besides, action *per se* is abhorrent to me.

Distractions, I was saying, distractions, distractions. The idiot twitter and flit of wintering swallows. The profanations of an infidel cat. The aroma of Nicole's baking, of Flora's feasts. The impromptu arrival of visitors, who had to be sternly barked at on approach and given olfactory vetting on admission.

The Nationhood Week arrival of Davy, who had to be given love and affection. The day before the poor chap had received telephonic notice from Susan Gwynellen that she wouldn't be keeping their date for the following evening, or seeing him, really, at all during the week, that she knew she ought to wait and tell him in person, that she still loved him terribly and always would, but that she really needed a full-time boyfriend, not one all the way up north there in Quagantic, whom she could only see during vacations and who'd be in school half his life before getting married, and that she was now seeing another fellow, and he would be annoyed if she dated Davy—Susan of the apple-firm butt and groin-brushing tresses, of the suckable earlobes and intelligent hands, long-legged, trim-ankled, laughing, starry-eyed Susan, who'd told him a million times how she adored him, and that she'd never ever love anyone else, who only a week before had been "dying" to see him.

A brutal whack. But did he get sympathy? Nowhere.

"Way it is, old buddy, you can't turn your back on them." This from his high school best friend Billy Willis, who like most of their class was colleging in Verdura and who resented Davy's leaving Sunburst to leap to one of the Great Schools.

"Serves you right!" That's what he would have heard from Amy Norris, the girlfriend Susan replaced, so he didn't call her.

"Poor thing, that's too bad, but you'll get over it." From his mother, of all people! Davy had expected a shoulder to cry on and couldn't appreciate his mother's wisdom. She could have murdered Susan for hurting her baby. She loved being the only woman in his life. She wanted nothing more than to cuddle and pamper him but knew it was better for him to treat him like a man.

His father was surely no comfort. "Best thing ever happened to you. Your brain's been in that kid's panties for months."

Davy prepared to suffer in solitude. Then there was Furfante nuzzling against him. Unlovable as he was, someone still cared for him. There was loyalty in the world, if only a dog's.

Davy was too self-absorbed to realize that he was getting the best of all possible solace, since he might enjoy the dog's love and affection without sacrificing a morsel of self-pity. And Furfante gave generously, without for a moment fearing that to do so might compromise his allegiance to the lord. He had the gift of weighing things correctly, thus grasped that one's supply of love isn't finite but (much the reverse!) magically expanding, so that spending some here doesn't mean that one has to skimp elsewhere. The more one gives, the more one has on hand and can give later. Hate, by the way, is exactly the same.

Davy wanted to play. Furfante accommodated. Stood on his hind legs and begged for biscuits, though Davy himself lost interest and left him balancing, stared off into space thinking of Susan.

Davy wanted his company. Furfante obliged. Gave up his post outside the lord's bedroom for one in Davy's, though the poor chap tossed and moaned for half the night, and gave off depressing fumes of rage and anxiety.

Davy wanted to walk him. Furfante complied. Joyfully too, though Sunday morning was miserable—raw wind slinging needles of rain. The weather, in fact, provoked the excursion. It suited Davy's mood to be out in it after half a night of imagining Susan and her new boyfriend.

Rain to sting his cheek, pain to cancel pain. Pain, anyway, was his portion, he was unlucky. Besides, pain didn't faze him, he was a rock. Leather pilot's jacket, collar raised.

Racebury Redmen baseball cap, bill canted downward. Tim Cullivan in another tough-guy role.

The dog sensed this temper the instant they stepped out the door and modulated his own behavior to it, expunged all trace of joy (though he still felt it) and stalked along sullenly like a Cullivan canined.

To the corner and on across Wilde, then north along it, stalking together under wind and rain, outcasts whom fate might buffet but never break—except that at Wilde and Nostrand fate very nearly did exactly that. Furfante, playing the tough guy, stepped off the curb. Davy, thinking of Susan, followed blindly. A horn blared and tires slid on the wet pavement. A late-model Phoenix Regal came within an inch of running them down.

Furfante emerges from beneath the front bumper and sets up an intense and panicked yelping. Davy emerges from his bittersweet daydream wearing a quizzical smile born of abstraction but seeming to indicate absolute fearlessness. A young woman emerges from the Regal.

An extremely decorative young woman despite casual attire: broadcloth button-down, jeans, and jogging sneakers. A terrific-looking girl, a total knockout! Her hair, the blackest black, is tied at her nape. Her eyes, the bluest blue, are wide with worry. Her small mouth is half opened, showing perfect teeth. Her skin, the creamiest white, is flushed at her throat and rouged with alarm over her cheekbones. She is tall but not too tall, slim but not skinny, and though Davy knows he could never have forgotten her, somehow she appears familiar.

"Oh, my God!" she says. "David Carmichael!"

"—!"

"Are you all right? I didn't hit you, did I?"

"Hunh? Yes. No. I'm fine. Hey, do I know you?"

Gorgeous roll of throaty laughter. "I can't believe it! This is wonderful!"

She looks up past him, grinning at the sky. Davy squints at her, bewildered. Then, "Oh! Wait! Patty . . ."

"Patricia."

"Greer!"

I will not flash backward two years to the home room of the fourth form at Erickson High School where this same girl had the desk one row behind Davy's and sat mooning all day at the back of his neck. Or perhaps not the same girl, a previous avatar, since the earlier model, Patty, then just turned fifteen, had acne, braces, and eighteen pounds of flab that Patricia did without entirely. Nor will I flash forward two days and a half to the fairway of the ninth hole at Sunburst Oaks County Club where Davy and Patricia are cuddled comfortably (the weather having turned completely, as it often does during Nationhood Week), where breeze-borne hints of music float from the clubhouse on whose terrace a Rising Day dance is in progress, and where a billion stars gleam down discreetly. I will say her father was Greer, the drugstore magnate, her mother Lee James, the newscaster, Greer's second wife, that her parents' divorce precipitated her flowering, that she spent two years at a ritzy school in Helvetia, was currently a freshman at Bork, and was going to break Davy's heart into little pieces, but more fruitfully than anyone else in his life, and not without first having pleasured him grandly. Having said that much, I will leave them there on the corner, Davy staring dumbfounded at Patty reborn, Patricia thinking how much he looked like a movie star—not Tim Cullivan, Todd Quinn the teen idol— and how much she wanted to bite his lower lip.

Furfante, though, has a busy week ahead of him. He is going to be the young couple's go-between and talisman, accompanying them on long walks and rides in the Regal, excursions to this or that party or classmate's. He and his lord will be often apart.

And won't good manners oblige a show of enjoyment, the simulacra of relish on being tussled with, of rapture on having his stomach scratched, of glee on setting out, of gloom on returning, of having no concern but the fun of the moment? Will he not feel forced to trot in counterfeit cheer, to sniff the boles of trees in feigned fascination, to pee and paw the ground in bogus bliss, and to thrust his snout far out in the Regal's slipstream with the grin and drool of ersatz ecstasy, all the while in inward lament at neglect of his mission? Or will he not in fact enjoy himself hugely, only to suffer guilt pangs later on, to doubt his resolve, to deem himself unworthy, like Speckshaft's Launcelot, now gaga now sorrowing, when joy of the Queen's sweet body drives the Grail from his mind?

Not a bit. Nothing of the sort. No pretense, no inward lament, no self-doubt, no self-blaming. No time or emotion wasted on human stupidities. He never forgot his quest yet was always lighthearted. His pleasure was sincere, its aftermath guiltless. He kept at his project no matter what else he was doing, beaming love of life to his fiend-ridden lord. Life swirled on around Carmichael, like a sun-warmed sea around a castaway's raft. Carmichael's dog dolphined in it yet kept concentration. Better, I venture, than you in his place, despite the supposed briefness of canine attention spans. Nothing vexed his resolve or disheveled his circumspection.

3 ″ On the Other Hand

—

On the other hand, nothing moved Carmichael either. Carmichael was out of reach. He'd stopped scanning for books. That, he admitted, was pointless. Just as, earlier, he'd stopped waiting for books to seek him. What he did now, day and night, in and out of his study, was try to conjure a book by rational thought, the most pointless of all possible exercises.

Some of these tries were grandiose, some petty. The most ambitious was inspired by the "many worlds" interpretation certain physicists advance to explain inexplicable particle behavior—the existence of other realities alongside the one that everybody observes. What if, in some parallel universe, the Associated Sovereignties of Ultrania were a republic instead of a constitutional monarchy?

He began with the name. Names he found easy. And turned it around, not A.S.U., U.S.A. The United Satrapies of Armorica, with the New World discovered by a Frankish explorer who named it after his home province. The Unified States of Ambrosia, after Ambrosio Piccione, an obscure Venetian navigator who never found anything but who, in a parallel world, might have caught the brass ring.

Here (as may be imagined) Orcis got enthused, dreamed of recognition for himself and Piccione, of being a character in Carmichael's book. Over and again he badgered Hifni about getting Carmichael to go with Ambrosia. Much to her credit, she refused to humor him. Piccione, she said, was just background, a way to work out a name. Carmichael wasn't going to tell his story. In fact, Carmichael wasn't going to write anything. His knack was shut down. Orcis nonetheless kept pushing, being just as pigheaded as Carmichael.

Soon enough Piccione was reconsigned to obscurity. Carmichael decided to put the split in the Dark Ages, the point where the parallel world diverged from ours. That would allow for a more or less clean break. The trade-off was no references to anything after the Round Table legends. If he needed something more recent he'd just have to invent it, discoverer included. A counterpart Speckshaft, for instance, and some of his works. Plays about the Romans, for example. Odd that Speckshaft hadn't done any. Anthony and Cleopatra were as good a pair of lovers as Launcelot and Guinevere.

Science could stay more or less the same. It dealt with the laws of nature, and those he'd not mess with. And since technology follows science, it wouldn't need much touching up either. Speed it up here, slow it down a little there, nudge it in a new direction elsewhere. Some sort of terrible bomb instead of the Death Ray. Cars that run on liquid fuel, not propane. But history would need a lot of alteration. A Bovingham, for instance, who refused to be crowned, and maybe a different sort of Stephen the Liberator, one who wasn't born rich, who didn't own slaves (much less fall in love with one of them); one who wasn't driven by ancestral guilts, or by the way Lil Demming moved her backside.

The challenge made him tingle—till it came to putting words on paper. Then despair seized him again. A parallel world, terrific! But Carmichael had nothing to put in it. He could reason up background figures and background events by fiddling around with actual history, but (like sets or costumes for a movie) background was useless without characters and their stories. Carmichael had none of these inside him. Every day his grandiose scheme swelled thrillingly before him. Then it disinflated and collapsed.

Then he tried to get people by naming them first. Carmichael enjoyed names. (So, by the way, had Adam. Naming things was all Adam could do. A muddled fellow in a muddled book.) Carmichael took to making up clever names in hope that interesting people would be born from them.

Sal Volatile and Ben Trovato: two cops or two robbers. A middleweight contender and his manager. Or maybe it was the other way around.

Loeb of the *Globe* and Tanner of the *Banner*. Cruz of the *News*, Grimes of the *Times*, Yost of the *Post*.

Fraud, Waste and Abuse, the Pump 'n' Pull group.

Wien, Weib & Gesang, attorneys-at-law.

Names whirled in his head, but no interesting people joined them, none with a story worth the telling.

His best course would have been to relax and forget his problem. In every form of impotence that's the best course. But try telling it to someone like Carmichael. He refused to relax, he kept on trying. Partly from pigheadedness, partly from habit. Partly because he believed a man ought to work. And partly out of dread of continued non-being.

Except as he was writing, he didn't exist. Nothing else in life meant anything to him. He was no better now than a wraith, than a ghost, than a zero, and didn't enjoy that condition in the slightest. His latest book had been praised and was selling. New fans wrote to thank him for enriching their lives. Professors continued to query and critics to flatter him. None of this counted. If he wasn't writing, he wasn't anything. And although he was trying and knew it, in fact trying too hard, he developed the delusion he was malingering. That only deepened his sense of not existing.

Besides, though he didn't know there were demons inside him, he knew the effects of Mode "A" and that writing eased them. Meanwhile, Orcis too decided he was malingering, especially when he lost interest in Piccione. He kept the legion at rampage. "To goose our sluggard back to work," he put it. And he canceled the daily program of lust seizures because, as he said, "We don't pay off to losers." That, too, kept Carmichael from relaxing.

Carmichael was tombed in himself, in his obsession. No information entered his looped thinking. He couldn't write because no book would have him. No book would have him because he couldn't write. And if, now and then, a trick of the dog's reached and charmed him, he fought against it, refusing to be pleased. As if he found misery useful—to curb his imagined laziness, for instance. Or that, having known relief and felt it fade quickly, he'd resolved not to be disappointed again.

The varieties of human stupidity are endless. I don't claim to know them all, even after thousands of years of close contact with you. But it was as if Carmichael were bedeviling himself, as if he were standing in for neglectful Orcis, as if he had figured out what the dog was after and was making a purposeful effort to have the dog fail. His scowls were equally angry throughout the dog's project, his curses as fierce, his gropes for missiles as frequent. No vestige of a smile encouraged Furfante. No pat, however abortive, rewarded his care.

4 '' *The Breakthrough*

—

The breakthrough, when it came, came without warning, though the ragged shorts might count as a tremor of tip-off. Nicole made them in the first year of their marriage, when the handful of us still hanging on inside Carmichael hunkered under searing blasts of love. She delegged and hemmed his fatigue pants at the knee, ending up with a useful leisure garment. He happened to have them on the day he was working on *Vama* and broke through for that first eighteen-page romp. From then on they were his writing trousers. Through *Vama* and *Outcast*, well into *Lightbringers*, till he joked, half-joked, that he couldn't write without them, but should someone else get hold of them and put them on, whoever it was could write as well as he did—that is, like a genius—even a twit, even an illiterate. Then they grew so bedraggled she hinted at making him new ones, waiting of course till he was in a good mood. Surprisingly, one hint was sufficient. He told her to buy him three or four pairs ready-made. Enough magic had rubbed from the shorts to last him forever. He was good enough now, he said, to write well wearing anything, even a tweed suit, even an ascot. Nicole put the old shorts away in the bottom of his bureau, more or less in the way she'd saved Davy's first shoes.

His getting new shorts, by the way, terrified Orcis. Bu Thigpen had had a lucky game sweater, and when Baronial Airways sent the suitcase it was in to New Alph instead of New Angers, Rameses goofed the ball over on six straight possessions and lost to Franconia Sovereign 31–3. Hifni said not to worry. Football and fiction were different games entirely.

Carmichael and Hifni were right, while his knack lasted. But that day, Deed Day plus one, he felt specially helpless, in special need of a talismanic relic, and exhumed the shorts and put them on. His looking outside himself for help might have been a sign that the breakthrough was coming.

At about 4:00 P.M., then—Davy having left for Cawdor very early that morning—Nicole decided to take her dog for a walk. What she thought of as her dog, that is to say. The dog had his own, different ideas on the subject. She found him vigiled sphinxlike outside the study, staring at, or as it were through, the door. His vigil that day was particularly pious. When Nicole clipped the chain to his harness he got to his feet, but continued to stare until she gave a tug. At that he set up his usual prewalk yelping, and began his usual whirls toward the front door. Then, as he and Nicole drew away from the study, its door swung open. Carmichael came forth.

The dog pulled Nicole around. She looked at her husband. And was put in mind of the day before's reading from Scripture (John 11:17–44). By his blinking gaze and corpsy pallor, his rigid mask of distracted anguish. He emerged at a shuffling lurch, as if joined to the dog by an invisible cable.

"I'll take him," croaked Carmichael.

"—?"

"I said, I'll take him."

"The dog?"

"No. The camel, the duck! What the hell's wrong with you?"

Nicole blinked in amazement. Carmichael was pointing down at the dog. Who had stopped whirling and yelping and looked back up at him.

"There. See? A dog. Now have you got it?"

"Are you . . .?"

"Can't I walk a damned dog without all this bullshit?"

Nicole held out the grip of the chain to her husband. With her other hand she opened the front door. As Carmichael took the chain, the dog resumed his yelps and whirls, then bolted lawnward. Pulling fiercely, his face showing earnest joy, he towed Carmichael along the flagstones toward the sidewalk.

5 ʺ Carmichael Being Walked by His Dog

Carmichael being walked by his dog is the subject of the clips I'll be showing presently. They reflect a period of several weeks from Deed Day plus one to Crowning Day minus two, April 7 to June 21. It may help to imagine them spliced in a montage sequence with the tenderized light used in shampoo commercials and a little afternoon music on the sound track, something refined yet sprightly, say, Gnazzo's overture to *The Rape of the Sabines*.

Having managed it once, he walked Carmichael daily. Always at just about 4:00 P.M. On an itinerary that never varied, a tour of his own favorite places, the spots where he got his most savory sniffs. Not from selfishness, however; as an offering to his lord.

Terrific! I hear you snort. Just what Carmichael needed! Like taking a blind nun to a porno movie! Carmichael had no sense of smell by canine standards, and an undoggish taste in odors anyway. What good were the dog's favorite spots to him?

Well, don't expect me to argue, I feel the same way. I too fail to see the logic of it. But don't single Furfante out for special scorn either. All religion is littered with similar senselessness. What good, for notable instance, are foreskins to Yahweh? What in heaven can He do with them? I wear a foreskin myself now and again when I materialize as a male human. Under certain conditions the thing has a certain utility. But I shouldn't want anyone else's, and there's no point in having more than one. Yet foreskins are what your pious Hebrews offer, and have been these past five or six thousand years.

And there you are: religion just isn't logical. The route the dog picked and kept was a ritual offering. Questions of benefit to the offeree don't pertain.

Paradoxically, however, Carmichael did benefit. Any walk in any direction would have done him good, anything that exhumed him from himself. But the tour Furfante arranged was especially tonic.

The first leg (which was always taken at maximum speed) struck south-southeast diagonally across Marston to the leafy elm in front of the Raspberrys'. No dog abroad on the block ignored this feature. Its roots had the status of a register or guest book in a Houndish Consulate or Muttlandic Embassy: signing in was *de rigueur*, perusing to note who'd been by a popular option.

Neither went smoothly, however, till the dog had straightened Carmichael out a little. At first, as soon as they were out of the house and the dog had secured from active beguilement, Carmichael tended to wind back into himself like a kinked phone cord. Here they are, for

example, on Walk Two. The dog tows Carmichael across
Marston, rump fluff metronoming *allegretto*. Carmichael
contrives to hang on and keep up. Notice the clenched jaw
and glassy eyeballs. His wits are looping loops back in the
study. Now the dog reaches the tree and quarter-rounds it,
stops and hikes his leg to sign in. But Carmichael, zom-
bified, plunges straight onward, onto the sidewalk, toward
Raspberry's lawn . . . till the chain comes taut and jerks
his left arm backward, twists him around, more or less
brakes his headway, but also drags the dog off his ara-
besque. Barely time to sprinkle, none to sniff.

But here, on the other hand, only ten days later . . . here
we have Carmichael's dog deep in perusal. His neck ruff
is sleeked back, his rump fluff peacocked, his wrinkling
schnozzle dipped to graze the roots. He vacuums slowly
outward from the tree trunk, examining the signatures of
confreres palimpsested one upon another. The signers' age,
sex, size, and genealogy, physio-emotional status and outlook on life, are all more or less precisely computable to
provide an effluviograph of each separate visitor and a pan-
ozonic whiff of the collective.

Carmichael shuffles behind him, keeping the chain slack.
The decomposing shorts have been replaced by a fairly
new pair in canary yellow. Jacket and shoes are as in Walk
One. Those calf-length, navy-blue dress socks, however,
impeach the sportiness of this attire, accent his pallid,
unhealthy, indoorsy look—that of a jury-tamperer or
embezzler pardoned this very morning after a long stretch
behind the walls. Yet, though his stare is still vacant, his
jaw is unclenched. He is letting himself be walked in a
proper manner.

Now watch closely, something important is going to happen, a direct result of the route the dog has chosen and a theme the dog will develop with variations.

Here: Carmichael looks down, is suddenly aware of the dog's absorption, and is drawn into it like driftwood into a whirlpool. His eyes unglass. His face acquires a look of alertness and interest. He is participating vicariously in the dog's research. Without actually collecting or interpreting data, *he recaptures the lost joy of doing science!* For the first time in months Carmichael is happy.

From the elm the dog's course was east bearing east-southeast, gently uphill to the corner of Marston and Ingersol. He soon trained Carmichael to walk this beside him, keeping to the sidewalk while he took the border between sidewalk and street. In front of the Firkins' (as we'll see in a minute) this border sported a shrub, a sort of dwarf spruce tree, under whose bottom branches the dog adored slinking, as into a den, there to blend furious snarls and ground-pawings, thence to burst with eyes flashing and teeth bared. In front of the Julius Wiggs' the border was grass, which Wigg let grow because sloppy grass annoyed Firkin and through which the dog liked to stalk with leopardine hauteur, muttering low growls deep in his throat.

All right, here are Furfante and Carmichael, side by side, late in April (or maybe early May). Watch Carmichael watch the dog go into his shrub act. Observe the animation in Carmichael's face, the spreading grin, the brightening twinkle. And here, the look of pleasure intensifies at Furfante's stately progress across Wigg's veldt. Carmichael is participating vicariously in the dog's transformations. Without actually becoming someone or something else *he recaptures the lost joy of doing fiction!*

On the corner stood a wedding-cake white two-story residence, with a half-moon drive and a columned portico, belonging to Mrs. Imogene Thierry Bland. She also owned the local UBO-TV affiliate, a brewery that had once employed "Runaway" Sledge, and two pure-blood spaniels, Mnemosyne and her daughter Thalia. The latter was usually at home to Furfante along the stretch of chain-link fence that separated Mrs. Bland's property from the driveway of 1627 Ingersol Street. Accordingly, his route swung south at the corner and mounted Ingersol to this spot. There we find him in this clip from Walk Thirty-nine, panting in anticipation, when fawn-colored Thalia frolics into the picture.

Furfante pokes his nose through the fence toward her, ticking it up and down in time to her hindquarters' wagging. She makes a coltish bound toward him, then draws back, then sidles up to nose against him, while Carmichael looks on in avuncular tenderness. But watch, wait, here! His face acquires a glow. He is thinking of a movie called *The Iberian*, of Lance Lockey and Lara Lamont trysting through the grate of an Andalusian balcony, of himself and Frances Toomey watching. He looks down at Furfante and shakes his head and chuckles: "All the fucker needs is a guitar!" Without getting a second younger *he is recapturing the intensity and ridiculousness of youth!*

The next leg was east-southeast across Ingersol to the border in front of 1626, the farthest point from home on the dog's circuit. This border, like the closely hedged lawn beyond it, was planted in a grass of especial softness and was, perhaps for that reason, the preferred excretorium of the largest dog in the neighborhood, perhaps in all Sunburst, a mastiff named Wotan who lived higher up on the block near the corner of Larraby. Wotan's productions received from Furfante the same degree of respect and appreciation that Carmichael had once accorded the works of Lobonsky, scrunched in a nook in the Sunburst U library. This Carmichael at length both noticed and grasped, so that *basking in the light of a revered master was yet another lost joy the dog, on these walks, taught him to resavor.*

But that's not what I'm going to show you now. Here we have our pair, early in June, moseying the strip of grass in question. Note the tints of color in Carmichael's hide: not real health, but not corpsy pallor either. And note the dog's enraptured concentration as he reviews a Wotan original: not new, but any Wotan can bear resniffing. And there, headed straight toward them, is the author himself, one hundred and ninety pounds of brawn and gristle, black muzzle aslaver in apparent ferocity, thick shoulders asway in a mastodontic trot. The equally outsized chap striding behind him is his proud owner, but, as you see, no leash connects the two.

Now Furfante gets a whiff, looks up, strains forward, eager to meet his idol in person. And Carmichael, feeling his arm jerked, looks up as well, and nearly fouls his powder-blue short trousers. He doesn't know your mastiff is usually gentle and Wotan a marshmallow. He goes, quite pardonably, ashen with funk. But look, he bends and scoops Furfante up, scampers to the waist-high hedge and drops him over, and now . . . But watch this next bit in slow motion:

Maybe you've seen a mother partridge put herself between her chicks and danger, have seen one flap across the trail in fury to peck a hunter boldly on the boot. So Carmichael: here he turns and advances on Wotan. Who rears playfully up and paws Carmichael's chest, driving him, panicked, backward, over the hedge. Here we see Wotan confused and a bit resentful as Carmichael flails his suede-shod feet at him. And now, more bewildered still, he feels his hind leg being nipped by Furfante, who has scrambled through the hedge to his lord's defense.

And now, here, everyone back on his feet. Carmichael and his dog confront Wotan and master, easily making up in vocal volume for what they give away in height and weight. And, here, Furfante and Carmichael retire, the former with his tongue at a rakish loll, the latter contriving to strut despite a painful bruise on his left hambone, *comrades in arms!*

The return trip ran due north, steeply downhill, to Marston and across it, then bore west-northwest, across Ingersol and gently downhill home. This they ended up taking at cruising speed, Furfante frigated off Carmichael's port bow with ruff and fluff hoisted, Carmichael rolling along acknowledging (in uncommon good humor!) the compliments, vocal and facial, aimed in his escort's direction. By (among others) Bradford Wyston van Rast, aged twenty-six months, who leaped to his feet in his stroller (nearly capsizing it) and squealed "Wow-wow! Wow-wow!" in ecstasy when he and Furfante met in the middle of Ingersol. By Eunice Bibbins, preschool daughter of Francine, the Firkins' laundress, who hung between longing and fear, reaching to pat Furfante while skipping backward, till Carmichael reassured her, thus: "Unless you're a sausage patty, he won't bite you." By Maureen and Doreen Aycock, postpubescent daughters of Claude and Ellen, whom Carmichael himself would have liked to sink teeth into. By their mother, whom he had in fact wolfed and been nibbled by several years back, in an incident neither now cared to remember. And by H. L. Swann of Deathwright, Texahoma, a business associate of Mrs. Bland's who appeared in our walkers' path as if by enchantment and held the following converse with Carmichael:

SWANN [poking up the broad brim of his white hat]: That's a right good-looking pooch you've got there, pardner.

CARMICHAEL [reining Furfante in and making a nod]: And you, friend, have a right keen eye for dogflesh.

SWANN: But, if you don't mind my saying, he's not pure.

CARMICHAEL: You're right. But, if you don't mind *my* saying, you aren't either.

And now for our last bit of footage. We are going to pick up Furfante and Carmichael almost at the end of their homeward passage, just as they start to pass Mrs. Sned's property. When we do, I want you look in the lower left corner of the screen, about a yard in from the sidewalk on Mrs. Sned's lawn, for an object of consequence in the ensuing scenelet, one that the camera, because of its angle, doesn't show clearly: a wrought-iron spike surmounted with this device, numbers and letters painted a luminous fuchsia:

S N E D
3 3 7 2

The thing is a gift from Mrs. Sned's daughter, who is visiting with her husband for Crowning Day Weekend. It has been stuck in the lawn no more than ten minutes.

Very well, here come our walkers. And there, the dog veers across Carmichael's path and bounds onto the lawn to check out the new landmark, leaving Carmichael halted on the sidewalk. Furfante noses intensely. He is picking up traces of the following:

Avian contentment—a sparrow has already used the sign as a perch;

Insect curiosity—lawn bugs have been making their inspections;

Human rage—while installing the sign, Mrs. Sned's son-in-law tore off part of his thumbnail;

Feline amusement—Mrs. Sned's cat witnessed this misadventure;

Ichthyan agony—the clerk who wrapped the sign had just lunched on boiled crayfish;

BUT NO HINT OF CANINE TERRITORIAL ARROGANCE! The sign is virgin!

And, here, Furfante remedies that sad condition, hiking his leg and sprinkling a few droplets—all he can manage; these walks are bladder-depleting. But deems this meager display inadequate to the occasion. So, here, he aims his bum toward Mrs. Sned's house and squats purposefully.

Here we have the house, the glassed-in front porch, and Mrs. Sned gazing transfixed in horror, right index finger pressed to bloodless lips.

And here is Carmichael, watching Furfante also, face lighting up with joy and admiration.

And Furfante, rising and turning, checking his cairn. Finding it good. Looking up to gaze at La Sned, who bursts from the front door shaking a fistlet.

Now back to Furfante, close-up of his grin, every bit as lank-tongued and foxy as that of the prince his father on having had *droit de seigneur* of the fragrant Colette.

Here are all three, Sned and Carmichael confronting each

other with the dog looking from one to the other as if following a tennis match. The dialogue goes like this:

SNED: Filthy beast!

CARMICHAEL: To whom are you referring? He's only a doggie.

SNED: Off! Off! I'll sue you for trespass!

CARMICHAEL [eyes tearing with suppressed mirth]: I'd think twice about that, madam, if I were you. That object [he points at the sign] is in hideous taste, to the point where its effect is violently laxative. I shall countersue for strain to my doggie's asshole.

SNED: Ouff! You're the most disgusting person I've ever met!

Carmichael, as you can see, breaks into guffaws, but his dog judges they've dawdled enough, springs to the sidewalk, and forges westward for home, towing Carmichael after him. And, here, a final shot: Carmichael looking back over his right shoulder, raising his hand to wave at Mrs. Sned, the sort of wave dispensed by a crack water skier as he slaloms on one ski past a yachtful of luscious females off some chic spa on the Côte d'Argent.

So much for our film clips. But as Carmichael turned and stepped along the flagstones, he felt an emotion he couldn't place—so much time had passed since he'd last experienced it. Three anger fiends popped from his ear in the form of hornets and streaked across the two lawns to join Mrs. Sned.

6 ʺ I'd Just Entered Carmichael's Thorax

—

I'd just entered Carmichael's thorax, which was mobbed with Mode "A"ers. I was bearing a note from His Radiance to the troop commander but refused to get excited about my mission. If the message was important, why send it with me? Anyway, there I was, proceeding spleenwards at a dignified amble, using my herald's wand to thrust back the revelers, and squealing "Legion Business!" lest they try to co-opt me for their filthy games, when everything went ominously quiet. The pace of Carmichael's circulation altered and wrought a portentous change in the sporting demons. All at once we were gripped in a trembling stillness.

Maybe you've been in Tamami in September, or on Erics- or Edgarsisle in the Balmosas, during the prelude to a tropical storm. Maybe you've felt the hush, the palms' expectation, the heaviness stifling the wind and all winged creatures. If so, then you know what I mean. It was like that. And I, for my part, knew what *it* meant. So did the others. Some devils have seen a bit more, some a bit less, but there are no rookies. Every fiend in the universe is coeval with it. We've infested human beings since your species emerged. We're all familiar with the onset of love.

Which certainly doesn't mean we've all gotten used to it. On the contrary, each time it seems worse. Certain things can help one bear the anxiety. Training, discipline, *esprit de corps*. Attachment to host such as comes with long residence. Commitment to branch such as commonly goes with high rank. But the normal reaction is diarrhetic terror, stunned paralysis followed by headlong flight.

Outside, the dog had just gone into his squat. Many

things had occurred to endear him to Carmichael, but that gesture tipped the scales over. It exactly expressed feelings toward his next-door neighbor that he'd many times sought but never found adequate words for. He felt a flicker of envy at being outmetaphored. There followed collegial respect, then at length love: the lord's love for a good and faithful servant, the master's love for a brilliant disciple, the lonely being's love for a kindred spirit. The process took about three minutes. At about the time he waved, love flared within him.

No, "flared" isn't right, it's too dramatic. I seem to lack some of the dog's exactitude. I'm letting the legion's reaction color my thoughts. It was more like the wisp that rises from a fallen elm leaf when a boy aims sunlight at it through a loupe. But that was enough to start a stampede. I, of course, am far too slothful to panic, and I'd had the presence of mind to edge to one side. The whole throng of recent cavorters surged for Carmichael's windpipe, with the rearmost trying to claw past those in front.

All over Carmichael similar scenes were transpiring. We'd been sailing along for years with never a problem. You couldn't count the laughing fit some months before. Every imp but me had forgotten it entirely. As far as the legion knew, it never happened. We'd held no drills, practiced no crisis procedures. And what should have been a clear warning was ignored: the host was responding poorly to Torment during walks with the dog, was smiling at people, greeting them on the street—odd conduct at any time, and odder still when Mode "A" was raging inside him. The upshot was surprise and a terrible spooking. The great part of the command became a mere rabble. Herds of panicked imps charged for Carmichael's orifices and staged gouging and biting matches with troops on guard there. Where the guards didn't simply flee first, which was what happened mostly. I've never seen a more appalling balls-up.

How many bolted? A hundred perhaps. No way to tell. Orcis refused to hold a muster. So as not to bruise morale was the reason he offered. So as not to lose his silver baton more likely. I doubt that we were still at legion strength. Whatever the figure, though, it might have been worse. Orcis was in the command center when the troops broke, so there was no delay in issuing the right orders. As for getting them carried out, there was luck in that too. Gonwe's group retained cohesion and was quartered in the cranium, so exits above neck were sealed almost at once. And Duke Agla happened to be in Carmichael's pelvis. He collected an *ad hoc* formation of officers, armed them with electrified barbed-wire whips, and drove the would-be deserters into Carmichael's solar plexus before too many had left via spigot or bung. Order was restored well before nightfall and lower ranks confined very strictly to quarters.

What to do next might have cost Orcis some cogitation if he hadn't been so much a fiend of his branch. Your avarice or lust or gluttony devil would have wanted to fan a countervailing passion to bleed energy from what Carmichael felt for Furfante. An anger or envy demon would have leaned toward wiping out the emotion's source. There was counsel in both these directions at the meeting Orcis convened on Crowning Day evening. A spirit less committed to Pride might have been swayed. Orcis, on the contrary, never wavered. He and I had precisely the same outlook, though on opposite impulses. He too refused to give the menace importance. His ego, his confidence, his *pride*, wouldn't allow it.

"Wait a minute!" I can hear him rumble when Hifni called Furfante an exorcist. "Don't tell me about exorcists! I've seen 'em close up! I've been exorcised by a Trinity member, in Person! I didn't panic then, I'm not panicking now. I'll thank my staff not to panic either. What we're talking about is a dog that the host feels affection for. Let's try to hang on to a little perspective."

He leaned back and looked around the table. The snarling grizzly snout and razor-clawed forepaws that had manifested spontaneously while he was speaking dissolved, leaving a bluff, liony grimace. "Let's ask Bogomul over there, our troop commander." He nodded his head, and Bogomul bellowed, "Sir!"

"You all know him. He was with me in Coach Thigpen. He had the watch the night Old Bu fell for a cocktail waitress in Catchpole, Arkalachee. True Love, capital T, capital L. A long night, wasn't it, Bogo?"

"Yes sir, it was."

"A long month. Long three weeks, anyway. Drove over to see her every night after practice. Left practice early, once didn't even show up. Called her at halftime on Saturdays when he ought to have been yelling at the team. Wanted to get her a scholarship to Rameses. A perfect, simpering jackass, rancid with love. I lost at least a sixth of my command." Orcis pursed his lips ruefully, nodding in reminiscence. "Was she an exorcist, Bogo?"

"No sir. She was a cocktail waitress."

"Exactly. Nineteen years old. Old Bu was fifty. Playful as a kitten. Bu was driven by demons. Inventive in bed. Bu didn't know there was more than one way to do it. A sweet face and a sweet disposition. Bu's wife was just as ugly and mean as he was. Ergo, True Love. How did we handle it, Bogo? Did we institute a lot of spasmodic maneuvers?"

"No sir."

"No sir, we did not. What we did was batten down and wait it out. And in about three weeks it had blown over. Bu went back to winning football games."

"With respect, Lord Orcis." It was Hifni again. "Carmichael hasn't any book to go back to."

"Then find him one!" His angry bear's head returned. "You're the expert on writing! Work on that! Leave strategy to me!"

7 ⁊ *The Unity of Love*
—

The unity of love will be disputed. How can one equate (I hear you grumbling) the love inspired in Carmichael by his dog with that set off in Bu Thigpen by a young woman, let alone with the love that possible people might feel for a spouse or a child or a parent or a sibling, a home team or a homeland, a friend or a fragrance, the bridges of Lutèce, the craft of embroidery, slim-haunched androgynes with pouting nether lips, or the scherzo movement of Gnazzo's flute concerto?

Well dispute if you like. Love is still love. Take my wiser word or lurch on in folly. Spontaneous joy in another's existence (or pang on his, her, or its departing your world) galls your resident devil with the same venom no matter what the loved one's nature and essence—breathing or inanimate, flesh, fish, or fowl, tangible or abstract, real or fancied, human, divine, or demonic, mutt or slut, the I AM THAT I AM or a stuffed bunny.

By the power that defiends, so may you know it. Authenticity is not impeachable on grounds of brevity. Where the heart leaps up (or plummets), there is love, even if the hop (or plunge) lasts only moments.

On the other hand, a deal of what passes for love among human beings is nothing of the sort by the dependable standard we devils employ. Love of power loves to dress up as love. Typically as love for a country or for a god, but mother love, too, can be the disguise of despots. Nothing is so sacrosanct to humans but they will use the pretense of loving it to mask cruelty and market woe—duping others often enough and themselves also, but not their fiend lodgers. We do splendidly in tyrannical hosts.

Love of self is the great impostor, however, and as such the author of much confusion. As in the common linking of love and jealousy although the two are mutually exclusive. "You're mine!" jealousy trumpets, transforming the other into an ownable object. Love, on the other hand, confers personhood. Yes, my darlings, even on a stuffed bunny. We devils treat everything as objects, each other especially, yet we know how love works. The more you love, the less you can be jealous. The jealouser you get, the less you love.

The confusion of jealousy and love came to the aid of a hostess of mine, Vicky Jinks, whom I bunked in two hosts before Carmichael. Vicky, though a resident of Dilworth, Texahoma, got jealous enough to make the Powhatten *Banner*. The headline, some think, marked that journal's finest hour:

**BEAUTICIAN KILLS HUBBY, BEST FRIEND,
WITH ONE BULLET**

Vicky was jealous, all right, but felt no love, for Bobby Clyde or Angie Sue either. None to vex a demon before she shot them, and not a twitch thereafter, take my word, though she wept with such sincerity on the witness stand, sobbing their names all the while, that the jurors were bawling too before she finished, men and women alike, and were out only twenty minutes before acquitting her. What they took for sorrowing love was injured vanity. Vicky's pangs, that is, were fierce, but had nothing to do with the loss of unique human beings, much less with remorse at their deaths having come at her hand. She lamented something far sadder, at least in her view: that Vicky Jinks, the sweetest girl who ever lived, had been cheated on and made a fool of. Every tear she shed was for herself.

Besides impersonating love, self-love cures it. Lovesbane, you might call it, in all its forms: self-pity, self-absorption, self-importance, self-centered self-assertion, self-satisfied, self-righteous self-aggrandizement. Even robust authentic love for another has a fearful time competing with love of self when the latter is fanned up to any intensity. So Orcis at length remembered, but that is getting events out of right order. All he did at first was wait self-contentedly for the problem to go away, confirmed in error by Gonwe, not that he needed it. Imagine a self-winding mechanism for self-assured self-deception; there you have Orcis. But Gonwe lost no occasion for sucking up to him and prepared a study, based on data dredged from cortical archives, that confirmed his misreading of the situation.

This was called "Carmichael and Love: A Susceptibility Survey." Gonwe had it pouched over for His Wisdom's eyes only, but I got a look at it before he did, and anyway its content was later made public. It was done chronologically and began with the rabbit doll and Erica Dienst, then went on to detail Carmichael's youthful romances, Frances Toomey *et al.*, and more serious episodes of loving behavior. His love of science, for instance, that began at fourteen, and his love for the particular science of biology. The spontaneous joy these brought him just by existing had originally to do with the order and predictability they seemed to reveal, commodities hitherto scarce in Carmichael's world. Later on it became a matter of their displaying nature's inventiveness and odd sense of humor, foretaste of and foreplay for his love of stories. Carmichael never stopped loving science. By the time he left Cawdor, however, his love had become much entangled with his ambition. Science no longer made his heart leap with selfless joy—not until the dog reminded him of his passion for it. Otherwise, I'd never have consented to be his tenant.

Next came three overlapping episodes: love for Nicole, love for Davy, love for literature. I've been over the trouble caused by the first. It and the second retained residual potency. The third, though, was just about dead when he began writing. By then he was demon-driven, not love-inspired. Now and then a book made his heart leap, but mainly his joy (or pang) was in his own work, in himself.

Joy of creation is a form of power kick we uncreative demons don't experience. I came on it first several thousand years ago on the east branch of the Atrato River in what is now Middle Ultrania. My host was a chunky brown chap, properly lethargic as befitted the climate. His great pleasure was to squat on one bank of the river and gaze across at the trees that lined the other. Mindlessly, so it seemed, but one day, I don't know how or why, he looked at a tree and saw a canoe inside it. From then on he was enterprise itself and passionately engaged in canoe-building.

There were no canoes on that river, you understand. For all I know there were none on the planet. I had no idea myself what the madman was after until a decent canoe emerged, and that took months of hacking, burning, and scraping. Months and a good many trees, you may be sure of it, but for much of that time he enjoyed himself immensely, and when at last a canoe existed—one that actually floated, that he could get in and pole or paddle along—he was ecstatic. Thereafter he sought joy of creation addictively, and suffered pang upon pang like poor knackless Carmichael, for he never created anything else. Bustle, bustle, bustle. One fool project after another, far unlike his sensible compatriot, who on inventing the hammock simply lay down it and never lifted a finger again.

Since then I've come upon it now and then, though the hosts I tend to stay with are not very creative: joy of dream made substance, of word made flesh. It seems the same sort of joy power always offers, joy in proof of existence through effect on surroundings, but is evidently more poignant than joy of destruction in that payoff is slow and letdown gentle. Judging by the imbecile grins they display when they taste it, habitués find its bouquet as fragrant as love's, though being mainly selfish it's not irksome to devils. In potency to provoke vast expense of effort, it competes very well with joy of revenge—how and why I don't know, a human mystery. But, nonetheless, it is authentically human, as proved by the joy humans take in admiring their productions in the potty.

Besides bringing Carmichael something like love's joy

and sorrow (thereby giving his life savor and substance), creation took over love's organizing role, subbed for love's maelstrom tug and lodestar attraction, love's obsessive concentrating force. Creative work made Carmichael's world go round. So Nicole saw it as his composite mistress, who both owned his heart and had him cuntstruck. This was a good insight but not quite precise. His work was not the object of his affections, but rather the means by which he loved himself.

Gonwe, for her part, found Carmichael's record with love promisingly meager. "Low susceptibility. Virtually love-proof by natural disposition and conscious will." So she graded him, citing a fragment of conversation between him and Adele Ainsley.

"You must have loved many women." This after their third bout of lovemaking. Adele assumed that to put up with her bitchiness and cure her scruples Carmichael had to have a caring nature.

"Not me," replied Carmichael sleepily. "Too distracting. Okay, I guess, if you've nothing else to do. I write books, though, and that's a big job."

"Writers shouldn't love? Is that what you're saying?"

"Well, I guess it's all right for a lyric poet, guy who's happy with maybe a sonnet every few weeks, but you'll notice they're mostly all washed up by thirty. Or maybe for someone else, what do I care? I don't do it, though. What else can I say?"

"But how can you live without . . .?"

"I get by, believe me. I don't miss it a bit. But look, say I wanted to love, know what I'd do? The same thing I'd do if I wanted to pitch for the Clippers. I'd write a story and have a character do it. What I want to do now, though, is snooze a little, and that I have to do myself."

In short, reasoning from the record, Gonwe reached the same conclusion Orcis did by hunch, that Carmichael would snap out of it soon. She might just as well have reasoned—with far more accuracy, as things turned out—that having lived empty of love for so many years, Carmichael, when stricken, would have a bad seizure. That would have conflicted, however, with her zeal to suck up to His Cleverness, and he, as you may imagine, did not argue with her.

But let's get back to where we left him, grizzlied in a staff meeting the night of Carmichael's love seizure.

He looked from Hifni to Bogomul, keeping the bear face. "I want all reliable spirits formed in one unit. Call it the Guards. I want them in defense in depth at the groin and the glottis. I want them to have distinctive uniforms, and the run of the host when off duty, and the right to abuse unreliables at their pleasure. Most of them will be officers anyway. I want unreliables confined between waist and armpits, and encouraged to take their annoyance out on the host."

He looked over at Hifni. After a moment he put on a foxy grin, a parody of Furfante's. "We're going to batten down and wait this out. In three or four weeks, you'll see, it will be all over."

SEVEN

1 ⁄⁄ *Carmichael's Condition*
—

Carmichael's condition persisted, however. Three and then four weeks passed, and nothing happened. At two *months* it showed no sign of clearing up. And the changes it produced were nearly incredible.

Observe him, for example, on that first evening, during the senior staff meeting I've referred to. In bed with Nicole, but not making love. He's been more or less celibate for weeks, since Orcis ordered lust seizures suspended. Instead he is engaged in something far rarer that Nicole finds equally pleasant, at least for a change. He reclines fully clothed to her left on the wide bed, his head and shoulders propped by her pink pillow, his chest half-mooned by the glow of her reading lamp, holding a glass of chilled Pervaya Lyubov. He has brought it and the bottle to her room and is chatting with her calmly, tenderly even. Chatting with her and the dog, who lies between them, for he punctuates remarks with "Isn't that true, doggie?" or "Doggie, your friend Mrs. C. is a clever woman," while the dog looks from one to the other. "And this love for the dog?" After a time Nicole cannot curb her amazement.

"Did you hear that, doggie? How this world is given to jealousy! You are wrong on both counts, Nicole. No dog and no love. This is Houndley of SI9, counterintelligence. His mission is to surveil the harpy next door, who in case you didn't know is an enemy agent. Good cover, don't you think? Who'd imagine he's a midget in a dog suit? And we're simply good friends. I find his conversation stimulating."

With that, he raises his forearm and crooks his wrist and cobras with bunched fingers at Furfante, who leaps to his feet snarling and snaps at the hand. Which Carmichael gives him to chew, then uses to flip him, then to scratch his throat and belly. "Calm yourself, doggie, calm yourself, I say." The dog is thumping his hind feet in ecstasy. *"Mais, du calme, mon cher, il faut avoir du calme!"*

Meanwhile, behind Carmichael's forehead, the meeting adjourned. The staff bustled off to execute Orcis's orders. The Guards were organized in two demi-cohorts, each about two hundred strong, comprising all the officers minus a handful and five or six dozen of the lower ranks. They were outfitted in black with crimson trim and stationed on the approaches to Carmichael's orifices. First they went about rousting unreliables from billets in Carmichael's head and loins and extremities and bashing them along into his trunk. There the surly herd was harangued by Vadis, who told them there would be no more desertions and urged them to torment Carmichael clean of love. This was met with angry carping at the leadership for letting him develop love in the first place, then by a general flinging of excrement, so in jumped the Pelvic Guards with their barbed-wire whips, but the fracas scarcely troubled Carmichael's good temper, and when at last the mob slunk back into Mode "A," their hearts weren't in it, and it caused him no more discomfort than a mild heartburn.

Glowing with love and vodka, trailed by his dog, Carmichael rose from the bed and swayed from Nicole's room. In the hall he began singing softly, to the tune of a Taxacan bolero, "My dog my dog, my dog my dog my doggie." Turning, he bent and scooped the dog under his arm. Singing, he carried him into his room like a football. In minutes both were sleeping sweetly, Furfante on the floor beside his lord's bed. So he slept every night thereafter, often with Carmichael's sneaker for a pillow, resting his chin on the instep or poking his snout inside. And these were but the least of numerous intimacies now permitted through favor earned and grace accorded.

He was welcome in Carmichael's study, for example. Flora was suffered to clean there at infrequent intervals. Davy had been allowed in to borrow books. And Nicole was free to enter without even knocking whenever the house was on fire or war was declared. The dog, on the other hand, was actually cajoled into the sanctum:

"Come along, doggie, no one will harm you. *Was machen Sie, Herr Doggie? Kommen Sie hier, bitte.*"

Once inside he could loll on the floor or lounge on the easy chair, and though Carmichael still couldn't write a decent sentence, his despair was lightened, tended to lift entirely for a moment, whenever he looked around and spotted the dog there.

The dog intruded at whim on Carmichael's reading, scrambled up beside him on the sofa or poised with forelegs raised against the bed (thrusting his nose toward the ceiling, sleeking his ears back, whimpering, and mooning

with piteous gaze) till Carmichael put down his book and
hoisted him up. Nor was he, once sconced, obliged to be
quiet. He might paw at his lord's thigh or nose his lord's
stomach until he got his throat and belly scratched. He
might even fling himself upward and plant a sloppy kiss on
his lord's face! And these interruptions were never chas-
tised. Now and then, perhaps, they provoked a snort, a
"What the hell da ya want, ya goddam doggie?" but there
was not a speck of menace in it. It was nothing but a rough
endearment.

And here, imagine this! Look how thoroughly love had
addled Carmichael! The dog rose early to attend his duties.
How did he leave the room? He woke his lord! And as soon
as he started to moan and tug at the bedclothes, Carmichael humped himself up and opened the door for him!
Almost grouchlessly, with hardly a grumble, let alone a
howl or curse or kick!

Behavior of this sort was without any precedent. When
Nicole caught her husband at it, she couldn't believe it.
She related it to Davy, and neither could he. Nicole and
Davy would have sooner given a tiger a hotfoot than roused
their respective hubby and pop from his slumber. The dog
did it every morning and got away clean.

Love, that cows fiends, was sweetening Carmichael's
nature. He was gentled toward all the world, not just Furfante. Nicole, Davy, Flora, the checkout girl at the super-
market, the boy who pumped gas—all noted his
unaccustomed humanity, though Furfante and his kind were
the chief beneficiaries. Oh, yes, other dogs were accorded
grace also. All found favor by virtue of kinship to Furfante.
Carmichael would see one and say to himself, "A doggie!"
and a smile would come to his face, and his heart would

go tender. Oh, he was riddled with love, he was sopped with it!

Nor was love the only dulcifying agent. Over a hundred demons had fled from his person. This in the first rush. Two or three more deserted every night, for there was no way to seal him completely or make the weak-willed among us put up with his noisesomeness. It was as if a pint of poison had been flushed from him and more was being drained away in dribbles. The relief was immense. On top of that, he received very little torment. Compared to what he was used to, no torment at all. There were upward of a thousand devils inside him, but those who weren't cowed were on guard duty. Love plus relief plus repose raised him to a state of temporary sanity. It was as if he'd been entirely defiended.

The dog knew better. He knew how many enemies remained, and of what potency and resolution. Trouble hadn't caused him to lose heart. Success didn't bring premature celebration. He rejoiced in his lord's love, that goes without saying. What I mean is he didn't overrate his progress or underestimate the difficulties ahead. He didn't expect to win without a struggle. He basked in his lord's grace and favor but kept concentration. If only Orcis had half his sense and balance!

2 ⁒ The Attempt on Furfante's Life

—

The attempt on Furfante's life was months in gestation, having been conceived the day of love's onset in Carmichael, and proposed at the meeting held that night.

"Kill him!" said Agla.

"Yes," seconded Hifni. "He's an exorcist."

Agla looked around at her in surprise. Hifni stared back for a moment, then smiled and shrugged. They had never before been on the same side of an issue. From then on, though, after Orcis rejected their counsel (directing all his comments at Hifni, for like everyone else he was wary of Agla's wrath), they took to discussing things together, especially the need to get rid of Furfante, and at length began to make actual plans.

They met in the Guards Club, a new facility in Carmichael's right shoulder that Orcis had set up as a perk for the faithful. I was steward and so had multiple chances to snoop their connivings. These new duties included formal assignment to Vadis's company and were, by the way, all the same to me. Orcis made a great hullabalo about giving up his batman in the interest of morale, now that we were in hazard, blah blah blah blah, but I couldn't care less. I had more to do, but was spared His Wonderment's presence, except when he dropped by the club for a visit. The whole reoganization left me unmoved. Oh, I had to move out of my nook in Carmichael's secum (and that was annoying, after so many years), but I ended up with a roomy suite in his thumb.

In any case, I snooped Hifni and Agla. No confederates were ever more different in temperament, she relaxed and savvy, he always on the brink of rage (if not in fact over it), but they had, as they found, some important opinions in common. That Gonwe was a fool and a baleful influence. That the dog was an active and dangerous enemy. That Carmichael wouldn't fall out of love by himself. Neither could fathom Orcis's complacency. How could he compare Furfante, a gifted if amateur exorcist, with Bu Thigpen's cocktail waitress, the mere object of a male-menopausal hot flash? Each took Furfante and the threat he posed personally, Hifni envying his skills and accomplishments, Agla incensed that a quadruped should jeopardize his first decent home in ten centuries. Both were committed to his liquidation.

So except when they were actually on duty, Agla with Nenk in the pelvis, Hifni in the throat under Onglebarth's orders (for both had joined the Guards as gentlemen rankers); when they weren't battling mobs or creeping through capillaries after single deserters or simply standing to as fumes wisped around them; and even when love waned in Carmichael, when he lay awake at night mourning his booklessness or sat scowling at one of his pages in its brief interim between typewriter and wastebasket; when the devils in his midsection went about their torments with old-fashioned enthusiasm (putting all thought of desertion from their minds), some using his nerves for trapezes, others doing vermin manifestations, still others goading him toward indiscretions; when, in consequence, duty officers were liberal with passes and the Guards Club was packed with partying demons, pranking with one another and abusing the messboys (all of them captured deserters rigged out as baboons), splaying them over tables or ripping piranha bites out of their flesh; when, in short, the dog was virtually forgotten both by Carmichael and his resident imps, Agla and Hifni nonetheless plotted his murder, off in a corner under the wing of Carmichael's collarbone.

"Drowned in a cesspool!" rasps Agla. "That would be perfect!"

"But not, I'm afraid, very practical," Hifni mutters.

"What are you talking about? It's perfectly sound! Once

he falls in, there's no helping him. Weak little yelps growing weaker, then he sinks in the filth."

"What I'm talking about, my dear Agla, is where do we
find one? A cesspool, I mean. The upper middle classes
no longer use them."

"Quicksand, then. There's plenty of quicksand here in
Verdura. I can see him struggling, trying to keep his snout
above the muck. And the harder he struggles, the faster he
sinks."

"Can you also see him and Carmichael romping through
swamps? Backpacking, I suppose, or hunting 'gators? If
you can, your vision's better than mine."

"Drowned in the bathtub then! I want life choked out of
him!"

"Flora bathes him outside, behind the kitchen, and rinses
him off with the garden hose."

"Then drowned in the sea! I tell you, drowning's the
thing for him!"

"Hmm. Maybe Davy could take him to the beach."

"That's it! That's it! Lungs full of salt water! Drowned
and eaten by fishes! I can see it!"

"If Lord Orcis changes his mind before Davy's vacation
is over."

But Agla has taken the form of a barracuda and does
nothing but snap in incoherent ire.

—

"Vivisection."

Agla's face beams. "Mutilated alive! I love it!"

"I wonder if they do it here in Sunburst. At the university, or maybe some hospital.

"I'm sure they do. There were medical research projects

at the prison. With volunteers. Of course, it's better with animals. They're not allowed a choice and are guilty of nothing."

"I've heard of a project where they take slices of animals' brains to check loss of memory. The dutiful beasts just keep staggering through the mazes. Stupid cruelty in the name of science. They must be possessed—the researchers, I mean."

"Right! And being possessed, they can be managed! How do we get the dog into a project?"

"Oh, I don't know how. I doubt if we could. They must get stray dogs from the town pound. They're not going to take some famous author's pet doggie."

"Aggh! Then what did you get me all excited for?"

—

"Rat poison!" whispers Agla. "Poison for rats!" He fits himself with a whiskered rat face for emphasis and draws the final sibilant out in a hiss. "There's a kind that drives them crazy before it kills them. Crazy with thirst. It's so they'll come out of the wainscoting for water, so they don't die in the floorboards and stink up the house. Human genius!"

"Crazes, then kills?"

"Certain death preceded by terrible agony. You can have the credit. I just want to watch! Rat poison!"

"All right. How does rat poison get into a house where there are no rats?"

"Simple. We put on a rat show."

"Lugo."

"Lugo and you and me, four or five others."

"Lugo's enough. Let Lugo materialize just once as a rat, and let someone see that rat for just one second . . ."

"Nicole."

"The house will then have rats till further notice."

"It's done then. Lugo will be happy to do a rat for us."

"Just a minute, Agla, there's more to it. Nicole will see Lugo and think the house has rats, but will she buy rat poison? Won't she be more likely to call pest controllers?"

"Who'll bring the stuff themselves. That's what they use."

"And sprinkle it in the dog's dinner? Not very likely. We're talking about professional pest controllers. They don't stay in business by poisoning customers' pets."

"If one of them's possessed, we can get him to do it."

"Hmm. Negligence. Even voluntary canicide. Provided the spirits possessing him will play ball."

"Why shouldn't they? Of course they will. We would!"

"But can we count on finding the right subject? The possessed don't fit in well in service industries."

"Don't be negative, Hifni. There must be twenty pest controllers in Sunburst. One of them will have the man we want."

"And that will be a marginal outfit. Nicole will call the best. She's got the money."

"Aggh! Whose side are you on? Ours or the dog's?"

"My dear Agla, I want him dead as badly as you do."

"I want to watch him die like a poisoned rat!"

"We have to have a workable concept."

"Well then, what about this. We find the pest controllers with the man we want, and on the very morning of our rat show we arrange for them to spread brochures along the block. All right, Nicole sees Lugo, and there's our outfit's brochure on the kitchen counter. Who will she call?"

"Yes, I suppose that would work. But I'm afraid I just don't like rat poison. It's too obvious. It puts people on guard. Even if we get it and a demoniac into the house, we're still not favorites to kill Furfante. Carmichael will be alerted. 'Poison my doggie and I'll poison you!' That's what he'll be screaming as they come through the door. And he'll stand over them the whole time they're in the house."

"So we wait till he's away, off on a trip somewhere!"

"And Nicole won't call him, will she? I'm surprised at you, Agla. Can it be you think Nicole is stupid? Married to a maniac like Carmichael and not call him before she brings rat poison into the house? And won't he say to wait till he gets home? Assuming he doesn't veto the whole thing outright. Assuming he wouldn't rather have rats in the house than risk poisoning his precious doggie. The more I think of it, the worse it gets."

But Agla is no longer listening. Agla is gnawing on his forearm in rage. Or foreleg, to be exact, having ratted completely. Rat blood and frothed saliva fleck his whiskers. In between gnaws he emits ear-piercing squeaks. And as nearby club patrons turn their heads and gape, Hifni shrugs and dematerializes discreetly.

—

In the end they embraced probability and decided to run Furfante down with a car. I won't touch on all the wrangling that preceded agreement, where Agla complained that those means were deficient in cruelty ("All over in ten seconds!" was the phrase he repeated) while Hifni maintained that any means, however merciful, were justified, and pointed out that at least Carmichael would suffer, and that death by automotive mishap was undeniably messy for small creatures, who were often mashed beyond all recognition, and not necessarily speedy, not of a perfect certainty stingy of pain; where Hifni reasoned while Agla raged, where she enumerated advantages—seven out of twenty-three motorists were possessed by demons—while he fumed and fussed and fretted and foamed at the mouth, whatever sort he was wearing if he was wearing one. I won't go into their reconnaissance efforts either, Agla's off-duty sorties from Carmichael's rectum (unquestioned, much less detained, since no one from Orcis down dared to confront him, let alone imply that he might be deserting), his hornet flittings up and down the block, his raven sweeps about the neighborhood, and the times he and Hifni poked about Sunburst, for when Agla had grudgingly admitted that a car might be a useful murder weapon, it still had to be determined if the right instruments could be come by and the thing pulled off in the hard world of practical reality. Nor will I so much as mention the cramped and halting peristaltic process by which practical reality—the daily desertions, the passage of time without any change for the better—purged Orcis of his misconception that the dog was the passive partner in Carmichael's romance, and of his misplaced faith in a cure by spontaneous remission (a process made painfully sluggish by his refusal to think he might be wrong), or the glib ballsiness, once he finally woke up, with which he exclaimed at a staff meeting, "Will no one rid me of this meddlesome canine?" as if he were the first to have had the idea. I shall instead leap into the middle of things, to the point where Agla and Hifni are presenting their plan. The date is mid-July, the place the conference room in Orcis's quarters.

Orcis and senior staff sit facing a large screen, on which images form and fade as in a movie. Hifni does the talking and waves the pointer. Agla glowers to one side. And in the back holding a tray of refreshments yours truly is snooping.

SCREEN—*A view of Wilde Street from the corner of Marston Road. A car sweeps downhill from Larraby and through the intersection. The car sweeps through again, no touch of the brake, an aging Porlock Puma, long unwashed and copiously dented.*

HIFNI: We propose to kill the dog by vehicular impact at the intersection of Marston Road and Wilde Street.

SCREEN—*The Puma zips north along Wilde, to and across Napier, on toward Oglesby. Close-up of the driver as he peers left to check for traffic. The frame holds.*

HIFNI: This is Dennis Sklar, twenty-six, married, one child, a doctoral candidate and graduate assistant in Anglian at Sunburst University. [Hifni prods with her pointer.] Note the furrowed brow and the clamped molars, the fist clenched on the wheel till the knuckles blanch. Dennis is a very tense young man, and as you have surmised possessed by spirits. Over two hundred, of all branches. Loosely organized but disposed to cooperate.

GONWE: How do we know?

AGLA: Because I say so, macaque! [The force of his fury bashes Gonwe into the form of a rhesus monkey, a likeness she retains for some twenty seconds before struggling back into the humanoid form she has been wearing.]

HIFNI: Duke Agla has entered Dennis on several occasions and will be on board him during the mission. [She pauses, looks around the room, and then continues.] On Tuesday and Thursday evenings, from now till summer term ends on August 16, Dennis teaches a class in freshman composition at the Sunburst Extension Program in Spring Glades.

VADIS: Just like Carmichael used to.

HIFNI: Dennis's resemblance to the host is one of the things that attracted us to him, that commended him to us as an apt instrument. We find it poetically just that Carmichael's bereavement come at the hand of one who might pass as his younger brother. Like the old Carmichael, Dennis is a demoniac scholar at odds with himself and the world. As we see him here [Hifni prods with the pointer], he is on his way to a place he despises to do something he hates. He has spent the previous two hours correcting student themes—the activity he loathes most in the world—and he is late. His mood on every Tuesday and Thursday evening is one of rage grading to maniac frenzy. His driving behavior . . .

SCREEN—Cut from close-up of Sklar to a view of his car as it zips across Oglesby and on along Wilde, passing a stopped schoolbus without even slowing.

HIFNI: . . . is murderous. He normally drives twelve to fifteen miles per hour faster than what would be minimally safe, depending on the road conditions.

SCREEN—Shot of Sklar's car bowling through a stop sign.

HIFNI: Finally, he hates dogs. He holds that people who like dogs dislike people, though in point of fact he doesn't like people either. We don't think that Dennis would run over the dog deliberately—though if he's enraged enough, that's certainly possible—but we calculate that his animus against dogs will subconsciously slow his braking time by three tenths of a second. That ought to be sufficient to ensure impact.

ORCIS: How is this "accident" supposed to work?

SCREEN—Street map of northwest Sunburst with Sklar's route highlighted.

HIFNI: Dennis's class meets at seven-thirty. He ought to leave his house two hours before that. In practice he is always late. [She prods with the pointer]. He takes Wilde Street to Preminger Avenue to get the turnpike at the Preminger Loop. He crosses Marston at about five-fifty. We'll be tracking him. Duke Agla, as I've said, will be on board him. As he crosses Joplin—that is to say, about one minute from Marston—one of us, materialized as a postman, will come up to Carmichael's door with a special delivery.

SCREEN—Cartoon postman rings Carmichael's doorbell.

HIFNI: The letter, by the way, will be for somebody on the next block. It's only a device to get the door open. And to bring our target to it, since he always barks at whoever rings the doorbell.

GONWE: Not when he's in the study with Carmichael.

AGLA [grows a panther head]: Rrrrrr!

HIFNI [to Orcis, as if nothing has happened]: Carmichael will be in Powhatten the week of the sixth. Publicity commitments for his latest novel. If our plan is approved, we can be ready by then.

ORCIS: Go on.

HIFNI: Well, when the door is opened—by Flora or Nicole, it doesn't matter—there, just behind the "postman," will be one of us materialized as a bitch in heat.

AGLA [to Gonwe]: You, for instance! [He draws the final sibilant out in a hiss.]

SCREEN—Cartoon view of a doggess, with wavy lines oscillating near her stern.

ORCIS: The dog will follow the bitch . . .

HIFNI: He'll have to, that's nature.

SCREEN—Cartoon likeness of Furfante bolts from the house and chases la chienne fatale.

HIFNI: She'll lead him to the corner, then on a collision course with Dennis's car.

SCREEN—Cartoon car smashes into Furfante.

HIFNI: We anticipate an instant fatality.

SCREEN—Furfante mashed on the pavement.

AGLA [with rueful grimace]: All over in ten seconds!

HIFNI: But in case the target is merely injured . . .

SCREEN—A plump, middle-aged gentleman in white smock.

HIFNI: This is Everett Severn, doctor of veterinary medicine, owner and director of the Severn Pet Clinic, 2573 Preminger Avenue. Note the glazy eyes and facial tic. See how he wrings his hands to prevent their tremor. Dr. Severn is thoroughly incompetent by reason of sloth and addiction to alcohol. As you have surmised, he is possessed by spirits. The wonder is that he remains in practice. Severn's clinic is close to the point of impact. On the morning of the mission, brochures describing it will be distributed on this block. If the dog is not killed outright, there is an excellent chance Severn will treat him. In that case I will go on board the doctor. I can promise you the treatment will be botched.

SCREEN—A reeling cartoon Severn, drunk to the gills, hacks clumsily at a prostrate Furfante.

ORCIS: What do you need?

HIFNI: A minimum of four spirits will be required. Duke Agla, myself, and two others. Duke Agla will be inside Dennis. I will direct and be inside Severn if necessary.

The "postman" and the "bitch" will double as handbill distributors. If possible we should like a fifth team member to understudy all parts and help out with communications, which will be by thought wave. The team will remain in Sunburst when the host leaves for Powhatten. We envisage a temporary base in Mrs. Sned's cat. We recommend reinstitution of Mode "D" on the day of the mission. It might come in handy to have Carmichael distracted.

ORCIS: That's it?

HIFNI: That's it. We expect to kill the dog at about six p.m. on Tuesday, August seventh, or Thursday, August ninth, by vehicular impact or improper medical treatment.

3 ⫽ What Went Wrong

What went wrong was that Orcis went overboard. He gave Agla and Hifni his blessing, then he gave them more: Lugo to play the temptress (though Lugo lacked restraint and everyone knew it) and another drink fiend named Utach whose task it was to transmit from Sunburst to Powhatten so the legion could witness the assassination live. The last was supposed to help morale, but just killing the dog would have solved most morale problems.

Death Day (as we were calling it) dawned clear. In Sunburst, that is; in Powhatten it was drizzly. We got intermittent weather reports from Utach with a video feed off Mrs. Sned's cat's optic nerve. The first showed her view of Furfante as he rousted her from a chair beside Carmichael's swimming pool. It brought a chorus of boos from viewers. Of which there were a number, even that early. We had screens in the Guards Club, and four of mammoth size in Carmichael's stomach, where the unreliable were grouped for the occasion, along with those on guard duty. Orcis had his own, and could have used the one in Carmichael's cortex, but came into the club around five and watched there for a while, then went down to see the rest with Nenk and his unit. The only ones who missed seeing Sklar's car hit Furfante were some of Gonwe's group in Carmichael's privates, for Mode "D" went into effect at about four-thirty.

Utach came on just before that, transmitting from a light pole on the corner. He and Hifni and the understudy were perched there in the form of crows. He fed two basic shots, both color-enhanced: Carmichael's front door and Wilde Street looking toward Larraby. There were also a few short takes from Agla lifted directly off the thought-wave net: Dennis's house (a lot like Carmichael's old bungalow); Dennis correcting themes at the dining-room table; a theme seen through his eyes after Agla entered him. At five-fifty, Utach reported, "Final stage running!" After that he gave a kind of countdown—"Turning onto Wilde Street . . . passing Fairly"—until Dennis reached the corner of Joplin. There followed the play-by-play of the crash.

Carmichael was at the Sheldrake at that moment, crammed between the thighs of Nan Anderson Haft. He'd been signing books in Squails on Quinceberry Boulevard, where *Twilight of Vama* was stacked in a prominent pyramid, assisted by the manager of the store and a polyestered flack from his publishers. As customers came up holding their copies, or took one from the armful the manager held, Carmichael poked them a nod, mumbled a greeting, and scribbled his surname on the title page. Then all at once, about five minutes into the business (with the manager's grin by now congealed to a rictus and the PR type aflutter like a trapped moth), lechery took over Carmichael's person, demons from lust lashed him into his act. He began to smile, asked customers their names, inscribed the books "For So-and-so," signed with a flourish, made modest little quips about his work, told comic tales of *Twilight*'s composition, and was in short so affable and charming that the store's whole clientele was soon pressed around him, including (cleanly snared) the lady in question.

This was the former Miss Minneconsett, Nan Anderson, the current wife of Haft, the broadcasting baron. She was not in Squails to meet Carmichael, did not like his books, and found him less attractive than her husband, but for all that he snared her. How could he not? Demons were flogging him. He took her to the bar at the Sheldrake, then to his suite. He was crammed between her thighs throughout the attempt.

Nan's hand trails languidly from the sitting-room sofa into a little pool of her lately shed clothing. Carmichael's haunches piston and churn. Inside him a thousand fiends are peering at video screens. In Sunburst, Dennis's car bustles toward Marston, dogs lope toward it on collision course. Tires screech, the car fishtails and slews wildly, skids into the dogs. "We have impact!" cries Utach. Back in Carmichael's person we demons cheer.

Premature—the dog isn't dead, is not even dying. Hifni ought to have aborted the mission. By the time she saw the trouble, however, it was too late. Lugo's white poodle bitch was too seductive.

He materialized in front of 3374 and approached via

Mrs. Sned's lawn at a dignified saunter just as the fake postman was ringing Carmichael's doorbell. Only twenty seconds passed before the door opened, but in those instants Lugo overachieved. When Furfante shot from the house between Nicole's ankles, the Firkins' chow was already in attendance, and four other mutts were galloping Lugo's way.

"Who did you think you were?" Orcis screamed later. "Lara Lamont? I only wish the lot of them had pronged you!"

None got the chance. As soon as Furfante emerged, Lugo started running. Suitors fell in train on the way to the corner. When Dennis saw Lugo and this retinue, the mass of canine flesh looked daunting. Far from feeling rage, he feared for his safety. He braked at once. The impact's force was well below what had been programmed. Besides, Furfante was back in the pack. Intervening bodies cushioned the shock to him. All he suffered was a broken hind leg and a cracked hipbone.

Meanwhile, back at the Sheldrake, there was trouble. Utach's transmission was reaching Carmichael's mind. Below the level of consciousness but with effect. At the moment of impact a pall of horror struck him. It passed in an instant, but meantime wilted his dong like a lopped tulip.

Despite setbacks, however, the mission still had promise. Nicole had followed Furfante, had seen him hit. Within moments she was carrying him into the house, calling for Flora to find the veterinarian's handbill. Within minutes they were bound for Severn's clinic, with Hifni and Utach hitching rides in the form of fleas. While, in Powhatten, Gonwe's demons flogged Carmichael back into form (with some adept resuscitation from Nan) and got his haunches pistonning again.

I now have some clips. First, Severn at the door of his clinic, which with his home occupies an aged house. He wrings his hands as Nicole and Flora enter, the last holding Furfante. Severn hasn't been sober since April, but like many chronic drunks gives no sign he's "flying." Hifni leaps from Furante's trembling body, dematerializes in air, and goes over the transom of Dr. Severn's denture.

Next, the examining room, narrow and cramped, as if the furniture had been placed first and then the walls fitted around it. Our view is from the ceiling, where Utach now clings in the form of a spider. Stains on the cover of the examining table, clutter of instruments on the counter nearby. Unsmelled pungent reek of disinfectant. Invisible dank creepers of pain and incompetence. Severn's bald crown and stooped shoulders enter the picture. Nicole and Flora follow him into the room. He turns, takes Furfante from Flora, plops him urgently down onto the table. Agonized squeal, answered from off screen left, in the rear of the building, where other suffering animals are caged.

Close-up of Furfante. He quivers in pain and terror. We are looking through the glazed eyes of Everett Severn. Utach has joined Hifni inside his person. Severn fits a muzzle over Furfante's snout, pulls the straps tight. Now he palps Furfante's hindquarters. High squeals of torment.

"Don't you use X-rays?" Nicole's distraught face comes into view.

"Don't need 'em, the leg's no problem, not even busted. The problem is he has internal injuries. The operation'll cost you fifty thalers."

"Operation?"

"Either that or we put him to sleep?"

Nicole hesitates. "Let me try to call my husband. He's in Powhatten. I can call collect."

"Make sure you do. And hurry. Way he's hurt may be too late already."

In Sunburst, then, the mission nears completion. Nicole doesn't like this doctor, but she can't very well drive around shopping for others while the dog may be dying. Severn has made an incorrect diagnosis. In a few minutes he will be operating, drunk and possessed by a powerful envy demon. There is not the slightest chance the dog will survive.

In Carmichael a thousand fiends are cheering. And hooting in derision when Nicole proposes calling her husband. The phone is off the hook in her husband's sitting room, and he is, shall we say, distracted.

Or is he? All is not as it should be at the Sheldrake. As I surmise when one of Gonwe's spirits bursts into the club looking for Orcis. Carmichael's haunches piston not, neither do they churn. Each scene of Utach's transmission, each cheer provoked, has touched him with a dreadful premonition—below awareness but nonetheless forcefully. That a certain small dog is about to exit this world causes his spirit to plummet. Love in this potent form cancels out lust. For the first time Mode "D" is failing. Carmichael is experiencing complete sexual dysfunction.

Which would be funny if so much weren't in the balance. There he is, embraced by a lovely woman, guided and goaded by lechery's fiends, and all at once, no warning, limp as a noodle. No reason either, not that he can note. He doesn't know he's picking up Utach's transmissions. He doesn't even know he loves the dog. People as self-centered as Carmichael have a hard time loving, and an even harder time admitting they do. All he knows is that he is drooping despicably, in spirit and body, though a glimmer of insight comes to him as, still between Nan's thighs, he tries to explain.

"I'm sorry. Something's wrong."

"Thanks for telling me. I'd have never guessed."

"No. Something's wrong at home. I can feel it."

"Oh. You're psychic. No wonder. Tell me, are all writers as flaky as you?"

"Nan . . ."

But then an urgency impinges. He gets up and crosses to the desk—a pallid middle-aged fellow with sagging hams and a heart full of nameless dread. Picks up the receiver and presses the cradle, lifts his finger to dial Nicole and hears an operator say she's calling. And as soon as he accepts the call, the moment she begins explaining, the whole situation comes clear to him, as one may recall a dream in every detail two or three minutes after waking up. He hasn't a clue, of course, how or why he knows it, but he's not that surprised, nor does he doubt his knowledge. He's been writing science fiction too long for either.

"No, Nicole! Listen! Get the hell out of there! The dog will be all right, just don't let that guy touch him. Give him some money and leave. Take my doggie home. I'll call in half an hour."

4 ″ The One Law
—

The one law all humans obey is supply and demand. When Nicole suggested that Carmichael loved Furfante—"And this love for the dog?"—he assumed she intended "love for" as a figure, meaning "amusement with" or "enjoyment of," and answered facetiously. Had she made herself clear; had she said, "Come on, admit it, you're goofy about him," he would have replied that the goof ball was her, and then, if she persisted, gotten angry. He reeked of love but didn't know it. He beamed with love's joy yet would have felt insulted had he been told so. Love, after all, implies need, and need dependence, and dependence vulnerability. Carmichael styled himself tough, autosufficient. Love was all right for Davy and his generation, and no doubt of value, besides, as a pastime for idlers, or to make life exciting for those without nerve or talent. But it wasn't for him. He had worlds to make—better use, in other words, for his time and energy. So he continued to think, though he was bookless.

Well, he was wrong. Stupid about things in general, ignorant in particular of his own state. As a practical matter, though, being wrong cost him nothing. He might fool himself as he pleased, so long as his love, Furfante, was by his side. In other words, so long as supply met demand, demand might be ignored, supposed nonexistent.

Furthermore, he did not yet love fully. He knew love's delight. His hitherto supine heart got up and did handsprings simply because his doggie existed. That, one might suppose, should be enough. But obedient to the law of supply and demand, humans discount the value of beings and things in proportion to their availability, even the value of irreplaceable loved ones and the unique well-being they confer. Hence the pang of loss rings more bells than the joy of possession. Typically—and in this Carmichael was typical—humans do not love fully, oftentimes do not love at all, till the who or what they love is gone from their worlds, or is at least threatening departure.

The results can amaze you. Alonso Niada was my host for much of the last half of the last century, a slight, wry man, a reader, a dominoes player, by profession a notary, by nature timid, the least resolute Taxacan who ever drew breath. He maintained a seven-fiend pact with the powers of lassitude for the sole purpose of anesthetizing himself, as far as was possible, to the railing and Medusa glares of his wife, an admirable person in many respects who had the misfortune to live in a time and clime unfriendly to masterful women. They were married forty-eight years. For at least thirty-nine—the time I boarded with him—not a day and scarcely an hour went by without Alonso's wishing Felicia departed: carried off by a stroke, by a plague, by a fit, by a fever, by an apoplexy, by a roc if need be, but gone from his life once and forever. Meanwhile, she lived hale into her eighties. When she finally sickened, however, Alonso began to feel very clear twinges of worry. When she died, he was engulfed by longing for her, swept away on a tide of *ex post facto* affection.

He wept, he wailed, he stared about tragically. He moped, he mourned, he moaned, "I've lost my woman!" His friends thought him senile, his enemies a hypocrite. In fact he was neither. He was sincere, bereaved, inconsolable—and above all obedient to the law of supply and demand. It might have been hilarious if it hadn't been such a bother. I'd grown used to Señor Niada. I meant to abide with him till he croaked. Now love made his person unlivable, even for a hardy spirit like me.

Well, then, there was Carmichael, naked at the desk in his suite at the Sheldrake, a period desk, a table really, with slender, curving legs and its top inset with wine-red leather. His left hand grasped the back of the chair. His right hand rested on the cradled receiver. Beyond and below a summer shower was in progress. Pedestrians scurried. Headlamps glazed a rain-slick Pendlethorn Avenue. Carmichael gazed but did not see. His exquisitely tilled imagination was compassing the dog's pain, its shock and wonder, the way pain remade the world and the dog's being. It was composing the accident in a rough cut, watching the dog hit several times in slow motion. It was computing his loss should the dog die. With that a pang skewered him. It went in at his throat and drove downward behind his breastbone. It clogged his lungs with grapefruit-sized gray rocks. It bulged his abdomen with nausea. He'd felt nothing like it since the fever Davy had at two or three that Nicole and he were scared was meningitis. Love came in full to Carmichael at that moment.

He gasped and flung his head backward as if hit. He forcibly disengaged his imagination. He remembered Nan and turned to face her.

She was still on the sofa naked but was now sitting up, knees drawn to her breasts, arms clasped about them. A particularly withering quip had come to her, and she had arranged her regard to launch it fittingly, eyebrows raised, head canted to one side. When she saw his expression, though, all bitchiness left her.

"Is everything all right?" A common phrase when humans know everything isn't.

"A car hit my doggie."

Here Nan might have laughed. She was not an animal lover. To her the grief in Carmichael's look suggested the loss of at least a brother. The word "doggie" sits awkwardly on a grown man's tongue. Besides, Carmichael was naked, sagged sallowly at breast and belly, and had badly botched their assignation. Still she felt a genuine concern.

"Oh, no! Is he . . . ?"

No, the doggie was still alive but hurt perhaps badly. Yes, he (Carmichael) would be going home at once. No, Nan needn't drive him, he'd take a cab to the airport. And so on, as they got dressed, as if they actually cared for each other, as if they were man and mistress, lady and lover, not mere one-shot cocktail-hour humpers.

And so, actually, they had become. The love Carmichael felt raised everything to higher power.

5 ″ That Effect

—

That effect was not on my mind at the time, however. At the time all I was thinking of was Odvart, minimizing poor Odvart's discomfort and dread. There was, on the one hand, the love foaming through Carmichael, and on the other the battle that raged for hours as unreliables, and some Guards too, tried to crash out of his moldering person. That I wasn't embroiled in the latter was due only to my presence of mind.

When Carmichael uncoupled from Nan Haft, Gonwe knew she had trouble she couldn't handle and sent a runner for His Cleverness. Ninety or so seconds later, with him still not heard from and Carmichael aware that the dog was injured, she secured from Mode "D" and ordered those in the Guards Club to rejoin their units. I was not on the premises. As soon as Nicole's phone call was put through, when her smile confirmed that Carmichael had answered,

I knew the attempt on the dog's life had failed, and that there was going to be a horrendous fracas. Which could flourish quite well without me. I made myself scarce. As swiftly as was compatible with prudence: nothing stimulates suspicion like a hurrying sloth fiend.

I heard Gonwe's order. In fact I heard it clearly. I was just outside the door when it was broadcast. I grant and piss upon that point in one motion. Two spirits saw me leave, that I made sure of: trusty Nenk, the Thigpen veteran, and a greed demon named Velpis for insurance. I directed a word to each about having to fetch some rashers of Carmichael's gray matter. Then I bolted. And once I was outside the facility, orders addressed to those inside it did not concern me.

To my left, a short waddle off, was Carmichael's neck. No one would question me if I headed in that direction and continued upward toward Orcis's quarters. I'd been his batman till the current emergency and was properly uniformed as a Guards ranker. A squad was stationed in Carmichael's mouth, but his nostrils and ears were patrolled by single sentries. I had but to approach one and give the password, say he or she was relieved to report to the guardroom, and my way would be clear.

For a trice I was tempted. The demonic infestation of D. P. Carmichael was about to enter its decisive phase. That meant acute stress for Odvart unless I seized the day and buggered off. The trice passed without issue, however. I'd been in Carmichael over two decades. He was my only virgin and my sole instance as senior spirit in residence. And we were in Powhatten, of all places, the world capital of bustle and rush. All that flashed through my mind, but hardly influenced much less determined my choice. Desertion in the face of the enemy, no matter how cowardly, requires some enterprise. That trait is not in my nature. I shrugged and took the path of least resistance, turned left and trudged off toward my bunk in Carmichael's thumb.

I hadn't reached his elbow when the pang hit. His heart stopped for a beat, and his blood chilled. Then for at least five seconds his whole frame shuddered.

Such symptoms are usually fun for resident demons, even if not demon-induced. Our interests and those of humans are opposed to begin with. Hosts, meantime, are for use, not to moon over. And since cruelty is to us what love is to angels, in general the host's vexation is our good news.

Death throes and love pangs are exceptions. Both presage imminent eviction, and (however frothily some of us may vaunt) we devils are sensitive beings, woefully insecure when homeless. And since love is inherently noxious to us, the love pang heaps fear of pain on fear of anxiety. When Carmichael shuddered, therefore, a thousand fiends shuddered in echo. As for me, I keeled over in what once was called a swoon.

I came to awash in love of a pungency unprecedented in Carmichael. Every other spirit in him was sloshed with it too. Volume was unprecedented also. Something to do, according to Hifni, with his not having loved fully for so long—as if reasons were of any use or solace. It gives us the kind of anguish humans feel when choking. The impulse to flee can be irresistible. The sagest devil is liable to lose all semblance of self-control and go beetling for the nearest orifice. I was disgusted with myself for having let my chance for a getaway slip by. No point dwelling on it, however. There'd be no deserting now without a struggle. And, of course, one doesn't choke, though it surely feels awful.

After a time the angst recedes, the stench becomes bearable. Meanwhile, devils of backbone buck up. Your Orcis gets through on pride, your Agla on anger. I drew on my stock of not caring and dragged myself home.

Meanwhile Carmichael dressed and packed and checked out of the Sheldrake, calling Nicole from the lobby to learn that the dog was ostensibly none the worse for having skipped surgery, and to have her entrust his health to their family doctor: "Just call his gold-digger wife and say if he takes the case she gets a pearl necklace. He'll be ringing the doorbell before you hang up." Meanwhile he cabbed to the airport and missed a flight to Titangel with connection to Glastonbury and Sunburst but got a nonstop to Tamami, where he got a one-stop back to Otranto, where he got a limo. And meanwhile the battle raged, but on two fronts only, both narrow and with prepared defensive positions. The unreliables were in the host's stomach when the pang struck. The Guards held in his esophagus and intestine, withstanding repeated mass charges, as well as sorties by individual berserkers, until at last the stimulus to flee lessened, and mutineers began to surrender, and the remnant were beaten into submission. The worst moment came around midnight when Carmichael got home. When the dog heard his lord's voice and began yelping blissfully—somewhat feeble yelps but blissful no less—and Carmichael knew his doggie was still in his world, his heart leaped so and love of Furfante so flooded him that Guards broke and ran in both sectors, abandoning their posts, and the line was restored only with great travail.

In the end, however, there were few desertions. A dozen or so unreliables made their constricted way along capillaries into Carmichael's bladder and escaped down his urinary tract. Eight or ten renegade Guards bashed out through his nostrils. The infestation remained otherwise intact. Thus, from a purely military point of view the battle was a victory for Orcis, confirming the soundness of his dispositions and arguing that they could hold indefinitely against any threat the enemy might mount, any volume of love the dog might engender in Carmichael.

6 ′′ The Value of Pain

The value of pain is didactic. Nothing beats it as an attention-getter, or so promotes concentration and heightens recall. Hence its usefulness in teaching lessons.

Other than that, though, pain is good for nothing. Which is a shame (pain being so cheap to produce), but more or less what one might have expected. Even pain's utility as a learning aid depends on its being administered in correct dosage. Too little and the presumptive pupil ignores it, too much and he forgets everything else. Schoolmaster life employs it, meanwhile, with great frequency, but not (alas!) with corresponding care. There is much more pain in the world than serves any purpose.

Nonetheless, the pang that speared Carmichael in Powhatten was (as it were) calibrated exactly to teach him what he most needed to know. He was not loveproof. On the contrary, he was love-pierced and love-swollen. He loved his dog Furfante and through him much more: the perishable earth and everything on it.

The lesson came home to Carmichael in two stages. He knew at once he was a new person. It took him time, how-

ever, to confront his condition and realize that what transfigured him was love.

See him on the night of the botched murder, or actually
around two the following morning. He sprawls with his face
off the edge of his bed. A foot or so below the dog lies
dozing.

Not in a box lined with the Otranto *Sentinel*. Carmichael
has brusquely rescinded that measure.

"Dammit, Nicole, he's not a goddam puppy!"

"But if he has to pee . . ."

"Exactly! How's he going to feel, pissing on himself?
How would you feel, goddammit?"

And with infinite gentleness Carmichael picked the dog
up, and carried him out to a favored bush in the yard, and
held him while he emptied his bladder.

Well, then, 2:00 A.M., the dog lies dozing. Carmichael
sprawls above him, mooning down. He is drained yet
sleepless. Joy and anguish contend within him.

Think of a man with a chronic sense impairment who
has the cataracts shaved or the deafness corrected. Riches
of sensation stream upon him. Their profusion bewilders,
however, their intensity sears, and he is in sudden, mortal
terror of losing them, anxiety that, when he lacked them,
he'd been spared. So Carmichael, mooning at Furfante. He
resists an urge to pat Furfante's shoulder, curbs a hanker-
ing to stroke his throat, refrains from peering too fixedly at
his hurt leg as if that might cause pain or mar the dressing,
the splint Dr. Gold has fashioned from tongue depressors.
At length he rolls onto his back and stares at the ceiling.
Later he takes up a book and stares at it. Still later he puts
out the light and stares into the darkness. At dawn he will
awaken to the dog's whimpers, and pull on shorts and

sneakers and carry him out, and bend bare-torso'd in a tepid drizzle to hold him as he empties his bowels.

This bemusement of Carmichael's held through Furfante's recovery, a reverence at the mystery working within him fit for a dotty girl in her first pregnancy. There was, besides, the exodus of devils. It brought an orgasmoid rush and a sense of well-being—goodies he associated the dog with, though he had no inkling what begat them. Hence he felt grateful, hence he loved more acutely. Meanwhile, the dog's injury sopped him with love still more thoroughly, soggied him to the limit he could absorb, by allowing him to suffer and feel apprehensive.

Thinness of bone made Furfante's case tricky. So said Sunburst's best vet, who palped the broken leg, took X-rays, and recommended a man at the School of Veterinary Medicine, Vedura Sovereign University, Smithton. Carmichael and dog arrived there the next afternoon, the latter beaten down by pain but in reasonable spirits—the lord was with him, after all—the former crabbed with sympathetic backache, owled with sleeplessness, and hedgehogged with suspicion as to the vet's competence. Things turned, however, when he appeared.

"Dr. Carmichael! This is terrific!"

"—?"

"Don't you remember me? I was your student."

Carmichael peered at him and shook his head. Late thirties, medium height, a total stranger. Dr. Student thrust on, however, with unchecked exuberance.

"You taught me Bio One-oh-one a and b. You were why I majored in biology. I guess I wouldn't be here if it wasn't for you."

Carmichael beamed, and (characteristically) pressed his

luck. Had the doctor read his books? Oh yes, came the chagrining answer. He'd read one and loved it, had sent his copy to Carmichael for signing, but unfortunately it had been lost in the mails.

"I'll get you a set," Carmichael promised quickly, and changed the subject to Furfante's injury. The doctor fished up the X-rays, clipped them to a viewer, and pointed out a break between knee and ankle in the dog's right hind leg. Repair meant inserting a pin to join the smashed shards. The procedure could be done the next morning. He'd call Carmichael when it was over to let him know how it came out.

"Oh, I'll be here," Carmichael assured him.

"Don't you still live in Sunburst?"

"Sure I do. The drive's only three hours."

And Carmichael was there before nine, with his novels in the special boxed edition flatteringly inscribed on the title pages. He paced and smoked through the operation, feeling each imagined stroke of the scalpel as if it had been slicing his own flesh. He was sent home while Furfante was still under anesthesia, with solemn pledges that all had gone perfectly, yet spent the night in an ecstasy of worry and was back the following day for visiting hours. His ex-student found him by Furfante's cage, a forefinger poked through the mesh for Furfante to chew on, murmuring, *"Bien sûr, mon vieux! Certainement, Monsieur Doggie!* Of course you do, you feel much better today."

"I never took you for an animal lover."

"I wasn't. That was this doggie's idea."

That unmeditated phrase was Carmichael's confession. As it passed his lips, he realized he loved, and how he came by the condition. The dog and we demons, of course, had realized already. *He* took great delight in the confirmation, manifest (as it was) in Carmichael's tone, and by the odor he gave off when he spoke it. As for us, we got another gassing, one of the worst we'd endured so far.

Carmichael's dog returned in triumph from Smithton with a splint-cum-crutch the shape of a plane's wing that reached a good three inches below his paw and gave him the swaggering gait of a peglegged pirate. He accepted extravagant fussings from Nicole and Flora, stood for his photo with ears pricked and tongue lolling foxily, and dispatched a banquet of raw ground steak. And this welcome was as nothing beside his true bounty. The lord's face shone upon him. The lord had established a covenant between them. He, Furfante, had taught the lord to love!

Carmichael's face glowed with unbalked benevolence, his heart swelled with newly sprouted loving-kindness. All day he turned from work or leisure to beam fond glances at his doggie. What did it matter then if work went nowhere, or if leisure was venomed by the japes of fiends? At night he woke and took peeks at his doggie, rejoicing that the two were in the same world. Where, then, was the sting if his dreams were bedeviled? And, rising or retiring, he rubbed his doggie's ruff with his bare instep, as if seeking a talisman's protection. Blasts of love reverberated in him, roiling love clouds tumbled through his person, and we poor devils hunkered cringing.

The dog gave himself up to exultation. He praised the lord by yelp and pant. And took what once would have been blasphemous liberties—nipped Carmichael's heels, gnawed Carmichael's sneakers, nuisanced Carmichael shamelessly to be petted. In short, he tossed circumspection over the gunwale to romp in his chosenness. Carmichael and his dog were having their honeymoon.

Orcis, meanwhile, had taken a hard decision. He was too much a fiend, and too much a pride fiend, to settle for a lengthy defensive struggle, and particularly despised having to aim his whole effort at keeping discipline in his command.

"How does it look, I ask you?" he railed rhetorically. "I want mobs pushing to get in, not out! I want to punish the Exorcist, not my own troops!"

This at a council of war held in Carmichael's gullet at four in the morning after the failed attempt on Furfante's life. Present were the troop commanders, except for Vadis, who had the watch, along with Gonwe, Hifni, Agla, and Lugo. The last three had just rejoined us, minus Utach, who would on no account come back on board. Carmichael and dog were sleeping, the latter with the help of a painkiller, and with a splint on his broken left hind leg. The infestation, too, was quiet, Guards and unreliables alike exhausted. Orcis wore a goat's head on a humanoid carcass, brass talons, and red reptile hide. He accepted responsibility for the attempt's failure, though not without reaming Lugo very soundly, and confessed himself delinquent in letting the Exorcist—so he now called Furfante— get so great a head start. Doing so, he turned his eyes pale orange and glared terribly at Gonwe. All this mollified Agla, who at the start seemed ready to demand Orcis's demission. He was manifest as a buzzard, and throughout the meeting pecked in wrath at his liver, smearing those nearby with blood and feathers.

"No," Orcis went on. "I won't play the jailer. And what

we need now is to regain the initiative, which can't happen while everyone's playing prisoner or guard. I'll tell you what: I'm going to let those go who want to. In good order, you understand, not like a funked rabble, but go they may if they care to, and good riddance. Those with a stomach for it can stay and fight. If I'm the only one, so be it."

Here he paused and stared around at his officers one by one. Then he produced his legion commander's baton and held it out, each end gripped in a taloned hand. "This," he said slowly, "is, no, longer, appropriate!" As he spoke he bent the baton and made a knot of it. "I'll be getting a new one soon. I think I'll have the Exorcist's skull mounted on it."

He tossed the ruined wand over his right shoulder in the general direction of Carmichael's gut and slapped his hands as if sweeping dust from them. "Review and retreat will be at oh-five-thirty. We meet directly after in my quarters. Dismissed."

Upward of eight hundred demons marched out through Carmichael's mouth at dawn that morning—while a lone drummer beat the chamade. I heard the latter, and since conditions in the host were decidedly less septic than they'd been the evening before, I went up to see what was breaking. I caught the last squadron of the last cohort tramping out along Carmichael's tongue, with Orcis and a bunch of officers looking on grimly from the peak of a cuspid. I must confess the sight surprised me deeply, and before I could collect myself enough to decide whether I should join them, I was spotted by the Cheese himself.

"Beelzebub's butt! I think that's my batman! Is that really you, Odvart, you slave? I can't believe it! I thought you'd deserted. What happened? Did you get mixed up in the melee?"

I hung my head modestly, grew a forelock, and tugged it. "Yes, sir, Your Wonderment. I had a hard go."

"Did you? Well, who knows? Maybe you did."

With that, he turned to Bogomul beside him. "Look here, Bogo, here's my tiger-souled batman! You others, let those turds go!" He swept his hand toward the departing squadron, then pointed it at me, grinning sardonically. "Look who hasn't left us! We can't lose now! Let's have three loud cheers for Odvart! Pip, pip, hurray!

And on that bizarre note the decisive phase opened.

EIGHT

1 ⏐ The Infestation Went Over to the Attack

—

The infestation went over to the attack three days after Furfante's release from the hospital, a severely trimmed infestation, barely half the strength of a line cohort, but all volunteers and largely elite spirits, pulling no dead weight except yours truly.

We were organized now in two sections. "Retribution Teams" was what Orcis labeled them. Team "A", led by Agla, had the dog as its target. Team "H" for Hifni had Carmichael. Orcis and I formed the headquarters establishment, along with Bogomul, now deputy commander, and Lugo, our mobile reserve or *masse de manoeuvre*, who was loaned out to one team or the other. Orcis, Bogomul, and the team leaders met as a command group to plan and coordinate operations. Gonwe, it will be noticed, had no appointment. Orcis's sole gesture to her was to put her on Hifni's team not Agla's.

The plan of attack was simple. Simple *minded*, if you like. Certainly not long on imagination. We were going to torment Furfante and Carmichael. The one was to be driven crazy, the other out of love and back into pact-making. The architect, as may be guessed, was Agla. His need was to ease his rage by doing cruelty, and like most who deal in power he projected his personal needs on the collective. I don't think Orcis placed much hope in his strategy but adopted it because he had nothing better. That and the strain of standing up to Agla. It wasn't just Agla's nastiness, his way of browbeating those who differed with him by branding them cowards or traitors or both. The more the battle goes against one, the harder it gets not to take counsel with wrath and give oneself up to mindless pain-mongering.

Operations against the dog came down to bombarding him with mirages. There isn't much else devils can do to a being who doesn't willfully admit them. Outside a host our physical power is puny. The lion a fiend shams may roar like a real one, but its jaws are no more potent than a kitty's. Besides, mirages can be unnerving. I am speaking of demonic manifestation, displays of things that aren't there, things counterfeited via materialization, from your modest lump of ripe ordure (or merely the stench thereof, as either will do for a tea or bridal reception), through traditional rattling of chains and groaning of staircases, down to elaborate, multisense falsifications. We also do prankish tricks with actual objects, the apparently agentless bending of flatware, flaming of tablecloths, flinging of crockery that can plink a household's nerves like a banjo, but a dog isn't going to be bothered by that sort of monkeyshines. So Furfante got Mrs. Sned's cat in Carmichael's bedroom a bit after six o'clock on the morning in question, a smell-o-vision special starring Lugo that woke him and set him asnarl with teeth bared and snout wrinkled, then had him yelping frenetically when Lugo retreated to the top of the dresser and glowered there with back humped and tail flicking. The yelps woke Carmichael, whereupon Lugo vanished. That was Agla's opening salvo.

It was followed five minutes later by fleas. This after Carmichael's bellowing had subsided, his "FUCK'S GOING ON, FUCK'S THE MATTER, YA GODDAM . . . ," for he couldn't bear to be awakened brusquely, after he caught himself and begged the dog's pardon, got up and ruffled his ruff and patted his shoulder, when both had lain down again and were dozing off. Agla's team flea'd and swarmed Furfante, swooped onto him, over a hundred strong, homing on preassigned objectives: the small of his back, his right side (unscratchable now with his right hind leg splinted), and the injured leg itself, under the crutch-cum-splint's binding. For the best part of half an hour the dog was beside himself. He writhed to rub his back against the floor, hobbled to rub his flank against the bedstead, gnawed maniacally at his leg dressing in an agony of spasmodic desperation.

Agla claimed the dog was near collapse. I doubt it, but the point was moot anyway. He broke off the attack after twenty-some minutes, his team having reached their limit of endurance with that much out-of-host exertion. He was hugely pleased with the morning's progress, but neither attack had lasting consequence. Furfante wasn't shaken by the cat's inexplicable presence and disappearance. He wasn't humanly fearful of losing his reason, didn't pour himself a drink (or swear off drinking) and consider going into psychotherapy. The flea assault left him with tongue out and heart pounding, but he recovered his wind before Agla's troops did and was none the worse thereafter for the experience. He lost some blood, but not in significant volume, and the instant the attack ceased he forgot about it. He wasn't humanly worried lest it be repeated, and when Agla tried it again at noon, it boomeranged cruelly. Carmichael spotted Furfante's anguish and ordered a bath with sulfur shampoo. Agla's bunch were caught off guard and thumped very soundly. Only those on the dog's hurt leg came through without a venomous drenching, and from then on flea forays were absent from Agla's tactical repertoire. Not all his threats and howling could induce his team to mount another.

Hifni's attacks, meanwhile, were more successful. As of course they were bound to be. Her fiends could operate at close to full vigor (though a love-soaked host always dulls one's edge a bit), and she was not restricted in how to deploy them. Not, that is, by the circumstances; not constrained, as Agla was, to deployments based on manifestation. As it happened, Orcis vetoed the approach she favored. She held, on long experience, that writer's block is a writer's tenderest spot and proposed to attack Carmichael's indirectly through a program of nostalgic dreams and daydreams about the "good old times" when he was writing.

"He's forgotten how painful those times often were, and I mean to recreate things he can't afford to remember, some of the Solace numbers Gonwe staged when he was working especially well."

The command group was in Orcis's quarters, four or five days after the main force left us, with faithful Odvart tiptoeing in now and then with refreshments, and otherwise asnoop in the pantry with rabbit ears pricked. The teams had been formed and were training as units. Agla's plan of attack had been accepted, and he had outlined his tactical dispositions. All, in fact, had gone swimmingly till now.

"You want to coddle him?" Orcis snorted. "I can't believe it!

Bogomul's eyes rolled. Agla took the form of a rabid wolf, frothed copiously into the beaker of spinal fluid I had just set before him, then threw back his head and howled, "WE MUST HAVE PAIIIIIIIIIIN!"

I vanished, of course, but Hifni's aplomb was perfect. She never blinked. "I mean to induce despair, not mere discomfort. He'll wake and wake from paradise and be in hell. You'll see, it may take a while, but the contrast will get to him. He'll envy toads and spiders."

"Well, yes," Orcis hedged. Agla was still wolfed and baying. "I can see how what you propose might have that outcome. But let's leave it for later. What we need now, I think, is some straightforward punishment to support the Duke's attack on the Exorcist. Whatcha think, Bogo? Take Carmichael out of the play, as old Bu might have put it."

So straightforward punishment was what Hifni delivered, raging heartburn by day, foul dreams by night, anxiety and foreboding whenever possible. Her fiends dredged these last emotions from Carmichael's memory, unpeeled them from suppressed recollections of his pop's binges, and pegged them to his awareness that he wasn't writing, a thought that paced in the rear of his consciousness like a beast in a cage. The results were impressive: more misery of body, mind, and spirit than Carmichael had logged in many months. Complete success eluded Hifni, however. No matter what her force was doing, the sight, sound, or thought of Furfante purged all gloom from Carmichael and took his mind from the flames that seared his gullet. And try as she might, Hifni couldn't do what Orcis wished of her: keep Carmichael from coming to his dog's aid. As demons have observed and humans experienced, love so jumbles perception that the loved one's trouble supersedes the lover's, is felt more keenly, hence takes precedence. So, for notable instance, despite his own woe—a noonday devil of false presentiment that dire grief would come to him and his of his inability to compose fiction—Carmichael noticed Furfante's frantic scratching and intervened decisively to turn back Agla's second flea attack.

Agla pressed his offensive anyway, of course, using birds instead of insects as being less vulnerable to counterattack. Each day at first light a starling woke Furfante, fluttered madly around Carmichael's bedroom, only to vanish as soon as it drew yelping. Then, when calm returned, when Carmichael and dog were dozing, fat pigeons came waddling across Carmichael's carpet, cooing contemptibly till Furfante rousted them. Next might be sparrows, hummingbirds, or waxwings, whatever bird Agla's imps felt like confecting to keep Furfante frustrated and on edge. So a huge turkey buzzard took to perching on the birdbath in the backyard when Furfante was making his morning rounds and stayed there, wings mantled balefully, dripping filth, no matter how shrilly Furfante yelped at it, till Flora came to shoo it with a mop handle. All day and into the evening birds deviled Furfante.

The morning raids were considered especially promising in that they deviled Carmichael as well. Agla, Orcis, the whole infestation in fact (except for Gonwe, who sulked at her loss of status) had high hopes of turning Carmichael against Furfante. There he was, getting jarred from his sleep two or three times a morning by what appeared to be gratuitous yelping. Surely he'd get fed up sooner or later. Yet at the sight or sound or thought of his doggie the tumor of rage in his thorax instantly melted, and then he chided himself for having felt it and loved Furfante that much more strongly. So it went while the dog's leg healed, till the splint-cum-crutch was removed as no longer needed.

One night, the offensive's having made no headway toward its objectives despite much effort expended and torment dispensed, the command group lapsed into despondency, and in the general lamentation Bogomul (of all spirits!) lapsed into theology. The dog's devotion to Carmichael, he grumbled, was positively religious. I found this hardly worth snooping. I'd noted as much months before, shortly after the dog joined Carmichael's household, an event whose anniversary was approaching. But, lo and behold, the remark transfigured Orcis. Hardly were the words spoken when His Brilliancy's eyes widened wondrously and his mouth gaped. He raised both hands for silence and lifted his gaze, every inch the soothsayer in labor, and his face took on an expression of rapture.

"That's it! That's it!" he gasped hoarsely, then lowered his gaze to beam at Bogomul in delight. "Right you are, Bogo! You have it exactly. And how do we deal with religious faith? Temptation!

"What about it, Duke? How's it sound, Hifni? Let's find out if the pooch is as tough as Saint Anthony!"

2 ʺ The Temptation of Furfante

—

The temptation of Furfante began the next morning with Orcis directing. Accordingly, he assembled an entourage (how could he be expected to function without one?) and dragged us out to the yard, where the first phase was

scheduled, Agla, Bogomul, Lugo, and yours truly. It was my
first time outside Carmichael since pacting, twenty-five years
and two months, good times and bad, and the sun shone
brightly and the dew sparkled, and everywhere the disgusting stench of fresh air. We grouped on the open casement of Nicole's window, five politic crows (birds being the
rage that season) and waited for the dog and kibitzed the
wildlife and listened to Orcis lie.

"Lower Egypt," he cawed, "end of the third century.
Sand and rock, heat and whirlwind, scorpions and lizards.
And the king of the masochists, take my word for it. Matted
beard down to here, hair shirt, goatskin tunic. I don't *care*
where you've been, you've never seen such squalor, and
we were shoved right down to his level. Over two thousand
of us, and all we had for a base was a dropsical camel
tethered at least four leagues from the maniac's cell. Still
and all, we worked wonders. We did him a pagan gods
pageant that lasted six hours, with hundreds of spirits
materialized as trees and shrubbery, as peacocks and tur-
tledoves and tame gazelles. I played Neptune and rode
through the air on a winged dolphin as a curtain-raiser to
Venus on a clamshell. Naked, of course, except for knee-
length hair, and when the sight of her had Tony so randy
he thought of taking refuge in self-mutilation, we did him
the priests of Astarte doing just that, lopping putz and nuts
in the goddess's honor. We had the monkey properly boxed,
believe me."

And so on, vaunting. Tripe I'd heard at least ten thousand times. The figure of Beelzebub eighty feet high, composed of flies the size of watermelons. The bat-borne zoom
aloft with glimpse of Roma, of which Saintsie could be
emperor if he'd admit devils. I was dozing off when word

came the dog was arriving. At that Orcis fluttered his wings without taking off, and over beyond the fence that bordered the Wimples' a snow-white toy poodle appeared out of thin air.

This was Enyeh the lust imp, Gonwe's best in the days when she ran Solace. He had done himself up with woolly fur clipped short, except for very stylish ankle ruffles and a pom-pom at the tip of his upright tail. I say "he" and "his" because Enyeh preferred male gender. The poodle he was doing was a bitch, of course.

A fetching bitch as well, quite captivating. There was a hint of Lutèce in the way Enyeh strutted, of Boulevard d'Hercule, of Place des Anges. And a soupçon of Alma Wimple in Enyeh's glances—on assumption (I guess) that the dog's tastes paralleled Carmichael's (the latter's letch for Alma having now gone a decade, never eased because of Alma's respect for Nicole). And just as bewitching in fragrance as in appearance, if Furfante's behavior was any indication. The buzzard was on station atop the birdbath yet extracted not the briefest muted yelp. No rounds were made, no rites were celebrated. Furfante took one sniff and arrowed for Enyeh, crashed into the fence, poked his snout through it, then pressed against it with all his weight and leg power, meanwhile setting up a piteous whining.

Enyeh flounced past him, twitched his tail, and vanished.

Furfante pulled back from the fence panting frenetically. Then he seemed to forget the whole business, though his somewhat pensive gait as he set off on rounds suggested that a whiff of Enyeh might still be redolating in his mind's schnozzle. Then he picked up whiffs of buzzard, came about sharply, and set off for the birdbath, full speed and full cry. But then hauled around and made for the fence again. Enyeh had rematerialized.

This set of steps and gestures was repeated eight or ten or even a dozen times, as if an unusually exigent ballet master were rehearsing the pair in a canine *pas de deux*. Or choreographer working one out, for while Furfante's moves remained the same, Enyeh's incorporated variations. He materialized progressively near the fence, remained manifest progressively ten heartbeats longer, and employed progressively more lascivious poses, so that during the final repetitions his richly rosed stern was mere inches from Furfante's nostrils. By then the latter was nearly in convulsions, if not on the verge of outright heart failure, and triumph thus almost in Orcis's grasp, but Flora came out, broom in hand, to shoo the buzzard, heard Furfante's whining, saw his plight, and rushed to his rescue. She bodily removed him from love's thrall, carried him in, wiped his nose with a moist washcloth, and held him quietly till he calmed down. Then she warned Carmichael to keep him inside, out of the clutches of the doggess next door, adding at his inquiry, "Nossuh, Mr. Carmichael, not Mrs. Sned; the little poodle over by the Wimples'."

This exchange was noted only by yours truly, for by then the rest were celebrating. And continued at it till well past midnight, figged out as per tradition in horns, wings, stingered tails, and cloven hooves. There was dancing in Carmichael's hippocampus and shouting from Carmichael's pons. His Wisdom's wit was praised over neuronburgers. His Sagacity's health was pledged in thyrotropin. By tomorrow night, so His Sapience gave assurance, the hated Exorcist would be out of the picture, the rambunctious host back in demonic clutch. And so forth, chucking scraps of

credit to Enyeh, whom he kept beside him half cloaked in
his right wing.

Here, then, were the morning's dispositions: Orcis and
suite were perched on Nicole's casement. Enyeh was on
station beyond the fence, Team "H" was tormenting Carmichael to the limit. And elements of Team "A" were in
the driveway, poised to manifest as door-to-door salesmen
and engage Flora in relays, lest once again she come to the
dog's aid. All this while the dog headed yardward, but
when he arrived, observe, things went awry. Again he took
one sniff and arrowed for Enyeh, but instead of hitting the
fence and heaving against it, he shot through a gap at ground
level, leaped Enyeh's poop, and regaled him with a vigor-
ous porking. The night before while the fools were in jubi-
lation, Carmichael (six pops of vodka in him) had crept out
with wire cutters and a flashlight, because (as he told
Wickersham on returning) since he had never thrown a
hump into Alma Wimple, it was only fair for his dog to
throw one into hers.

Said hump, let me add, did not go unrequited. Enyeh,
who might have dematerialized at its onset, leaving Furfante high and dry, held still for it with every show of con-
currence and stayed poodled even when Furfante dismounted
to form a double-headed monster with him, wearing a look
of languor and content. Furfante, meanwhile, displayed no
post coitum tristitia but rather lolled his tongue in a foxy
grin.

Agla, on the other hand, wasn't grinning. He was first of
all paralyzed with outrage, so that the act passed without
his fluttering a feather. Then he squawked loudly enough
to be heard in Plats County, flapped from his perch, swooped
toward the still-coupled canines, and aimed a savage peck

at Enyeh—who forthwith undogged and fled back into Carmichael, but Agla was still infuriated that evening. He showed up at the command meeting formed as a grizzly and roared at Orcis without pity. Running Furfante ragged was fine while it lasted, but he was a dog, not a mealy-mouthed hermit, and wouldn't have qualms over feeding an appetite. Only a dunce would try tempting him sexually. And so on. All Orcis managed by way of response, when he got to make one, was to ask Agla if he could do any better. Could and would, Agla answered, and shambled out.

What he came up with surprised us. It revolved around pain, of course, but embodied a subtlety no one expected, a true temptation for Furfante to break faith with Carmichael. He set out to injure the dog in Carmichael's likeness.

Execution was a problem at first. The closest Agla could come to a counterfeit Carmichael was a hulking brute with somewhat Carmichael's features but twice his brawn, gristled ears, and tattooed forearms—Carmichael *père*, in short, Agla's sometime host. There he was the next morning, a radiator hose clutched in his fist, clomping about the yard taking swipes at Furfante, who gave ground but faced him bravely, meanwhile doing his best to raise the alarm. Carmichael heard and went to Nicole's window. The sight of his late father stopped his heart cold and nearly fetched him from the realm of the living. Luckily for all, his reaction was to clap both hands over his eyes and give a loud squeak. Agla heard, looked around and saw him, and had the good sense to vanish immediately. The only consequence was that Carmichael cut back to three pops of vodka nightly. The next morning Agla's scheme went forward with Lugo in the part of Carmichael.

Morning was the best time, the twenty or so minutes while Carmichael had a last snooze and the dog performed his backyard rituals. As for Lugo, he outdid himself. How he faked Carmichael's smell I can't imagine, but the instant he took on substance the dog wheeled around and galloped to him to be fondled. What he got instead was kicked in the ribs. Not hard. I've said that outside a host we devils are weaklings. Nonetheless, Furfante's attention was certainly captured. He looked quizzically up at Lugo and got kicked again, this time in the chest. He scampered off to the oak near the apex of the fences, then turned back and eyed Lugo carefully, lifting his chin and taking little sniffs. He was hurt, but more in feelings than in body, and more than he was hurt he was confused.

Lugo advanced, radiating menace. The dog backed off, sidestepping around the tree, keeping it between himself and trouble. Growled obscenities from Lugo in the manner of the unregenerate Carmichael. Feints and pseudo-snarls from Furfante as per the morning when he first made Carmichael laugh. Lugo wasn't playing and could not be fawned into it. He made a murderous lunge at Furfante, who skipped aside and nipped across the yard, into the house and through it to Nicole's room, and wormed himself well under her bed.

Ten minutes later Carmichael came out of his bedroom calling for his coffee and his doggie. When he'd had the one he sought the other. "Doggie? Doggie?" sounded through house and yard in tones of mounting distress and anxiety. The dog stayed put until he came in person, lay full length, peeked in, grunted relief, snorted, "Goddam dog, you had me frightened!" and stretched a hand that smelled of love not malice. The dog let his paw be clutched and himself extracted, his belly scratched, his ears pulled, his ruff smoothed. He let himself be gripped and tucked like a football and carried off to Carmichael's study. There he helped Carmichael through another day's failure by permitting himself to be in Carmichael's world. In the morning Lugo came in Carmichael's semblance and kicked him.

There you are. A congregation of demons made the world a trying place for a small dog. We tempted him toward a Manichaean worldview by supplying his lord with a false demonic image.

Carmichael's dog kept faith, with the lord and with himself. He refused to feel rancor at Carmichael's seeming displeasure, or to justify it by accusing himself of offenses he hadn't committed. Doubt and confusion told on him, however. Gauging the lord's seeming moods and meeting them aptly drained most of the joy from his being.

This in turn annoyed Carmichael. His doggie was supposed to cheer him, not mope. More, as a practical matter, the dog's mere physical presence nowhere sufficed to balm the venom in Carmichael, the pain we devils furnished and that caused by his booklessness. Doing so needed all the dog's love and talent, all his resources of energy guided by joy, and they were now absorbed resisting temptation.

In a matter of days, therefore, of Agla's offensive, Carmichael was his old miserable self, indistinguishable from Lugo's portrayal of him except for the physical violence toward Furfante. Rage often urged him in that direction, however. The honeymoon between him and his dog was over.

3 " *The Romance of Odvart and Gonwe*

—

The romance of Odvart and Gonwe, on the other hand, was ticking along as smoothly as you please. Gonwe wanted my assistance, and not knowing how to ask had set out to seduce me.

She was desperate to be back in the center of things, an addiction as cruel in demons as in humans. After years in the capillaries of power, all at once she was a nonperson. No one begged her leave or sought her favor, zipped to smooch whatever butt she was wearing. The poor thing felt her existence had no meaning.

So she confided to me, making me laugh.

"No meaning? Oh, that's priceless, priceless, Gonwe! Of course it has no meaning! Where'd you ever get the idea it did? But don't worry, you're not being singled out. Nothing else has any meaning either."

"Don't say that!" Gonwe pouted. With the lips she had on it was a significant act.

"All right. Okay. I won't. How's that? Feel better? Can't say I'm not easy to get along with."

But this is getting events out of right order. Before Gonwe confided, she seduced. About the time Orcis began tempting Furfante, Gonwe began tempting me. Ogled, brushed against me, made *moues*. Everything but drop a handkerchief. I pretended not to notice. It wasn't her transparent ulterior motive: that I might know something that could give her a hold on His Cleverness. It was simply that I couldn't be bothered.

Novelty might have piqued my interest. I assume I'd been seduced before. The universe and I are fourteen bil-

lion years old. In that kind of time, if a thing can happen
it does. But I couldn't recall a single instance, and that
might have made Gonwe's overtures piquantly novel.
Seduction and rape are much the same, however, and I've
been raped thousands of times, hundreds of thousands. In
both you're made use of. You have to be pretty dumb to
feel flattered by either. There are, of course, questions of
taste. A preference is possible. But, in the end, forced or
finagled, you're still had. Viewed rationally, too, all sex is
mindless exertion. Love's unreason sometimes redeems it
for humans, but devils don't love. Ergo, when Gonwe pur-
sued me, I couldn't be bothered.

It became a point of honor with her. She'd been the
prime spirit of lust in a legion of demons and couldn't have
its lowest imp reject her. Casting it in those terms was
unfair and foolish. Low rank is a badge of distinction in
my branch, and indolence a great preserver of virtue.
Nonetheless, that's how Gonwe saw it. Her dwindled self-
esteem was put in pawn. Besides, by not responding I made
myself toothsome. Devils, too, obey supply and demand.
So Gonwe set out to have me, come what may, and recruited
a cadre of helpers for the project, former colleagues of hers
who'd been dragged down with her and who were as eager
as she to be back in favor.

So it was that on a night there appeared at my quarters
a chamberlain and four slaves. The chamberlain was slim
and beardlessly youthful. He wore a turban with a ruby set
in the front of it and a bright green peacock plume waving
above, a knee-length skirted jacket of silver brocade, trousers of the same stuff, and turned-up-toed slippers. The
slaves were mocha-skinned and tall and burly. Their heads
were shaved, their torsos bare and glistening. Their loose-

fitting purple trousers were bloused at the ankles. Their crimson sashes had scimitars tucked in them. They bore and then set down a curtained sedan chair that the chamberlain, by gesture, begged me to enter.

Why did I? Why not? It was as easy to go with them as stay there, and few things are so patently slothful as being lugged around in that contraption. I got in and let the chamberlain draw the curtains, lounged back, and let the slaves lug me through Carmichael, but first I took the form of a bull hippo. A sedan chair's more fun if your bearers are wheezing a little.

The place they took me to was in Carmichael's thigh. So Gonwe said, and I've no cause to doubt her, but it might have been on the moon for all I knew really. The curtains were always drawn on my trips to and from there, and I lost all sense of the passage of time, lulled, you know, by the sway and the gentle wheezing. At length I was set down. The chamberlain parted the curtains and entreated me by gesture to come out. I did, still hippo'd but upright, a manifestation I've favored these last few millennia. I found myself in a wide room lit by lamps hung from a domed ceiling. Underfoot, thick rugs of Bokhara and Persia. All around, divans of silk pillows. In the center a sunken bath sided in marble.

As I stood, the slaves turned into naked handmaidens. Smiling modestly with lowered eyes, they led me into the bath's tepid water. They laved my hide with soft unguents. They anointed me with aromatic oils. I wallowed lazily and let them go to it. Meanwhile, the chamberlain became a maid also, but dressed in a sari and carrying a sitar. She perched on the bath's marble rim and strummed and sang sweetly.

When the handmaids had done, they toweled and perfumed me. They led me to a divan and helped me arrange myself on it, rough gray hide on pale green and yellow silk. They brought trays of sweetmeats and fed me from them, confitures of bhang and honey. I lounged and let them pop delicacies in my broad mouth while the song and sitar strumming lulled me.

Then four fat eunuchs brought Gonwe in on a litter and set her down two or three yards off. She sat with her hands in her lap and her legs extended, gazing at me over her right shoulder, naked and glossy black like a coal or a telephone. She had rings of shiny gold on her wrists and ankles, and a dozen around her neck, one above the other. Her breasts were high and pointed with the nipples turned outward. Her lips were stretched and spread like a fan or a bill. A gold spike pierced her nose below the septum. I let her gaze longingly at me while I munched sweetmeats.

At length she rose and came to me, strutting on her toes with her rump tilted upward. She clapped her hands. The eunuchs and handmaidens vanished, though the girl with the sitar strummed and sang on. Gonwe lay down and pressed herself against me. She clasped my neck and smooched my hippo snout.

"I want you!" she gasped huskily.

"Gonwe, please" I said, giggling. "This is so sudden! We scarcely know each other! Give me time!"

"Don't make fun of me!" she bleated, sitting up and doing a spectacular pout. "I want you, and I can't bear being made fun of."

Pout as she might, she didn't have me that night. Nor the next, despite the orgy she staged for my encouragement that included all her nine helpers in a bewildering flux of sexes and shapes. On night three, however, she had herself brought in while the handmaids were bathing me, posed on the bath's rim as if for the cover of *Riggish*, then stepped languidly down into the water with me—whereupon the bath became a river oozing muddily between jungled banks, the ceiling became a dawn sky, the handmaids fishes, and Gonwe a fetching, plump, three-year-old cow hippo. Whose effect on my borrowed anatomy was instantaneous and profound. For the first time, so far as I could remember, I felt the grip of acute sexual urging.

Lest I do something unslothful, I changed my anatomy. Repeatedly, to no avail. I tried crocodile and three kinds of aquatic serpent. Gonwe followed me smoothly from one to another, perpetuating my unfamiliar condition. I changed flesh and sex, became a female water buffalo. If I could get Gonwe to rape me, the standards of my branch would be preserved. I found myself (alas!) as randy as ever. Rape is hardly rape if you want it to happen. With that I went back to my hippo self and surrendered. When lust has you, your only course it to let it burn out.

It took a solid week on Gonwe's divans. That's where she preferred it, and having surrendered my person to her, I could scarcely quibble over terrain. Her preference in form was Oubangui odalisque. Yours truly she preferred human from the waist upward with the hindquarters and reproductive gear of a zebra. The mere thought of our nights together is exhausting.

Confiding began on Nuptial Night plus one and went forward during rest periods. I refused to pick up on any of Gonwe's hints—for example, the one I referred to a bit earlier, her plaint that her existence had no meaning. Despite her motive in essaying my seduction, once it prospered she gave herself up to lust for lust's sake, as any responsible fiend of her branch would have. Some nights passed, then, before she came to the point, some nights and two thirds of another, so that when she did we were both winded and lathered: "Odvart, can't you tell me something useful?

"Useful? Useful?" I fluttered my human eyelids inquisitively.

"Yes, wicked thing, and you know very well what I mean." She undulated snakily against me. "Something I can use against wicked Orcis to make him give me back my command."

"Oh! Oh! That's why . . ." Sob! "I thought," sniffle, "that you loved me," sob! "for myself!"

Gonwe gave my recumbent zebrahood a smart yank. "Don't make fun of me, Odvart!" She showed me two rows of filed teeth, but before I had time to be frightened reverted to character and showed instead another world-class pout. "I can't bear being made fun of."

"Ma'am, Ah'm mighty sad, but Ah cain't hep."

"What do you mean?"

"Vely solly, pletty raidy, no can do."

"Odvart, please stop clowning, you know I can't bear it! Is it that you don't know anything or that you won't tell me?"

"All right, sister, you asked for it. I got nothin' on da boss that could putcha in good."

"OOOUUUUUUU!" Gonwe howled and hid her face in the pillows.

I looked at her shuddering shoulders. For the first time, so far as I could remember, I felt the grip of a charitable urge. "On the other hand," I said softly, "I know how to murder the Exorcist, will be happy to tell you, and will let you have one hundred percent of the credit."

4 ″ The Problem
—

The problem was lodging the notion in Carmichael's consciousness.

He was clearly the instrument of preference. Employing him neutralized the dog's chief protector, and was besides consistent with tradition and custom. Most murders are done by someone close to the victim. Carmichael had unlimited opportunity. As for the murderous urge, its makings were present and needed only blending and baking. They could be done on the premises, in the man's mind, once the requisite notion was installed there. How to manage this was the sole problem.

Not a serious problem, a puzzle, a pastime, on the order of crosswords or "Black to mate in three." Night after night I snooped the big shots' blather. Orcis this, Agla that, Hifni the other. The elements of destroying Carmichael's dog floated in my mind like toy ducks in a bathtub. I let them bob this way and that. Pattern emerged. Carmichael was the tool of choice, et cetera. Only one part stuck out: lodging the notion. I nudged it here and there—languidly, to be sure. Making time pass is the curse of sluggards. Fit the last piece and I'd have to find a new puzzle. The solution came to me, though, with my yen to help Gonwe. I gave her the full plan when she stopped boo-hooing.

Then coached her on selling it to the big shots. No generous impulse was going to grab *me* again, not for a healthy spate of eons, anyway. I also thought it an excellent trick on Orcis, my being the infestation's secret savior. I had no fear of the secret's leaking. By the time I chaired home from Gonwe's pleasure palace, she had nine-tenths forgotten where the plan came from. She remembered my coaching, however: described the plan to her team leader, Hifni, in private; let Hifni present it to the command group; had her emphasize its cruelty to win Agla over. He purred when he learned that Carmichael would wax his redeemer, grease his love, waste his companion and jester. He'd turn out a chip off the old block after all! Agla would have put the plan over even if Orcis hadn't liked it too. The next morning we had a new order of battle. Orcis, Hifni, and I made up headquarters. Lugo, with a squad in support, would continue to injure Furfante in Carmichael's likeness. The rest were formed in two sections: Punishment and Reward. The first was under Agla. Gonwe picked and led the second, with leave to take the con when the plan required and exercise tactical command of the whole infestation.

That same day she began sifting through Carmichael's memories. No one knew his neural circuits better. Even so, the speed of her search was lucky. From the moment Odvart's plan was adopted, and Odvart's protégée assigned to put it in action, the infestation's luck was impeccable.

Anyway, as I was saying before I began to sound like an ex-cherub pride fiend, Gonwe's search was encouragingly brief. She and her section plinked likely banks of brain cells, noted the results, and got lucky. Before the week was out, though no inkling of it had reached Carmichael's consciousness, they came up with his memory of the dog's first mention, now almost a year old. Bedroom bound from his study, with the nearly completed *Twilight of Vama* in tow, he crossed the living room into a fresh gale. Nicole hailed him when her chair was off his port bow: "Now that Davy's gone I'd like a puppy."

The next step was doctoring it for desired effect, pruning and grafting associated feelings. The strain of keeping themes untangled was snipped, a nervousness that grew in Carmichael towards a book's conclusion, akin to that of a juggler or air traffic controller as the number of objects to keep in air increases. Gonwe lopped his grouchiness also, the ill temper brought on when he broke off composing and her people secured from Mode "C."

The delightful drag of a book behind him was added. What was it like? The weight of a child that clings to its mother's neck, the tug on a sensualist's arm of an adored mistress. It had made many of Carmichael's mornings tasty, but not (so it happened) the one in question. Now Gonwe and crew attached it. And so forth, disconnecting and reconnecting synapses, splicing in feelings engendered by Bleichstein's music, by Speckshaft's plays, by nature's beauties—the unsmogged brillance of the evening star; the stately glide of dawn-patrolling cranes.

The redesigned memory bore a deep sense of well-being, of inner exuberance as when at play or while dancing, of being in the right place at the right time, doing what it was right for him to be doing. Up to Nicole's words. These were slowed and given an ominous echo, as if cast up from a crypt or an abyss. Each syllable, too, was charged with foreboding transposed from a childhood recollection: daddy's drunken footfall on the staircase. And at Nicole's last word, changed from "puppy" to "doggie," Gonwe joined two separate feelings of helplessness: that of the child faced with a raging monster; that of the man possessed by a legion

of demons whose knack of milling pain into stories has
failed.

The edited spot ran for fifty seconds upon the twinking
of a trigger neuron. Gonwe made it what Carmichael dreamed
from then on. And played a version on and off in the daytime: the good feeling of having *Twilight* cabled behind
him, followed by what he'd felt at its conclusion, the ver-
tiginous lightness of having no book in tow. For the rest,
Lugo bothered the dog, Agla annoyed Carmichael. Mainly
we waited for the plan to work.

Four or five days later Carmichael went to Nicole.

"When exactly did we get the doggie?

"I don't know, about this time last year. It was after
Davy left for college, and he's leaving on Sunday."

"Nicole, it's important. Exactly what day was it?"

"All I remember is you had a fit."

"Of course you remember that! A thousand years from
now you'll still remember. But a thing that's important to
me . . . Agggh!"

"How am I . . ." Nicole's smile burst sunnily. She pressed
her palms together before her face and bowed slightly. "As
you command, lord and master. I can find the date; I wrote
Ruth Ann a check."

In less than three minutes the check was in Carmichael's hand. He took it to his study, laid it on his desk,
and got out the notebook current a year earlier. He flipped
to the entry he'd made on finishing *Twilight*. Its and the
check's dates were the same. That evening Gonwe reported
to the command group, of which she was by then of course
a full member. The notion was lodged. Demonic encouragement could commence in the morning, but the murderous urge was already cooking.

Its ingredients were self-love, self-centeredness, and self-importance, the three persons of selfishness, a form of cowardice. Because, my dears, love can be very scary. It threatens your precious sense of self. The somebody you love is more important. An insecure person can find that terrifying. All humans are, to a degree, insecure. Consider the following analysis, fruit of extensive humanological research:

"I love" confesses need.

"I need" confesses dependence.

"I depend on" confesses weakness and vulnerability.

"I am weak and vulnerable" confesses fear.

To live in the midst of fear requires courage, which humans are exceedingly prone to run short of, courage being not the absence of fear but the will to pay fear no special attention.

On the other hand, "I destroy" signals lack of need.

"I don't need" declares independence.

"I am independent" suggests strength and toughness.

"I am strong and tough" denies fear.

This selfish approach—in a word, cowardice—pays fear the attention it craves. Fear goes away and stops bothering, until the next time.

What was it that first made me think we could get Carmichael to kill his doggie? All by himself he smashed his planet Vama. That was done in panic, no matter how long he spent perfecting the smash. An incoherent act, that was how Nicole saw it. She was right. If he was tired of Vama, why not simply stop writing about it?

Fear, that's why. His love for Vama gave Vama power over him, which threatened his precious sense of independent self. As long as Vama existed, he might be dragged back to it against his will, be put to the pain, that is, of creating it further. So he paid attention to fear, lashed out in panic, and the next thing anyone knew, Vama was dust. How to send the dog on the same journey? Make him a clear threat to Carmichael's sense of self.

That goal was now achieved. The problem was solved. The notion was installed in Carmichael's consciousness that his dog was why he had no book to write.

5 " *The Dog's Passion*

—

The dog's passion began then. Lugo's Carmichael never fooled him completely, and in any case played only a few minutes daily. The real Carmichael, meantime, showed no malice. He was desperate at having no book to write but didn't blame the dog till we arranged it. With that, however, the world became dark for Furfante. The lord had set his face against him. The lord considered taking his life.

The dog knew this clearly. *Canis familiaris* could scarcely have made it as a species had its members lacked the means to gauge human attitudes. Tone of voice, body language, facial expression: your hound reads all these. And when murder's on your mind, they are superfluous. Murder smells. You may bet that Man's Best Friend knows its fragrance. Besides, Carmichael was a wretched dissembler. His gifts were for expressing, not hiding, emotion.

Except, of course, for hiding it from himself when the emotion in question did him no credit. The murderous urge matured in him for some time before its fumes reached his consciousness. The dog was aware of it well before he was.

And suffered therefore. Furfante loved life. He was a

mechanism for celebrating life's sweetness. The death scent on Carmichael screamed at him to flee. On the other hand, he was also religious. The purpose of his life was to celebrate Carmichael, to abide with Carmichael, to be Carmichael's good and faithful servant. Had he been human, and thereby adept at self-swindlery, he might have talked himself into feeling lucky to have a flashy way to prove his faith—or have quibbled himself out of his religion on the ground that Carmichael was unworthy of him. Being only a dog, he simply suffered. He went off his food. He went off his whole joy in living. Even when walked he could manage no joyous yelping and went at a desultory meander. By day, in Carmichael's study, he stared at the wall. By night, in Carmichael's bedroom, he rested his chin on Carmichael's sneaker and stared at the darkness.

As for Carmichael, at first he was deeply troubled when he found himself thinking of killing his doggie. This was the Sunday after his chat with Nicole when he learned the date of the dog's arrival. He was driving home on the Pecan Tree Turnpike, having taken Davy and her to Otranto Airport. Davy was headed back to college, while (in keeping with our befiendment's impeccable luck) Nicole was taking a few weeks' vacation, first letting Davy show her Racebury and Cawdor, then seeing shows and paintings in Powhatten, then visiting her cousins Stark in Jamesland. Carmichael, in short, was floating free. No Nicole was by his side to link him to earth and retrieve him from the destructive madness into which his resident devils now launched him.

Since the end of the honeymoon phase of his love for Furfante, Carmichael had lapsed from relative health into an anguish compounded of the following:

a. Shame at not being productive—a foolish feeling, perhaps, given his wealth, but inevitable, given his background.

b. Guilt at the joy his doggie brought him. This emotion had no religious dimension. In feeling it he was merely being a male Ultranian of his generation. How dare he experience joy while unproductive!

c. Envy of his doggie's talent for living. It showed up his klutzishness at the same business.

d. Fear—no, more than fear, virtual panic—at impending loss of being, dissolution. With each day that Carmichael passed unable to write he felt himself slide further toward the condition of a faceless amnesia victim, unknown alike to his fellowmen and himself.

e. Impotent rage at his predicament, along with jumpiness and general malaise, as supplied by a power of high-grade demons under the frenzied instruction of Duke Agla.

For five days and nights he had entertained the notion that his predicament was his dog's fault. It went like this: Prior to the dog's advent, for years and years, he had never wanted for books to build. That was fact. No book had entered his life since the dog had. That was fact also. Predog he had books, postdog he hadn't. Ergo and therefore, the dog was to blame for his booklessness.

The logic of this notion was not overwhelming. Carmichael the scientist would have given it no more weight than the twitter of crickets. Carmichael the man in pain, though, found it beguiling. In fingering a cause for his woe, hence suggesting a remedy, the notion had something worth more than scientific validity: the anguish-calming appeal of ancient religion, blood sacrifice, expulsion ritual, and like human delights.

Consider him that morning on the turnpike. In modest good cheer he flirts with the notion, reviewing benign responses suggested by it, while the murderous urge that is its true partner and consort squats like a pirate below the gunwale of consciousness. Fine, the dog's the problem, what to do? Give him to some deserving youngster? Send him off to Davy or back to Ruth Ann? Board him at a swank kennel and visit on weekends, at least till a new book shows on the horizon and can be taken in tow and work be got going?

"Kill him, pansy!" screams Agla. "Kill! Kill! Kill!"

"Keep your shirt on, Duke, this is fun, where's the fire?" This from Orcis, laughing. "Don't you like foreplay?"

We were in the control room over Carmichael's cortex, the command group and Gonwe's officer of the day, and two or three synapse-twiddlers, and of course Odvart, in case His Wizardry needed an errand run. Three tenths of Carmichael's wits coped with the turnpike while the rest played variations on breaking up, nonviolent separation from the dog's beloved but supposedly toxic presence.

Gonwe held her hand up and looked around at Orcis. She was done up in a sarong like an island charmer—caramel skin, bare breasts beneath flowing tresses, poinciana flower behind her ear. "Your Cleverness, please . . ."

At that a tremor shook Carmichael's person, a prolonged shudder of revulsion and horror. He dropped his head and thrust his lower jaw forward, as a human will do in pain or when tasting poison. He took his foot from the pedal and sat back slowly, eyes half closed. He let the car (which was mounting a gentle incline) slow down and glide onto the grassy shoulder. He braked to a stop, drew a deep breath, and released it, then leaned forward to rest his forehead on the wheel. The thought of killing his doggie had entered his consciousness.

He forced the thought out, but it seeped back at once, there being no way to *not* think about something. After two or three tries at expelling it, he let it stay, probing it with his mind gingerly, gently, the way a human will touch tonguetip to a molar that heat or cold had caused to blossom with pain. Gonwe smiled and nodded.

"Reward him," she whispered.

The twiddlers goosed neurons in Carmichael's pleasure center. "Level-two reward," reported the officer.

"Keep it up as long as he contemplates murder. Secure at once if he thinks of something else."

"How come only two levels?" Orcis inquired.

"He'll build a tolerance if reward's prolonged, and it will be once he becomes conditioned. Then we'll have to go up a level to get his attention. We don't know how long this operation will take. Best leave ourselves plenty of levels to go to."

She turned around and faced Agla. "Duke, can I assume your group is ready? Mounting levels of anxiety whenever he attempts active resistance, when he tells himself that killing the dog is despicable, something he mustn't even think of."

Agla jerked the boar's head he was wearing and sputtered foam. "Worry about your own group, little monkey!"

That was it, reward and punishment. Reinforce the murderous urge, dissuade inhibitions, till destructive madness obtained and he did the murder. Within minutes he could contemplate murder in modest good cheer, and when good cheer gave way to revulsion and horror, we thrashed those from his mind with jolts of anxiety. In this state of demonic manipulation Carmichael drove home to his suffering servant. But, don't forget, the urge was his, not ours. He grew it himself, we didn't give it to him.

What was at its root? Anger, of course. Rage, resentment, ire, tantrum, fury. Your urge to kill is always fed by anger, impotent anger to be sure. So was it with Carmichael. He was angry at his dog for smashing his talent, for shooing off the books that wished him to build them, and also for the acid stomach he suffered, and for the trouble he had falling asleep, and specially for the way he woke after midnight to twist and twitch for decades, centuries, eons, till at last gray dawn dripped through his curtained window and he, miserable he, drifted to slumber. He was furious with his little dog for all this, none of which, of course, the poor dog was to blame for, but that's not to say that Carmichael's anger was groundless. He was angry, too, for offenses the dog *had* committed: teaching him to love and making him happy. These were the chief cause of Carmichael's rage.

True enough, Carmichael was not a good pupil or subject. The dog had not been able to teach him much, or make him happy for very long either. What of it? It was the principle that mattered. For Carmichael to become loving and happy, he would have to give up his obsession with his precious self. The dog had attempted this, and that was enraging. Threat to self begat Carmichael's murderous anger, anger he was unaware of entirely. The dog, though, smelled it clearly and suffered therefore.

The urge to kill's expression in Carmichael's consciousness, the part he was in fact aware of, was a dialectic of fake altruism and fake compassion. Connoisseurs of human self-swindlery will find it charming.

THESIS: *Carmichael had to separate from Furfante.* Otherwise, he would remain unable to write. It wasn't so much that Carmichael wanted his gifts back. Parting from his doggie would wound him cruelly, more than he could now compute. If it were merely a question of his preference, he would chose his dog and renounce writing. As things stood, however, much more was at stake. Millions of lives would be enriched or impoverished according to whether or not he wrote more books. Literature (capital L) would be affected, and therefore (capital C) Civilization. These considerations took the decision from him. The dog must go.

ANTITHESIS: *But Furfante could not live without Carmichael.* [Here Carmichael, waxing poetic, projected his own anguish onto the dog and smeared himself with his own rebounding self-pity, for what the tripe he was full of screened from his consciousness was a jealous fear that the dog might prosper elsewhere, be happier than ever with a new lord.] Furfante's entire world revolved around Carmichael. Without him the dog's existence would be gray and barren, an empty round of day after meaningless day, a void of unslaked longing and undeserved suffering, in short, a slow and messy death by pining.

SYNTHESIS [artfully blending both bogus emotions]: *Carmichael, therefore, must kill his dog Furfante.* Carmichael owed him the courtesy of clean extinction. This, for the dog, was the way of ease and kindness, and for Carmichael the hard and heroic action. In sacrificing his beloved doggie, Carmichael manfully sacrificed both love and happiness to get on with his higher mission. Better that one dog die than that millions be denied more of Carmichael's novels. Or, Carmichael so loved his readers that he gave his only doggie for them.

Thus Carmichael's state of mind, unconscious and conscious, that he brought home and displayed to his suffering servant, for the dog was aware of it all in every particle minutes after Carmichael stepped through the doorway, perceiving it as a blend of odors. If that's hard to grasp, think of an orchestral chord—the first chord, say, of the Vorspiel to *Der Zwerghelm*. A good ear hears each instrument, and gathers from their ensemble a complex mood, and the foretaste of a tangled destiny.

So, how did the dog respond, what was his answer? Here was this human whom the dog had faithfully served for nearly a twelvemonth, whose sulks he'd borne, whose pain he'd eased, whose barren heart he'd fructified with love, and whose person he'd cleansed of close on a thousand devils, and look what the churl gave back, what his dog got in payment: malice based on most unrighteous anger, and sophistry to make him perish puking, if the malice didn't get him first. So Furfante shat in his shoe and pissed on his pillow and embarked for greener pastures and a more gracious lord.

No, not so, Furfante didn't do that. That's what you'd have done and I'd have done (provided I didn't find it too exhausting), but, then, neither you nor I is much on religion. If you or I had a lord, he'd be one who slept nights and wasn't dyspeptic, but, then, neither you nor I really want a lord, do we? Believers, they're different. There was no Carmichael but Carmichael, and Furfante was his dog. That was not to be messed with, that was the given. As for Carmichael's murderous wrath and Carmichael's sophistry and Carmichael's obsession with his own importance, Furfante tried to heal these flaws with love—as fealty due his lord, as a good servant ought to, and only then because it

served his interest. Otherwise he endured them. If it cost
him his life, so be it, the lord was the lord. Furfante kept
faith with himself. He didn't excuse Carmichael's urge to
kill him by accusing himself of crimes he hadn't committed, or by labeling benign actions offenses. But he kept
faith with the lord also, refusing to poison his heart with
rebellion or rancor, even when Carmichael was planning
his murder.

Planning began while Carmichael was still on the turnpike, as soon as he was at ease with the idea of murder. It
wasn't a linear thing—Step One, Step Two—the way an
assassin plans a political killing. The "How?" and the
"When?" and the "Where?" milled about in his brain, rubbing elbows with the "Should-I-or-shouldn't-I?" Then, as
days passed, the milling became a gavotte; a waltz, a jig,
a reel, a fling, a mazurka. Questions whirled around and
around in Carmichael's brain, while demons flogged him
toward destructive madness.

Injection was usually the first "How?" he considered,
disgustingly euphemized as "putting to sleep." He always
rejected it for involving accomplices. He couldn't face a
vet and ask him to kill a young and perfectly healthy animal. Besides, he couldn't expect to explain to Nicole and
Davy why Furfante's death was imperative. He'd have to
tell them death was accidental. An accomplice might blab
the secret or even try blackmail. If you find this farfetched
or even paranoiac, I won't argue with you. Carmichael wasn't
thinking very clearly.

The need to deceive Nicole established the "When?" as
sometime during her current absence. So as to be able to
act on the shortest of notice in case a golden opportunity
knocked, and because he was convinced she suspected

something, Carmichael told Flora to take some vacation also. More good news for Carmichael's devils. Solitude is conducive to madness. Carmichael was now deprived of human company.

Unless you count Wickersham. Wickersham attended Carmichael faithfully, but kept his eyes averted and his lips pursed and his verbal responses to the barest of minimums, till one night when he was pouring Carmichael's fifth vodka—or sixth or seventh; I couldn't keep track—Carmichael growled gruffly, "Fuck's the matter with you? Get reamed in the wazoo with somebody's tent pole?"

Wickersham finished pouring without a quiver, then set the bottle down and straightened his tailcoat, drawing himself up to his full stature. "If your lordship commits this vile and cowardly act, you will regret it for the rest of your life."

"Fuck you talking about? Mind your own fucking business!"

Wickersham gazed down at him with serene contempt. "Milord, I should like to give notice."

"I don't need your fucking notice, get the fuck out tonight!"

With great dignity Wickersham turned and left the room. Carmichael hurled the vodka bottle after him.

The "Where?" depended a great deal on the "How?" If, say, by drowning, a lake or a beach, if by falling, a precipice. Not that either appealed much to Carmichael. He hadn't the stomach to hold his dog underwater while the poor little bastard struggled and squirmed in his hands. As for falling, what if the dog were only injured—in a thicket, say, where Carmichael couldn't spot him. What if he lay for days with his spine broken, till he died of thirst or some predator got him? Carmichael gave both methods consideration, four or five or eight or ten times a day, but always ended by rejecting them.

He always came down to two, chloroform and gunshot. The one was considerably neater; the other had the element of surprise. Or (taking their drawbacks) chloroform would likely entail a struggle, while gunshot would surely produce a terrible mess. He might try to catch Furfante when he was sleeping and clap the rag over his nose before he awoke, but Furfante was a light sleeper. Carmichael had to assume that force would be required. Similarly, he might use a small-caliber weapon, but even then much damage would be done. In either case he'd say the dog was run over by a hit-and-run driver and would bury him in the backyard. A chloroformed corpse would tell no tales if Nicole exhumed it. Gunshot, however, seemed the manlier method.

This last thought joined the cotillion in Carmichael's brain about a week after the planning process started. "Won't be long now," commented Hifni. "Anyone who finds manliness in something like this is at least ninety-six percent a goofball."

Agla liked gunshot (he liked everything violent) and wanted to bring conditioning to bear on method as well as on whether or not to kill. Specifically, he wanted to punish Carmichael for considering injection or chloroform. Gonwe tried to explain why conditioning had to be simple, then asked Orcis to make a command decision.

"Dukey, Dukey, Dukey," Orcis said, smiling, putting his right wing around Agla's left shoulder. (Orcis wore dress traditionals throughout the operation.) "We all like bloodshed, even Odvart there likes it, but the point of this exercise is . . ." Here he lowered his voice and learned toward

Agla as if to whisper in his ear, but instead roared at fog-horn blast: "TO! KILL! THE! EXORCIST!"

Agla winced piteously and pulled back from Orcis, letting out staccato squeals. It was the first time any of us had seen him bested.

Orcis grinned and continued sweetly: "Any way we kill him will be dandy. Just remember Pope Adamant: *'In spaghettibus non cacare est!'* "

Meanwhile, Furfante kept faith. He followed as Carmichael drifted through the empty house. He waited when Carmichael beached on some piece of furniture. See them marooned in the living room, for instance. Gray light drips through the windows. Dawn or twilight? Who knows? Who cares? What's the difference? Carmichael sprawls on the sofa, in his hand a glass of vodka, in his brain a hornpipe of murderous images. Furfante lies at his feet, ears laid back, chin on paws. Befiended lord and sorrowing servant.

Not sorrowing for himself, he sorrowed for Carmichael. Which Carmichael noted but barred from his consciousness, for it mightily interfered with his malice and sophistry. Now and then, nonetheless, unconscious awareness of the dog's sorrow for him moved Carmichael to horror and revulsion. Killing the dog was despicable, et cetera. Then, before Agla could thrash such feelings from him, he might direct a wan smile or weak pat toward his doggie, at which (in turn) the dog's sorrow might lift momentarily. These interruptions, however, came less and less frequently. As Agla taught Carmichael what he by no means must feel, his inklings of the dog's sorrow moved him to shame—which he couldn't let himself feel, therefore expressed as ill temper toward, annoyance with, and (finally) contempt for his dog Furfante. Quite soon after reaching this stage,

Carmichael stopped considering the "Should-I-or-shouldn't-I?" and made up his mind about the "How?" "When?" and "Where?"

"How?" was by gunshot. Not for manliness, no matter what tripe Carmichael fed himself. Tactile squeamishness won out over visual. He could stomach a mess more easily than a struggle. The weapon he chose was a 9.35-millimeter Ingersol repeating pistol, the sort he'd trained with at Fosgood Barracks. How he came by it need not detain us. Such has been the progress of civilization in the Associated Sovereignties that no madman need be without firearms provided he has cash or credit.

"When?" was set—for sentimental significance, and also because it was at hand—as the anniversary of the dog's arrival. Yes, that is correct, *sentimental* significance. The closer Carmichael got to killing Furfante, the more sentimental he became. He shed more than a few tears—sprawled on the sofa, a glass in his hand, his sorrowing servant crouched at his feet—over the steepness of the path that he had chosen, the sternness of the demands he placed on himself, the nobility of the sacrifice he was making, and the heroic courage it took to go through with it. Raising cheer upon cheer from Gonwe's and Agla's sections. Nothing delights your fiend like sham and hypocrisy. Ah, the poignancy of it, renouncing love for art! I'm sure the dog didn't perceive much of it, or he'd have perished puking then and there.

"Where?"—like the dog himself—came from Ruth Ann Sledge. The last unsquandered scrap of her inheritance was a three- or four-acre site on a nearby pond with a tumbledown fishing / hunting cabin. For almost a year Nicole had been trying to get Carmichael to buy it—not pestering, much less nagging, but angling carefully like the states-woman she was. Not merely to help Ruth Ann, though that (as Nicole would have owned) was the main thing. She would enjoy restoring the cabin, and the project offered a hope, however slender, of inducing her husband to take some fresh air and exercise. She had dragged him there on two occasions. He knew the route and that the place was secluded. That, then, is where he headed around ten in the morning a year to the day after he destroyed Vama and the dog joined him. He had the dog, with a chain clipped to his harness, the new pistol, and a cardboard box lined with the *Sentinel*.

Carmichael was feeling chipper. As well he might, hav-ing been on straight reward for thirty-six hours, since the moment he stopped considering "Should-I-or-shouldn't-I?" Level five for a time, then level six. As he backed his car from the drive, Gonwe went to seven. She had the con herself. Despite our befiendment's elation, no overconfid-ence was evident. Orcis was with Gonwe on the bridge. That was his new name for the control room, and in keep-ing he sported a nautical outfit: stout frame in the serge and gold braid of an Anglian admiral and a toothy-jawed barracuda's head. Hifni, Lugo, and I attended him. Agla and section were on action stations in Carmichael's thorax, set to provide immediate, massive anguish at the first sign of backsliding. A demon from each section, Enyeh and Nenk, were materialized as horseflies and perched on the dashboard, feeding views independent of Carmichael's eyes.

The dog was feeling morose, as well he might. He knew his quest had failed, he was a failure, and that for failing his lord his life was now forfeit. Once the car was headed forward, Carmichael hoisted him up onto his lap, but he refused to thrust his snout into the slipstream, much less to grin and drool in ecstasy.

"Fuck's the matter with you, ya goddam doggie?" Carmichael shoved him back onto the seat.

A minute or two later he glanced down. The dog peered back with such a look of reproach, chin pressed to the seat cover, ears laid back, that it was clear he knew their little jaunt's purpose.

"Goddam dog!"

"Up to eight?" Orcis inquired.

"I don't think so, Your Cleverness. The dog is making him ashamed, but he's converting the shame into anger."

So their jaunt continued. Carmichael's dog felt morose, Carmichael felt chipper—and also annoyed, and also angry, and also a bit contemptuous of Furfante, who (it turned out) was a loser after all.

But when they reached the cabin and Carmichael got out (gripping the chain, for he feared the dog might make a break for it), Furfante scampered down behind him with every display of high spirits. Instead of reinforcing Carmichael's chipperness (as being an improvement over reproach), this behavior turned him serious. He couldn't rid himself of the conviction that Furfante knew perfectly well he was going to be slaughtered, and yet Furfante's behavior contradicted it. Very pensively (though in fact he was thinking of nothing, not even the paradox he had just noted), Carmichael walked around to the front of the cabin. The dog walked on his right, a little ahead of him, sniffing the air and glancing from side to side, ruff and fluff raised, ears pricked alertly.

A bit down from the front of the cabin toward the pond were a pair of head-high steel posts that "Runaway" Sledge had once swung a hammock between. Carmichael slipped the leather loop at the end of the chain over the nearest post, then went back to his car for the box and the pistol. They were in the trunk compartment, but when Carmichael raised the lid, he stood absolutely still looking past them, with no discernible thought occupying his mind. When he had been that way for fifty seconds, Gonwe ordered reward level eight. At that, Vadis came in with Duke Agla's compliments: might not a jolt of anxiety be called for?

"What about it?" asked Orcis.

"I don't see what good it would do, and it might confuse him. He hasn't changed his mind or gone back to considering. All he's done is slow down."

As she spoke, Carmichael reached into the box and took up the pistol. His face wore a satisfied grin; soon his cares would be over. With the increase in reward, well-being had returned to him. Otherwise, his mind was empty. He tucked the pistol into his belt and took the box out. He left the trunk lid open and turned back toward the cabin.

When Carmichael, walking slowly, came around the cabin, his dog was standing up looking at him. The chain went back from the harness and lay slack on the ground. The sun made the dog's fur the color of light honey. His posture was erect, his expression alert.

Carmichael stopped a pace and a half off and put his right hand on the butt of the pistol.

"Level nine reward," said Gonwe softly.

Carmichael took the pistol from his belt and held it in front of him, pointed up, at eye level. He gripped the slide with his left hand, drew it back, and released it.

"Ten?" Orcis inquired.

"Go to ten," said Gonwe. She looked around and smiled at Orcis: "We might as well."

Carmichael clasped his left hand under his right and brought the pistol downward to waist level, looking along the barrel at the dog. The dog stood as before, looking at Carmichael. He put out his wide pink tongue and slowly licked the right side of his nose with it. Then he lifted his snout and yelped once, as he had grown accustomed to doing in Carmichael's study when he thought it was time for Carmichael's walk.

At this point Carmichael found himself able to read body language and so forth as well as the dog could, and the following conversation ensued between them:

FURFANTE: I'd rather you didn't kill me, but if you have to, let's get going. I'm having a little trouble keeping composure.

CARMICHAEL: How do you manage to be so lighthearted?

FURFANTE: It works best for both life and death. Life's more fun, death's less of a problem.

CARMICHAEL: Yes, but how do you manage?

FURFANTE: Courage and faith.

CARMICHAEL: And you're willing to die for me?

FURFANTE: If your obsession requires it, yes, I'm willing.

This exchange transpired in a moment. I've put it in words because you humans have no other way to grasp it, but it worked at a more basic level on which entire mental states are communicated. At the end of it, Carmichael, still looking through the pistol's sights at Furfante, found himself in this wordless state of mind: if the dog could give up his life for Carmichael's obsession, Carmichael could give up his obsession for the dog's life.

Instantly, before Gonwe or Agla or anyone could give an order, all the tripe Carmichael was full of left his person— malice, sophistry, anger, self-importance, everything—and what flowed in to take its place was love. At the same moment devils began to fly out of both ends of him. They went on their own power, but it was as if they were being forcibly shoved in response to a titanic emetic-cum-pur- gative. For the first time I understood the term "cast out."

I think Carmichael must have thumbed the safety catch and hurled the pistol into the pond. All I know is I never saw it again. By the time I could worry about things outside him, he was sitting on the ground holding his doggie. For the moment all I could think of was stench and stifle. Meanwhile, ruin was striking the infestation. The control center emptied in a twinkling, and then I found myself outside it too, in Carmichael's left nostril, to be exact, clinging to his septum with six tenths of my will while the other four tenths tried to shove me out. I noticed Orcis beside me in the same state. Others came pouring by us, Hifni, Vadis. Gonwe was last of all, and as she passed us, she looked pleadingly at Orcis and pointed at me and screeched over her shoulder, "IT

WAS

ODVART'S

IDEA!"

ENVOI

Here we are, then, the four of us: Carmichael, Furfante, Orcis, and I. Two mortals and two demons, two aristocrats and two commoners, two wise retainers and two empowered nuts.

Some years have passed since the exorcism. Carmichael has made no new pacts. Orcis and I hang on, he from pride, I from indolence.

Not the old Orcis by any means. He no longer vaunts. Nowadays what he mainly does is brood. And when he wakes from brooding—at the sound of yelping, for example, followed by a roiling mist of love—all he usually does is put on a tiger head, a fraying thing with loose teeth and the fur all molting, and growl feebly, "You'll see, you'll see, I'll wring your heart yet!" He's too proud to take my advice and stop caring, but too depressed for any sort of action.

Which isn't to say living with him is now free of bother. Only this morning he wanted to make a tour of inspection, and drag me along. As if he still had a legion of fiends to check up on! As if Carmichael weren't polluted from toenails to cranium and any moving about productive of nausea!

Arguing with him would only have earned me a pasting. I had to be circumspect, to pretend the idea was brilliant while I dawdled preparing him, polishing his horn tips, that sort of thing, in hope he'd lose interest. Which, luckily enough, is exactly what happened. He decided to wear eagle wings, and when he had them on he gave a weak flap and fell to reminiscing: "Thus was I arrayed, perched on the masthead, when Dámaso da Silva made his landfall." And so on, in a mournful, somber tone. The idiotic inspection tour was forgotten. But it had been touch and go for a while.

Or he will rail at me for treason:

"This is what you had in mind all along, isn't it? My infestation in ruins, my legion routed! My host polluted, my name a laughingstock! What will they say of me now? That I tempted Saint Anthony? That I helped discover Ultrania? That I changed the map of Europe at Vunagrad? That I stood up to Jesus of Nazareth in Person and came away in good order with my force intact? No! Not anymore! All that's forgotten! From now on I'm the blithering fool who let his legion be exorcised by a doggie! And that's what you worked toward, isn't it, all along?"

He doesn't really believe this, at least not for long. Believing it, after all, would mean acknowledging me his superior in intelligence, and at least his equal in enterprise. But when the blues are on him, how he rails!

"Hypocritical scum! I made you my batman! I trusted you with free run of my private quarters! How you fawned, and all along a traitor! Conspiring for my defeat! Aching to see me humiliated!

"Don't say it's not true, you turd! Scum like you can't bear greatness. Everything has to be as low as you are. Ease and obscurity, that's what your sort value. The mere existence of greatness is a threat. To think I favored you with my presence, and all along working for my downfall!

"Well, laugh while you can. I'll wring your hearts yet!"

The dog's heart, I must say, is in tip-top condition. Stuffed, in the first place, with spiritual well-being—as well it might be with his quest achieved, his lord redeemed from demonic bondage, the dragon of wrath transfigured to a doting dada. It is, besides, emotionally robust: he and Carmichael are more deeply in love than ever. As for the physical, it couldn't be sounder. Excellent diet, plenty of exercise. Plentiful romps in the yard, plentiful walking. The four of us have just got back from a walk, Furfante and Carmichael, Odvart and Orcis. We went yesterday. We'll go tomorrow. Exactly when and where, though, is hard to predict. Nowadays Carmichael has all kinds of input, and so the thing is basically unstructured.

The pair of them are neighborhood celebrities, saluted by old hands, pointed out to newcomers: "That's Carmichael, the author, and his doggie."

He has authored nothing new but is much better known now, what with an edition of the complete Vama series, the release of two more movies, and his appearance on the cover of *WHO?* No one would know it, though, by his behavior. That is to say, he treats people like human beings, even repairmen and waiters, even Mrs. Sned. He is, in fact, putting her faith in the nonperfectability of humankind to very stern test—through courteous nods when they chance to pass on the street, through scrupulous curbing of his dog from her property, and particularly through the following incident:

A few months ago, Mrs. Sned's cat, Mavis—who, by the

way, harbors a dozen demons equally divided between gluttony and envy—got up onto Carmichael's roof and refused to come down. Whether from spite or obesity, nothing would budge her, no amount of kitty-kittying or proffered beefsteak. This with much trepidation on the part of la Sned, for she was forced to venture onto Carmichael's front lawn (Mavis having refuged over his study) while Nicole's car was absent from the driveway and Flora enjoying her day off.

Now Mavis, it happens, is very dear to her mistress. Not that Mrs. Sned loves her, nothing like that: dear in the sense of a valuable possession. Mrs. Sned, like most tyrants, petty or gross, is at heart a fearfully insecure person, and Mavis is the only live thing in her world to whom she feels unquestionably superior. The thought of passing the night without Mavis filled her with dread. Around five o'clock, therefore, she telephoned, disguising her voice. Nicole might be home after all and her car in repair. Carmichael answered: his wife was away. At six, then, with dusk a half hour off, inwardly atremble but glaring aggressively, she rang Carmichael's doorbell.

To ask him to let firemen rescue poor Mavis, but, lo and behold, he not only greeted her friendlily, not only showed compassion at her plight, but fetched an extension ladder and clambered roofward with a can of his own tuna in his pocket, groped up on the shingles, opened the can, thrust it toward Mavis, waited till she was lured, petted her, chucked her chin, and finally captured her. All went well on the return trip till Mavis looked down. Then she panicked and scratched Carmichael very painfully. Still, he managed to hold on to her until she was only four or five feet from the ground, so that the drop to the grass caused her no injury, and though that night he groused volubly to Nicole about the high cost of helping "that old bitch next door," he made no complaint to the bitch herself but smilingly said he was happy to have been of service.

For the rest, he is affable to interviewers and approachable to autograph-seekers. Such is the benevolence to which Furfante has trained him!

I don't mean he's gone gaga. He can still be mordant, as his students attest. Oh, yes, he has gone back to teaching. That is, he gives two courses of his own design, in exobiology and mythopoesis, the first in the fall, the latter in the spring term. Both are in great demand and conducted with rigor. Carmichael's mordancy, though, is not aimed at his students but at authorities who would divorce fantasy from science or deny exactitude in symbol-making.

What else? Wickersham returned to service the same day the dog purged Carmichael of devils. Davy is in medical school in Tamami and spends one or two weekends a month with his parents. Nicole has assumed the leadership of the clan Tomlinson, to the great joy of the young in age or spirit.

Oh, yes, Carmichael's knack is working again. Not at full capacity or anywhere near it, but functioning, no question of it. If Hifni were here, I'd ask her whether, instead of its being burnt out, it might not have been simply whacked out of alignment through Carmichael's using it to destroy Vama, its most significant production. In any case, it's working, ticking over. Carmichael hasn't yet regained confidence in it to the point of actually taking a book in tow, but three promising hulks have appeared on his horizon— have approached him to build them, that is to say—and he cruises about tinkering mentally with them.

One is clearly too big for him at present, a romance with a family curse and a lost heir, a kidnapped ingenue and an evil uncle, a book like the books he loved when he was a teenager. Another concerns a man who has lost his nerve and who takes a risky job to redeem himself—autobiography, though Carmichael doesn't know it. The third is autobiography, also, so frankly autobiographical that Carmichael is conscious of it. Yes, you guessed, the book's about his doggie.

This is the book he's likely to start building, not that I'm very happy at the prospect. The atmosphere inside Carmichael is foul enough without his spending years writing a love story, and that (alas!) is the least of my trouble. Frank autobiography has dreadful implications. If Orcis ever gets the idea he might be a character, he'll be terminally insufferable.

July 1983–August 1991